CAMIE

ENTERTAINMENT

1

Christopher Speight

Black Viper

Christopher Speight

Black Viper

Acknowledgements

My first journey into the land of detective novels has been an exciting one to say the least. For some time now, I've been wanting to step out of my comfort zone and step into a genre that I've been reading since I began reading. This is my first detective novel and I hope you all enjoy reading it as much as I enjoyed writing it. Detective Franklin Stone awaits you. Enjoy the read. With that being said, I have a few acknowledgements I would like to give out.

First, as always, I acknowledge my Lord and Savior Jesus Christ. Without him, nothing is possible.

To my agent N'tyse. Thank you for believing in me. I appreciate all that you have done.

To my associate agent, Diane Rembert. You have rocked out with me since Chedda Boyz and I truly appreciate your support.

To Robert White. I truly appreciate your unbiased opinions of my material. Keep giving me the real.

To Jamoni Davis. Thank you for taking time out of your busy schedule to read my manuscript. I truly appreciate it.

To my mom. Thanks for all the support you have shown me. I love you!

To my sons, Deonte and Aaron. I am really enjoying watching the two of you become men. Keep up the good work!

Last but certainly not least, my wife Margo. Thank you for putting up with me. Love you!

Christopher Speight

Black Viper

Christopher Speight

Black Viper

1

As far as watering holes went, this couldn't be confused with a top-of-the-line establishment. A drab shade of chipped blue paint adorned the walls. The fluorescent lights dangling from the ceiling hadn't been cleaned in months. The dust covering them was so thick that, even when the lights were on, the ability to take notice of the quaint ambiance of the place was, at best, difficult. The floor was always sticky, due to the lack of attention from the lazy, part-time janitor. Under normal circumstances, such ineptitude would be just cause for termination. However, the owner, Victoria Baker, had promised her mother on her deathbed that she would look after her baby brother, Saffold. The siblings were polar opposites, from their looks to their demeanor. Victoria was a fiery redhead, who stood around five foot two with brown eyes and an average figure. On the other hand, her brother was rather athletic, with a physique that resembled an NFL quarterback. At six foot two, his sculpted body intimidated most men and caused most women to swoon. His light blue eyes, hypnotic and mesmerizing, enticed many captivated women into his web.

Over the years, Victoria had lost quite a few friends because of Saffold's pump 'em and dump 'em strategy. In addition to his womanizing ways, Saffold was also a raging alcoholic and occasional cocaine abuser.

He was so prolific at drinking that he would sometimes challenge the bar patrons to contests, which he'd easily win. The reward for his victories were often free shots or drinks.

Although Saffold only worked three days a week, he could be found at the bar nearly every night hustling free drinks or trying to seduce women.

Despite the warnings of his sister, it wasn't unusual for Saffold to take a different woman back to his place for a night of fun. Although she knew that the women were essentially playthings to him, Victoria did breathe a sigh of relief when he left with them. On more occasions than she cared to remember, his drinking had led to an altercation with someone in the bar, which led to a fight, which, in turn, led to someone having to be paid off to keep the matter out of court. She was growing tired of cleaning up his messes, but her promises, and her sense of obligation to keep them, bound her to the point of paralysis.

As the clock moved closer to closing time, a faint smile morphed across Victoria's lips. Today was her brother's birthday. Knowing him as she did, Victoria did not doubt that he would be looking to celebrate by drinking plenty of booze and then searching out a willing female to cap off his night. She just prayed to God that he would find someplace else to do it.

"Knock, knock," a familiar voice called out to her from the doorway. Her smile grew twice as big when she looked up and saw the love of her life, Kevin, standing there. Immediately she dropped the ink pen she'd been using to complete her paperwork, leaped to her feet, and flew across the room into his arms. Before he could get another word out of his mouth, she had firmly pressed her lips against his. They were quite the odd pair. Not only were they an interracial couple, with Kevin being African American, but they were from entirely different backgrounds. Kevin Broadnax had grown up surrounded by money. His father was a prominent real estate developer who owned many apartment complexes and houses.

When Kevin was just a teenager, his father began laying the groundwork for him to thrive and succeed in the real estate market. By the age of twenty-five, his net earnings had climbed to over $200,000 a year. Now, just a few weeks shy of his twenty-ninth birthday, Kevin's net worth was somewhere around half a million dollars. Of course, he wasn't about to share that information with Victoria just yet. His father and mother had always told him that the only way to know if a person's intentions were sincere was to allow them to think you didn't have anything. Once people knew that you had money, greed took over. But Kevin loved her and would be all too happy to share his fortune with her, when and if they ever tied the knot.

Victoria, on the other hand, grew up somewhere between the middle and lower class. Her family didn't struggle to live, but after paying all of their bills, they had very little left with which to do anything. Her mother, Rosemary Baker, was hellbent on not wanting her children to live paycheck to paycheck. She took out a $50,000 life insurance policy on herself and stipulated that it be divided equally upon her death. While Saffold blew the majority of his money on fast times and even faster women, Victoria opened up the bar and began carving out her niche in life. She and Kevin met a year and a half ago and soon began dating. Saffold was furious, insisting that his sister break it off and stop interacting with a "coon." His bigotry only pushed Victoria further into Kevin's arms, much to her brother's chagrin.

"I guess you just couldn't wait to see me, huh?" she asked when her and Kevin's lips finally parted.

"I think we both know the answer to that."

"Indeed, I do. I guess you missed your little snow bunny, huh?"

"You have no idea," he said, wrapping his arms around her and pulling her close to him. After embracing for what seemed like forever, Victoria grabbed Kevin's hand and pulled him toward her desk. She then pushed herself up and sat on the edge. She licked her lips seductively as she pulled Kevin between her legs and wrapped them around his waist. Things were just beginning to get hot and heavy when they heard someone clear their throat.

"Excuse me, Miss Baker, but you told me to let you know if your brother showed up. Well, he just showed up."

Victoria sighed. She was hoping that she wouldn't have to deal with Saffold's bullshit tonight but apparently fate wasn't on her side.

"Is he drunk?"

"Well, he's not as drunk as he usually is, but he's still pretty tipsy."

"Okay, thanks Wendy."

As the barmaid turned to walk back to her post, Saffold staggered toward her. He gave her the onceover, blowing a kiss in her direction.

"I guess you had to come and report to the boss lady that I was in the building, huh, Wendy? Hey, how about a kiss for the birthday boy?"

Wendy tried to ignore him but Saffold wouldn't let her. As she passed him, he slapped her on her behind. Wendy responded by slapping him across the shoulder.

"Keep your hands off of me, asshole!"

Saffold roared with laughter. His face morphed into a mask of hatred, however, when he noticed Kevin.

"Well, well, well, if it isn't Buckwheat!"

Kevin's fists balled up at his sides. His nostrils started to flare as his hate-filled eyes focused on Saffold. He truly wanted to strangle the man.

"What's the matter, boy? You got something you wanna get off your chest?"

"As a matter of fact, I do," Kevin said, making his way toward Saffold.

"Knock it off, you two," Victoria said, grabbing Kevin by the arm to hold him back. "Saffold, what the hell do you want?"

"What do you mean, what do I want? It's my birthday, sis. I want you to come out here and have a drink with me."

"She's busy," Kevin stated, a smug look on his face.

"Wasn't nobody talking to you, boy." Saffold punctuated his statement by pointing his finger at Kevin.

"Oh, I'll show you a boy."

Kevin balled his fists up and took a step toward Saffold. Although Saffold was built like an athlete, Kevin *was* an athlete, having run track and played college football. He'd put on a few pounds over the years, but he still frequented the gym regularly. In short, Saffold *looked* the part. However, Kevin *was* the part. Victoria knew this, which is why she didn't hesitate to jump in between her brother and her lover. With her hand planted on his chest and a worried expression on her face, Victoria looked up at Kevin with pleading eyes.

"Please baby, let me handle this," she implored him. Saffold may have been a racist jackass, but he was still her flesh and blood, and she had no desire to see him in the hospital.

"Just wait for me in the car, okay?"

Kevin stood there for a few seconds, glaring at Saffold. After cutting his eyes at Victoria, he reluctantly let the matter drop and headed for the back entrance. Saffold opened his mouth to hurl even more insults at Kevin, but a cold look from Victoria froze his tongue. As soon as Kevin was gone, Victoria whirled on her brother and slapped the taste from his mouth.

A confused and shocked expression washed over Saffold's face. As far back as he could remember, Victoria had only put her hands on him one other time. That was when he'd gotten drunk at a family gathering and called her out of her name.

"Damn, sis, what the hell?"

Victoria's eyes narrowed into slits. Her chest heaved in and out as she tried unsuccessfully to suppress her rage.

"Let me tell you something once and for all. I am *sick* and *tired* of you acting like Kevin is a second-class citizen just because he's African American! He is *my* boyfriend, and you may as well get used to it, because that's not going to change! So, either get used to it, or find yourself another job!"

Saffold looked at his older sister and smirked. He too had been standing at the bedside when his mother made Victoria promise that she'd look after him. He was getting ready to remind her of the promise she'd made to their mother, but something in her eyes told him that she meant what she'd just said. The grin slowly evaporated from his face and was replaced by a disgusted frown.

"Dad would turn over in his grave if he knew that you've taken up with a N—"

"Don't you *dare* say it!" Victoria yelled, cutting off his racist remark before he even finished it.

"It's true, and you know it! He'd be as pissed at you as I am!"

"Well, seeing that I'm a grown-ass woman, there would be nothing that he could do about it, just like there's nothing *you* can do about it now!"

Victoria fumed, doing her best to keep from shaking. For the life of her, she just couldn't understand why her brother was such a bigot. If memory served her correctly, Saffold dated an African

American girl when they were in high school. Maybe it was a phase. Or maybe it was Saffold wanting to taste the forbidden fruit that their father had stressed to them to stay away from. Whatever the reason, she didn't feel that way, and she never would.

Saffold stood defiant, folding his arms across his chest. He snorted out a sick-sounding laugh as he took inventory of the situation.

"So, let me get this straight. You're willing to fire me—your only sibling—because I disagree with you keeping time with a N— African American? You're willing to just throw our relationship in the trash for *him*?"

Victoria rubbed her temples. Saffold was starting to give her a migraine. She took a deep breath and prepared to explain her feelings to him…once again.

"Saffold, if you disagree with my relationship with Kevin, that's fine. You don't have to. But as God is my witness, you *will* respect it. And I'm going to have to insist that you keep your snide and racist comments to yourself."

Tears formed in the corners of Victoria's eyes. Ever since she and Kevin had started dating, she'd had to endure this. She hoped that her brother would have a change of heart, but she should have known better. The jokes Saffold and his father made about African Americans while they were growing up should have been a clear indication of how he would feel for the rest of his life. Saffold took one look into his sister's eyes and his heart sank. Although he'd suspected it all along, he was now convinced of it. His sister was in love. Deep love.

"Fine sis. If that's what you want, I'll just stay out of your life."

Saffold turned to walk away but stopped when he felt his sister's hand on his shoulder.

"Saffold, I don't want you out of my life. I just want you to respect my relationship."

"Yeah, okay. Whatever you say, sis."

Saffold made up his mind right then and there that he would have to look for another job. He wasn't about to deceive himself into thinking that he could accept his sister dating a Black man. Although he'd put up with it for over a year, Saffold no longer had the intestinal fortitude to continue doing so.

"Saffold, you and Kevin really do need to find a way to coexist."

"Oh yeah? And just why in the hell would I ever get close to that fudge bar?"

Victoria was quiet for a few seconds. She wanted to light into her brother for his degrading comment but decided that the best revenge would be the answer to his callous question.

"Because I want my child to grow up with both his father *and* his uncle in his life."

When Saffold turned back around and saw his sister rubbing her stomach, he nearly passed out.

Christopher Speight

2

Kevin was so ticked off, that he had to stop himself from punching the windshield literally. He'd tolerated Saffold's racist ways and condescending attitude for close to a year and a half and it was beginning to weigh on him. Although he did love Victoria, it had crossed his mind on several occasions to break it off with her, just to avoid the humiliation and ridicule that Saffold continuously heaped upon him. Feeling like he needed something to calm his nerves, Kevin leaned to his right, opened his glove compartment, and took out an already opened pack of Newport 100s. It had been nearly two weeks since he'd last smoked a cigarette. It was a nasty habit that he'd been trying to kick for the last six months.

Now that Kevin thought about it, the only time he ever smoked anymore was when he had to suffer through the angst of being around Saffold. Quickly shaking one from the pack, Kevin slid it between his lips and lit the tip. The cancer stick came to life as the dull white end instantly turned bright red. Kevin took a long, deliberate drag before letting down the window and blowing the fumes out into the air. Thirty seconds later, a calm washed over him as he leaned back on the headrest and closed his eyes. Although the nicotine had done its job, Kevin was still pissed. He would like nothing more than to waltz back inside and punch Saffold in the face.

Being a Black man in America, Kevin was no stranger to racism. In high school, he'd seen his share of racist jokes and quotes inside the lavatory stalls. He'd even been called the N-word on the football field, which resulted in a huge fight between the two teams. Oddly enough, Kevin was the only player to be ejected from the game. When his coach inquired about why his player was the only one being thrown out, he was told that it was because Kevin had incited the entire spectacle. The coach took one look at the all-white officiating crew and walked back to the sidelines, shaking his head. He glanced back over his shoulder and caught a glimpse of the referee smirking at him. He wanted to get mad, but he knew that it wouldn't do him any good. After the game, he pulled young Kevin to the side and tried to explain to him why he was seemingly being targeted. Kevin cut him off immediately, stating that he already knew. Kevin had nearly fallen asleep when he heard the car door open and close. He opened his eyes to see the love of his life slide into the passenger's seat. The two of them stared at each other for a few seconds before Victoria spoke.

"Sweetheart, I'm sorry about my asshole brother. I know that he's a racist prick, but please, just be patient with him, okay?"

"Patient? Baby, did you just ask me to be patient? Victoria, for a year and a half, I have put up with his racist comments, anti-Semitic views, and intolerant attitude. I'm sorry to tell you honey, but I'm running out of patience."

Victoria placed her hand on Kevin's leg and rubbed it gently. She could tell by how tight it was that her man was extremely tense. Knowing what it took to calm him down, she squeezed his leg as she rubbed. Kevin smiled.

"I know honey. But just so you know, I just told Saffold in no uncertain terms that I wanted him to cut out all of that racist crap and respect our relationship."

"And do you really think he's going to do that?"

"He'd better if he wants to continue working in my bar."

This surprised Kevin. Although she hadn't confided in many people about the bedside promise that she'd made to her mother, she had however confided in her lover.

"Really? You'd fire him, even though you made that promise to your mother?"

"Sweetie, I'm pretty sure that my mother would feel the exact same way if she knew Saffold was being such an ass. But it isn't just for my mother," Victoria said, smiling.

"Oh no?"

"Of course not silly. I love you and I'm not going to let my brother or anyone else ruin our relationship."

That was all Kevin needed to hear. He knew that Victoria loved him, but he often wondered if she loved him enough to set her brother straight once and for all. Now he knew, and it warmed his heart to know that beyond a shadow of a doubt, he was number one in her life. With love filling his heart and lust filling his loins, Kevin threw his arm around Victoria's neck and pulled her mouth to his. They melted into each other and shared a powerfully sensual kiss. It lasted much longer than either of them intended. They were so engrossed in each other's love, they never even noticed they were being watched. A heavy tap on the window quickly broke their embrace. When they looked outside, their eyes landed on the hardened face of a police officer. The officer snatched off a pair of cheap shades revealing cold, dark, eyes.

"Does this look like the Holiday Inn? The Hilton? The Motel Six?" the cop asked through the window. Kevin and Victoria quickly separated. Victoria fidgeted in her seat, while Kevin straightened himself out and lowered the window.

"Uh, hello, Officer. I apologize for what we were doing. We were just—"

"I know what the hell you were doing! And out here in a parking lot is not the place for it! Now get the hell out of here before I run both of you in for indecent exposure!"

"Indecent exposure?" Victoria shouted, while looking at herself.

Both she and Kevin were fully clothed, so she couldn't understand the threat. Kevin cut his eyes at her. He wanted to avoid the problem that he was sure was coming. Slowly, he turned his head back toward the window and saw that the officer had ceased walking back to the patrol car and was coming back to his.

"So, you have a problem with something I said, little lady?" the officer asked.

"No, no problems," Kevin quickly said, attempting to defuse the situation.

The officer continued to stare at Victoria for a few extra seconds before heading back to the police cruiser. Only when the officer got into the vehicle did Victoria have the nerve to speak again.

"This is horseshit! The only reason that cop harassed us is because a Black man was making out with a White woman!"

"Huh? How did you come to that conclusion?"

Victoria shrugged her shoulders. There was no real validity to her claim, and she knew it. It was just the disgusting look the officer gave them that caused her mind to matriculate that way.

"Damn, I guess that cop is going to wait until we leave," Kevin said, after looking in the rearview mirror and seeing the cop sitting behind the wheel, staring daggers at them.

"Oh shit," Victoria said, looking around.

"What's wrong?"

"I left my purse in my office. I'll be right back."

Victoria got out of the car and made her way back to the rear entrance of the bar. From her vantage point, she could see her brother staggering out the front door. The two of them locked eyes briefly. Victoria smiled and rubbed her belly. As much of an ass as Saffold had been, she just couldn't resist reminding him that she was about to have a child by a Black man. Saffold responded by waving his hand at her and spitting on the ground. A slight smile of satisfaction spread across her lips. After grabbing her purse, she was just about to leave back out when her shift manager called her name.

"What is it, Greg?"

"Sorry to bother you, boss lady, but we're fresh out of tequila. Do you want me to go on a liquor run or do you want me to send Patricia?"

Victoria thought about his question for a few seconds, and quickly answered.

"You go. She should be able to hold it down until you get back."

"Roger that," Greg said as he turned and walked back toward the bar. In all actuality, Victoria wasn't completely comfortable with Patricia watching over her place, but the last three times she was sent to the store to get something, she brought back the wrong product. So, she chose the lesser of two evils. Just before Victoria walked back to Kevin's car, she stopped in the doorway and stared out. She smiled again while rubbing her stomach. Victoria had decided that today was the day she would tell Kevin that he was going to be a father. She was only six weeks pregnant, but it was enough to instill great joy in her heart. Although neither of them had seriously broached the subject of matrimony, they both knew that their relationship was trending in that direction.

"I think I'll tell him tonight after we make love," she whispered.

Victoria continued to rub her belly and smile as she made her way toward Kevin's car. Once there, she opened the passenger's side door and got in. She blushed as she looked down at the floor.

"You know, I'm really looking forward to tonight. I'm going to make it special for you, sweetie."

Without turning her head to look at him, Victoria sat up and let her temple rest on Kevin's shoulder. It was killing her to keep the pregnancy a secret from him. She took a deep breath and sighed. She hadn't looked at him since she'd gotten in his car. A small giggle escaped from her mouth. She couldn't do it. She just couldn't hold out any longer. She had to tell him.

"Babe, there's something I have to tell you, and I hope it brings you as much joy as it did me when I first found out.

Victoria was downright giddy. She could barely contain herself. She moved away from Kevin and sat back in her seat. Still smiling, she slowly turned to look into her lover's eyes. The horrific sight before her caused her to scream at the top of her lungs. As Kevin's head rested on the headrest, his open eyes stared at nothing. His throat had been slashed from ear to ear.

Christopher Speight

3

Bright lights hung from the rafters and shined down on the students of St. Joseph's High School. The high school's auditorium was packed as the young men and women got ready to reenact one of the most famous plays in American theatre history. The school's janitorial staff had done an extraordinary job of getting the stage prepared. They had the hardwood floors shining like they were new and there wasn't a piece of trash anywhere to be found on the red carpet. In addition to that, every piece of gum that had been stuck to the bottom of the seats had been removed. Smiles were in abundance as a little more than one hundred proud parents filed into the auditorium. None of their smiles, however, could come close to the man's sitting in the front row with his son and neighbor.

The smile on Detective Franklin Stone's face was so bright, that it could compete with the sun. His soul was filled with pride as he watched his daughter, Rhonda, perform on stage. For weeks, he'd been looking forward to the play in which she'd landed the lead role of Ruth Younger. The play, *A Raisin in the Sun*, also just happened to be one of his all-time favorites. The Lorraine Vivian Hansberry play, one of the most popular acts to ever grace the stage, had always given him a great sense of pride. He loved how it portrayed the strength of a typical African American family when they pulled together.

Franklin was so engrossed in her performance that his son Franklin Jr. felt he could take liberties messing around on his smart phone. His antics had gone unnoticed until a low snicker escaped his throat and alerted Sadie Malone.

Sadie Malone was a sixty three year-old widow who lived next door to the detective and his two kids. Because she got lonely at times, she was more than happy to lend an ear, as well as sage advice, to Franklin and sometimes even his kids. She'd lived on the street longer than anyone. She'd seen a lot and she'd been through much more.

Sadie loved kids but she and her late husband Al could never have any of their own. They adopted a teenager when they were in their forties, but it ended in disaster. Her name was Tanya and she ended up getting hooked on drugs and running away from home. Sadie had only seen her once since she left, at her husband's funeral. Sadie tried to talk to her after the funeral, but Tanya left without giving her a chance.

Sadie didn't know that Al had been abusing Tanya for years after they adopted her and that played a large part in her turning to drugs. Knowing how close Sadie and her husband were, Tanya chose not to tell her about the abuse.

"Frank Jr., put that doggone cell phone away and pay attention to your sister's performance. You can play around on that thing anytime," Sadie said, after elbowing him in the shoulder.

Sighing loudly, Frank Jr. turned his phone off and placed it in his pocket. With a twisted scowl on his face, he crossed his arms and glared up at the stage. It wasn't that he wasn't proud of his sister. He just wasn't interested in any of the things that she was.

"Boy, don't make me take that damn phone," Frank Sr. said, cutting his eyes at his son.

A sharp pain shot through his arm also as Sadie elbowed him in the shoulder. Sadie hated profanity, and every time Frank used it, she would either pinch him or bash him on the shoulder.

"Will you please watch your mouth, Franklin?"

"Oh, sorry Sadie," Frank said, smiling. Over the years, Frank had grown to care about Sadie very much. The status of their relationship could be described as aunt and nephew, although they didn't share the same bloodline.

"Dad, how much longer is this play? This crap is boring," Frank Jr. complained.

"Jr., what in the world is your problem?" his father asked.

"Nothing."

Jr. slowly sank into his seat. He was itching to get home so that he could call a young lady who'd gained his interest.

She was one of the prettiest girls in his entire school. He'd told her that he would call her at eight o'clock. The last thing he wanted was to miss out on dating her because he couldn't keep his promise.

Black Viper

He thought about going to the bathroom and calling her from there, but two things prevented him from doing so. One, there was no way that he would have any kind of privacy there and two, Sadie and his father would see right through the pathetic attempt.

"Well, to answer your question, we have another thirty minutes before the play is over."

"I wish both of you would be quiet. I can barely hear what's going on up there," Sadie said, giving them both the evil eye. Frank Sr. cracked a sly grin as he leaned over to his son.

"You'd better be cool unless you want to get beat up," he whispered.

Detective Stone turned his attention back to the stage and continued to enjoy the play. When the final curtain closed, he was so impressed with his daughter's performance that he nearly shed a tear.

"Dad, are your eyes watering?" Frank Jr. asked.

Detective Stone ignored his son as he continued to give his daughter, along with the rest of the teenage actors, a standing ovation. He was just as proud of her as he was his son during his boxing tournament.

"Oh brother. Can we go now?" Jr. asked. If they hurried, he could still get home in time to make his phone call.

"No. We have to wait on your sister. Boy, why are you in such a damn rush?" Detective Stone asked, drawing a hard pinch from Sadi.

He was starting to get annoyed with his son's lack of support for his sister. He didn't know what Jr.'s problem was, but he definitely wasn't going to stand for it. Before Jr. could answer him, Rhonda came running up to her father with a large smile plastered on her face.

"Dad! Mrs. Turner said that was one of the best performances she'd ever seen. She said I was a natural."

"She's right, young lady. You *are* a natural," Sadie said, as she twirled her forefinger around one of Rhonda's curly black locks.

"You really think so?" Rhonda asked. She was so excited that she could barely contain herself.

"I *know* so," Sadie said.

"Baby, I am so proud of you," Detective Stone told her.

"Now that it's over, can we—"

"Jr., if you say one more thing about leaving, I'm going to pull your tongue out of your mouth," Detective Stone said through gritted teeth.

"You know Jr. I don't recall Rhonda acting like this when she had to sit through two hours of your boxing tournament last month," Sadie reminded him.

Jr. looked at his sister and instantly felt terrible. Sadie was right. Now that he thought about it, his sister had always supported him and now that she wanted and needed his support, he was acting like a first-class jerk. Besides, he thought they were about to leave anyway.

"Sorry sis," he said, dropping his head.

"It's all good big bro."

"Now that that's settled, I think we should all go out to eat to celebrate the fact that a star was born tonight," Frank said.

Frank Jr.'s lips tightened, but he didn't say anything.

"Stop it Daddy. I'm not a star. At least not yet," Rhonda bragged.

"Well, you're a star in my eyes, and I would be honored to take my little thespian out to dinner."

After hugging his daughter tightly, Frank led everyone from the auditorium. He was still smiling when he got to his SUV. He opened the door for Sadie and instructed Jr. to do the same thing for his sister. Frank made it a point to instill chivalry in his son. He'd always treated his wife with the utmost respect and expected his son to do the same with not just with someone he was dating, but any female.

"Okay, young lady, where would you like to go to eat?"

Before Rhonda could answer her father's question, his cell phone went off. The smile he'd had for the past couple of hours slowly began to disappear. Frank listened to the caller intently before speaking. When they were done, he simply sighed deeply and shook his head.

"Rhonda—"

"You don't even have to say it Daddy. I already know."

"I'm sorry baby."

"It's okay. We can go out some other time."

Black Viper

Over the years, Frank Jr. and Rhonda had gotten used to the job snatching their father away during family gatherings. While Jr. had pretty much understood the scope of his father's job, it took Rhonda a long time to stop getting angry at his sudden departures. She'd come a long way over the last two years in terms of realizing that her father's job was one of the most important ones in the entire city.

"So, how many people died this time?" Sadie asked, a somber look on her face.

Christopher Speight

4.

Detective Amber Davis pulled up to the curb in front of Frank's house and cut the engine. She felt terrible about having to tear him away from his daughter's play but under the circumstances she had no choice. Their boss, Captain Snyder, told her in no uncertain terms that she wanted them on the case. When told that it was Frank's day off, Captain Snyder told Davis that she didn't care and for the two of them to get to the crime scene ASAP. She was only a few minutes from Frank's house when she received the call, so after calling him she knew that it would take at least ten minutes for him to get home from St. Joseph's High School. While she waited for her partner to arrive, Amber figured that she'd facetime her son and see what he was up to. She dialed the number and was treated to the shock of her life. On the other end of the phone was not her son Ryan, but a half-naked young lady with tight braids and the body of a fully grown woman.

"Uh, is there a reason that you're calling my man's phone?" the young lady asked, rudely.

Amber silently stared at her phone for a minute before exploding.

"*Excuse me*? Who in the hell are you and where in the hell is my son?"

The young lady's mouth fell completely open. In her jealous mind, some other female was trying to contact her man. She'd only been seeing Ryan for a couple of weeks, but just like the rest of the young ladies he was involved with, his charm had cast a spell over them that was hard to break.

When Amber sent Ryan to live with his father, she felt that it was the right thing to do. Being a detective was so demanding that she couldn't spend anywhere near the time with him that she needed to. For that reason, she sent him to his father, hoping that he would teach him how to be a man. But apparently, the only thing he was showing him was how to be a womanizer.

"Son? Oh my God, oh my God, I am so sorry, Mrs. Murphy."

Before Amber could correct her about calling her the wrong last name, she heard her son screaming in the background.

"Hey! I know you didn't just answer my damn phone."

Amber looked on as her son stormed into the picture.

"Give me my phone," he yelled, snatching the phone out of the young lady's hand. When Ryan looked and saw who it was who'd facetimed him, he nearly passed out.

"Ryan, what the hell is going on over there? Where in the hell is your father?"

"Oh, uh hey Ma. Ain't nothing going on."

"Where. . . in the hell. . . is your father?"

"He went out to shoot pool with a couple of his friends."

Amber reached up with one hand and rubbed her throbbing temple. She was starting to get a headache.

"Did he also tell you that you could have company while he was gone?"

"She was here when he left Ma, and he didn't tell her that she had to leave, so I assumed that it was okay with him."

"What? He lets you have company when he's not at home?"

Knowing that telling his mother the truth would only make her angrier, Ryan chose just to shrug instead.

"Boy, I don't care what your father said. Get rid of that slut, right now! And tell your father to call me when he gets in!"

Amber hung up on her son without saying another word. She wanted to choke the life out of her ex-husband for allowing her son to be so wild. She took a couple of deep breaths and tried to compose herself. Her partner would be there any second and she had to put on her game face. She glanced in her rearview mirror just in time to see Frank pull into his driveway. She sat in her car and watched as he walked his next-door neighbor to her front door. She continued to stare at him as he made his way to her car. Franklin Stone was a fine specimen in her eyes, but there was no way that she would ever tell him that. The department strictly prohibited fraternization of any kind, and the last thing she wanted to have happen was to lose her job because she had a crush on her partner. Amber unlocked the passenger's side door so her partner could join her.

"How bad is it?" Frank asked, reaching for his seat belt.

"Not sure partner. You know just as much as I know at this point. An African American male was found dead in his car."

"Who found him?"

"His girlfriend."

Detective Stone grimaced.

"I know right? That must be the sickest feeling in the world. I wouldn't wish that on my own worst enemy."

"Hey, didn't you tell Captain Snyder that I was off today?"

"Yeah, I did. You think she gave a shit?"

"I'm going to guess. . . no?"

"Ding, ding, ding. Give the man a prize, Johnny."

The two of them rode in silence for a few minutes before Amber vented to Frank about the way her ex was letting her son run wild. Frank was surprised. Usually, his partner never wanted to talk about her son, so it had to be bothering her in order for her even to bring it up. While listening to her, Frank simply nodded his head. He'd learned a long time ago that when women vented most of the time, all they wanted was for you to listen, not try to solve their problems. Today was no different. Amber didn't stop ranting until they got to the crime scene.

Christopher Speight

5

The wind blew slightly, causing the yellow police tape to ripple in the breeze. On lookers and innocent bystanders whispered amongst themselves as the gruesome sight sat in plain view for all to see. Sitting on a nearby bench, nervously smoking a cigarette was Victoria. It was the third cigarette she'd smoked since calling the police to inform them that the love of her life had been murdered. Her rational mind told her that smoking while pregnant was unhealthy for her unborn child, but she couldn't help it due to her circumstances. She needed the nicotine to calm her nerves. The image of her brother's smug look as they glanced at each other when she went back into her bar stuck vividly in her mind. Victoria didn't want to think that Saffold despised her relationship to the point that he would mortally wound her boyfriend, but with his racist attitude, she couldn't rule it out either.

"You okay, boss lady?" Wendy asked, carrying a coffee mug in her hand. When she got close enough to her, she extended the mug to her boss. "Here. I thought you could use a hot cup of coffee," she said.

"Thank you." Victoria gratufully took the mug from Wendy's hand and took a sip. As soon as the liquid touched her lips, she knew that Wendy had spiked it with some liquor. She glanced up at her barmaid, who just stood there with a sly smile on her face.

"Is it okay?" she asked.

Victoria nodded her approval and took another sip. Although they both knew that there wasn't a potent enough form of alcohol on the market to take her pain away, she was extremely gratified that someone had tried to subdue her heartache. Had Wendy known that she was expecting, there was no way that she would've given her alcohol. But in Victoria's eyes, what Wendy didn't know, wouldn't hurt her.

"Do you want me to try to get in touch with your brother again?"

Victoria thought about it briefly before shaking her head. She'd tried no less than five times to get in touch with Saffold but to no avail. She closed her eyes and immediately saw Kevin's handsome face. The memory was too much for her heart to bear as she burst into tears. Wendy quickly sat down beside her and threw her arm around her boss's shoulders. She'd been working at the bar for a little over two years and in that time she and her boss had become close. Since she was fresh out of rehab, Wendy desperately needed someone to give her a chance. Her saving grace came in the form of Victoria Baker, who, at the time, needed another barmaid. Victoria could have easily hired one of the other three applicants, but there was just something in Wendy's eyes that convinced Victoria to give her a chance. As Wendy was doing her best to console Victoria, she noticed two detectives getting out of their car and making their way toward them. She leaned down and whispered into Victoria's ear.

"Maybe we should go inside."

"Inside? Why?"

"It looks like the detectives are here."

6

Detectives Franklin Stone and Amber Davis had made this walk time and time again. It was a walk that neither of them ever looked forward to but because of their job description they'd had no choice but to get used to it. Amber took a deep breath as she pulled into the bar's parking lot and parked.

"You ready?" Frank asked her.

"I'm never ready for this," she said solemnly.

The two detectives got out and made their way over to Kevin's car. After pushing up the yellow tape and ducking under it, a tall, muscular, officer with black, curly hair and a neatly trimmed beard greeted them. His skin was the color of milk chocolate. His brown eyes were slightly slanted. Timothy Jordan had been on the force for a little over a year. He was an inquisitive young man well liked on the force despite being a relative newcomer to the precinct.

"Afternoon, Detectives."

"Hey Tim," they both said in unison.

"What's the story here?" Frank asked.

Officer Jordan shook his head as he reached into his breast pocket and took out his notepad. He calmly flipped through the pages until he came to the information that he was looking for. He stared at it for a few seconds before shaking his head.

"Gruesome man. Just plain gruesome. Apparently, the victim, a Mr. Kevin Broadnax, was sitting in his car waiting for his girlfriend, a Miss Victoria Baker, when someone got in the back of his car and slit his throat."

Frank and Amber followed Jordan over to Kevin's car.

"So, what do you think?" he asked.

"I'm not sure yet," Frank responded. He reached into his pocket and pulled out a pair of latex gloves. After putting them on, he reached for the door handle. Just before he touched it however, he stopped and backed away.

"Something wrong, partner?" Amber asked.

"No. I just want to check something else first."

Instead of opening the front door to get a closer look at the victim, Detective Stone decided to open the back door. He and Detective Davis exchanged glances when the door wouldn't open.

"It's locked?" Jordan asked.

"Yep. That means that the killer probably wasn't behind the victim when he or she killed him."

"Huh?" Jordan was confused. He didn't understand what a locked door had to do with anything.

"Tim, do you honestly think that whoever killed this man would be thinking about locking the door after committing a murder in broad daylight?"

Jordan thought about it and had to concede that it made sense.

"Damn, I guess that's why you guys are Detectives and I'm not."

"Don't be so hard on yourself, Tim. No one knows everything when they first become a cop," Amber told him.

Jordan watched closely as the two detectives opened the driver's side door and examined Kevin's body. Detective Stone looked closely at the victim's slashed neck, while Detective Davis looked around the car to see if there were any clues for her to pick up. After examining the victim's fatal wound, Detective Stone glanced down at the edge of the seat. Squinting his eyes, he zeroed in on a single drop of blood.

"Amber. Look at this," Frank said, pointing to the droplet. Amber trained her eyes in the direction of where her partner was aiming.

"I don't see anything."

"Look closer."

She leaned down and let her eyes sweep back and forth. It only took her a few seconds to notice the red spot on the fabric.

"Are you thinking what I'm thinking?" she asked Frank.

Jordan looked from one detective to the other.

Black Viper

"Okay, I'm lost again. Just what the hell are you two thinking?"

"Whoever killed this man did so from outside of the car," Frank told him.

An exasperated frown appeared on the officer's face. It was frustrating to him that he couldn't figure things out as quickly as the detectives.

"Okay, Detectives. Please explain to me how you've come to that conclusion."

"May I?" Amber asked Frank, the senior detective.

"Please do."

"Tim, look at the wound," she said, pointing to the victim's neck. "The starting point indicates that someone cut his throat from right to left. It stands to reason that when the blade was taken away from his neck, blood dripped on the seat. Add that to the fact that the back door was locked and voila! His killer sliced his neck from the outside."

"Ooooo okay. I get it now," Timothy said.

"Tim, did you call in the techies? We're going to need them to dust this car for fingerprints."

"Yeah, I called them about forty-five minutes ago. I don't know why they haven't gotten here yet. Do you think I should call them again?"

"No need," Frank said. "Here they come now."

"Well, let's get out of their way so they can do their jobs. Tim, fill them in on what happened over here. We need to talk to the victim's girlfriend," Amber said.

"Yes, we do. Where is she?" Frank asked.

"That's her sitting over there on that bench. Looks like she's about to leave though."

"No, she's not. We need to talk to her."

As Victoria made hurried steps toward her bar, Frank and Amber walked twice as fast to reach her before she went inside.

"Hold up a second, miss! We need to talk to you!" Frank yelled.

Although she wanted her boyfriend's killer apprehended and brought to justice, Victoria needed a break from talking to the police.

37

She was an emotional wreck and on the verge of having a nervous breakdown.

"Hey! Didn't you hear the detective?" Amber yelled. "He said stop!"

Had it not been for Wendy grabbing her arm, Victoria probably would've continued walking. The way she saw it, she had talked to the police once, and now it was time for them to do their jobs. On the other hand, Wendy knew that the best way to get cops to help was to cooperate with them, although she hated talking to them. As Frank and Amber approached her, a frustrated Victoria threw her hands in the air.

"Oh my God, what now? How many more questions am I going to have to answer?"

"Miss Baker, you really need to calm down. Now I know that you've been through a traumatic experience and may I say that we are very sorry for your loss. But we need to ask you a few questions if we are to get to the bottom of this," Frank said. He could tell from Victoria's puffy, red eyes that she'd been crying for quite some time. He had no desire to add to her pain but had a job to do.

"Miss Baker, you *do* want us to find who killed your boyfriend, don't you?" Amber asked with a raised eyebrow.

Both she and Frank had been on the force long enough to know that the first person to look at in a murder investigation was the significant other.

"What the hell kind of question is that? Of course, I want my boyfriend's murderer found!"

"Then you need to work with us instead of giving us a hard time."

"*Excuse* me?" Victoria said, tears now running down her cheeks. "How in the hell am I giving you a hard time?"

Wendy put her hands on her hips and glared at Amber. She was thoroughly disgusted by Amber's snippy attitude. Amber did a double take when she noticed how Wendy was staring at her.

"Is there a problem?" she asked.

"I don't know, *is* there? You're treating my boss like she's done something wrong, and we don't appreciate it."

Amber gave Wendy a hard stare.

"What is your name?" she asked while taking a notepad from her pocket.

"Why is that important?"

"Look, you can either give me your name, or you can go inside and wait until we finish questioning your boss," Amber said flatly. She wasn't about to have a pissing contest with this woman.

"Wendy. My name is Wendy Lomax," Wendy said after a brief hesitation.

"Okay. Everyone calm down please," Frank said, raising his hand. "Once again, Miss Baker, we are sorry for your loss and please understand that no one is saying that you did anything wrong. We just need to ask you a few questions. We will do whatever we can to find out who committed this heinous act, but to do that, we need your help. Anything you can tell us about the incident could quite possibly lead us to find the killer."

The look of sincerity in Frank's eyes seemed to make Victoria feel better. After cutting her eyes at Amber one last time, she led the two detectives into her office. Once they were inside, she plopped down on the sofa and exhaled.

"What do you want to know?" she asked, sniffling.

Amber opened her mouth to start the questioning but quickly closed it when Frank held up his hand indicating that he would take the lead. It was clear that Amber didn't like it as she jammed her pad and pen back into her pocket and crossed her arms. Frank gave her a stern look as he took out his own notepad and pen. Typically, Amber was sympathetic during an interview, but today was different, and Frank felt that he knew why. He made a mental note to talk to her about her behavior later.

"Where were you when Mr. Broadnax was killed?"

Wendy's eyes narrowed into slits. A disgusted laugh escaped her mouth as she shook her head.

"Really, Detective?"

"I'm sorry, ma'am, but it's a question we have to ask."

"Whatever," Wendy said, with a flip of her hand. "Sounds like an accusation to me."

"Well it's not, and please stop trying to tell us how to do our jobs," Amber chimed in. "The more you interrupt, the longer this is going to take."

Wendy let out another disgusted laugh, but remained quiet.

"Miss Baker? Could you answer my question, please?"

"I was in here. We were sitting in his car, getting ready to leave when I remembered that I'd left my purse in the bar, so I came back in here to get it. Then when I went and got back in the car, I started talking to him. A few minutes later, I looked at him and saw that he was dead," Victoria said, starting to cry again.

"Sooo, it took you how long to discover that he was deceased?" Amber asked. Both Victoria and Wendy shot her a contemptuous glare.

"Hey, I'm just asking," Amber said, holding up her hands in surrender.

"Look, when I got in the car, I had a few things on my mind, so I didn't look at him when I first got inside."

"Miss Baker, did you noticed anything suspicious after discovering the body?"

"What do you mean?"

"Well, for instance did you see anybody lingering around? Or did you see anyone running away? Did you see a vehicle driving away? Did you notice a vehicle sitting there that wasn't there when you went back into the bar?"

"No, I'm sorry, but I didn't see any of that." Victoria said.

"It's okay ma'am," Frank said. He was trying to keep Victoria from losing her composure.

"Are you feeling nauseated, Miss Baker?" Amber suddenly asked.

"No," Victoria said, shaking her head.

"Are you sure? Because I notice how you keep rubbing your stomach."

Frank had noticed the same thing but was going to wait until the end of the interview to bring it up. Victoria's eyes darted from Frank to Amber.

"Oh my God, maybe she's hungry, Detective."

"Or maybe she's pregnant," Amber blurted out.

Wendy popped her lips and rolled her eyes. She didn't know why the detectives were giving Victoria a hard time when she was the victim. She was just about to give them a piece of her mind until she noticed the look of guilt on her boss's face.

"Victoria? Are you pregnant?" she asked. Victoria responded by slowly nodding her head slowly. A few seconds later, she burst out crying again.

"And now my child is going to have to grow up without a father," she said.

Frank allowed her a few minutes to compose herself before continuing.

"Okay, Miss Baker. I just have a few more questions. Did your boyfriend have any enemies that you know of?"

"Enemies?"

"Yes, enemies. In other words, is there anyone that you know of who would want your boyfriend dead?"

No matter how hard she thought about it, only one person kept coming to mind, and that was her brother, Saffold. Both detectives stared at Victoria as she debated in her mind whether to tell the detectives how much her lover and her brother hated each other. But at the end of the day, Saffold was her brother, and she couldn't betray that bond.

"No, Detective, I don't," she lied. Although the detectives didn't believe her, they let the matter drop for the time being.

"If we find out anything, we'll be in touch. Thank you for your time," Frank said and motioned for Amber to follow him as he left.

"So, what do you think?" Amber asked.

"About what?" Frank responded in a surprised tone.

"You think she had anything to do with it?"

"I seriously doubt it. The woman was pregnant. I doubt very seriously if she killed the father of her unborn child. Plus, I feel I can read people pretty good, and the woman I talked to in there was in a great deal of pain."

"Maybe," Amber said, shrugging her shoulders. "She could've been acting though."

"Really? You mean to tell mean that you think she was acting?"

"Hey, you never know. I mean, let's play devil's advocate for a minute. Picture this. She goes out to his car to tell him about their impending bundle of joy. But when she tells him, he's not as happy as she expects him to be. As a matter of fact, he gets downright pissed off at the news. She's shocked at his reaction but after the initial shock wears off, she gets just as pissed off as he is. An argument ensues and he tells her that he feels she should get an abortion. She refuses. He laughs and tells her that it doesn't matter anyway because he just won't claim the little bastard. Hearing that the love of her life not only doesn't want to be a part of her life, but he also doesn't want to be in the child's life sends her into a rage and before you know it," Amber said, as she ended her statement with a throat-slashing gesture. Frank laughed for a few seconds before blowing a hole in her theory.

"Nice deducing, except for two things."

"Oh yeah? And what would they be?"

"Well, for one, the victim's neck was slashed from right to left, and two, the killer was standing on the outside of the car when he or she committed the murder."

"Yeah, well I'm still working on that part."

"Keep working," Frank said, smiling.

7

After leaving the crime scene, Amber dropped Frank off in front of his house. Although he kept an air of professionalism while he was on the job, Frank was slightly perturbed because he couldn't figure out why Captain Snyder had pulled him in on his day off to investigate a murder. Surely, she could have found another team of detectives to handle the situation. Had his partner called him just fifteen minutes later, he would not have even answered his cell phone because he would have been at a restaurant enjoying dinner with his family.

As he walked up to his front door, he looked at his watch. It was almost nine o' clock and he'd missed a date with his wife. It was a standing date that the two of them had every Friday at 7:30 p.m. Although he was slightly disappointed that he hadn't gotten to spend any alone time with her, he was still happy knowing that they would all be together the next day as a family.

As soon as Frank entered his house, the aroma of baked chicken, sweet potatoes, collard greens, and macaroni and cheese drifted through his nasal passages. He backed out of the doorway and shot a glance next door. Standing in her doorway, giving him a radiant smile was Sadie. Frank closed the door, walked across his porch, and leaned on his banister.

"Now, you know you didn't have to do that, right?"

Sadie simply shrugged her shoulders. Truth be told, she enjoyed cooking. Outside of spending time with her husband when he was alive, cooking brought Sadie more joy than anything else in the world. To keep her sanity after he died, she started cooking meals for Frank and his family whenever his job called him away. As time wore on, Frank tried to get her to stop. It wasn't that he didn't enjoy her cooking—quite the contrary. Sadie's cooking skills were better than anyone's he'd ever encountered, including his wife's. The truth of the matter was that he was starting to feel guilty. Sadie was cooking for him and his family so much that, in his eyes, it was equivalent to having a full-time job. The last thing he wanted to do was be accused of working an old lady to death.

"I cooked this yesterday. All I had to do was heat it up. I was going to surprise you guys after the play, but I didn't know at the time that you were going to take everyone out to dinner," she laughed. "Just my way of saying thank you for inviting me."

"Sadie, as much as you've filled our stomachs with your delicious food over the last couple of years, you don't owe us anything."

Sadie crossed her arms and stared at him.

"Detective Franklin Stone, are you trying to kill me?"

"What do you mean by that?"

"You know good and doggone well that, if I tried to eat all of that food by myself it would kill me. So, I figured I'd put it to good use by sharing it with my favorite family."

"Well, thank you Sadie. I really appreciate it."

"Don't mention it. I just left your house a few minutes ago. Rhonda was doing her homework and Jr. was on his cell phone talking to some girl."

"Talking to some girl? How do you know that?"

"You're not the only one with detective skills," Sadie said, laughing. "Besides, I heard him call the person on the other end of the phone, 'baby', so I have to assume that it was a female. . . unless there's something that you haven't told me about him."

"Not at all. That boy is all male. As a matter of fact, I have to slow him down sometimes. I swear, that seems to be all that's on that boy's mind nowadays," Frank said as he turned to go back into his house.

"Frank, are you okay?" Sadie asked. The concern in her voice caused him to stop in his tracks.

"Yes, why do you ask?"

"Because today is Friday."

"Oh. Yeah, I'm okay. We have family time tomorrow, so that will make up for it. I just hope she's not mad at me," Frank said and disappeared inside of the house.

8

Bitter cold bit at Frank's ankles as he went out to the curb to retrieve his morning paper. He'd tossed and turned all night thinking about Kevin Broadnax. Something about the case that bugged him, but he couldn't quite put his finger on it. Unlike his partner, Frank had no suspicions that Victoria Baker killed her boyfriend. In his opinion, she was a broken woman who was going through her own private hell. However, the one thing that did bother him about her was how she'd hesitated when they'd asked her if her boyfriend had any enemies. A slight hesitation wasn't unusual, but Victoria's hesitation combined with the look on her face when he asked her, had raised a few red flags for him. After careful consideration, Frank decided not to press her on the matter at that time.

After scooping up his paper, Frank went back into his house and headed toward the kitchen. He looked at the clock on the wall and knew that he didn't have much time before his kids came downstairs looking for their breakfast. It was Saturday, so he knew exactly what they wanted to eat. It took him all of ten minutes to grab the box of pancake mix out of the cabinet, the eggs out of the refrigerator, mix it together in a bowl with water and put it in a hot skillet on the stove. After getting that together, he went back into the refrigerator and took out a pack of bacon. He quickly peeled eight slices out of the pack and put them in the microwave.

When all the food was ready, he made three plates and set them on the table. No sooner had he done this, Jr. came downstairs, sniffing the air. The traveling aroma had invaded his sense of smell and made its way down to his stomach.

"Yeah, pancakes! *That's* what I'm talking about Dad."

"Boy, don't you know how to say, 'good morning'?"

"Oh, my bad, Dad. Good morning."

"Good morning. Where's your sister?"

"I don't know. Probably taking off her ugly mask," Jr. said, laughing. Before Frank could admonish his son for his remark about his sister, Rhonda trotted down the stairs and showed her father that she didn't need him to come to her defense.

"At least I can take off my mask. Your ugly is permanent," she said, bumping his shoulder as she brushed past him.

"Don't look at me," Frank said. "You started with her first," he added, when Jr. gave him a "Did you just see what she did" look.

"Man, you get on my nerves," Jr. said, frowning at his sister.

"Good," Rhonda said, sticking her tongue out at him.

"That's enough you two. Hurry up and eat your breakfast so we can leave."

"Are we going to see Momma today, Daddy?"

"Why do you ask that every Saturday? Don't we always go on Saturday?" Jr. asked, annoyed.

"Ain't nobody talking to you, big head."

"Hey, didn't I say that was enough?" Frank said, more firmly this time. "Yes, sweetheart, we are going to see your mother today."

The three of them remained quiet as they ate breakfast, each of them lost in their own thoughts. Frank saw the sadness in his kids' eyes, and it caused his heart to ache. They missed their mother terribly. Although she'd been gone for nearly two years, neither of them had gotten used to her not being there.

Frank collected the plates when they finished eating, rinsed them off, and put them in the dishwasher.

"Okay, guys. Go upstairs and get dressed so we can go," Frank told his kids.

He waited until they were upstairs in their respective rooms before sitting back down at the table and massaging his temples. Saturday mornings were always a tough time for him. Knowing that he was going to see his wife always put him through a myriad of emotions. Taking a deep breath, Frank got up and made his way to his bedroom to get dressed. Since he'd already laid out what he was going to wear, it only took him five minutes to dress. When he finished, he went into the living room to find Jr. and Rhonda waiting for him on the couch.

"Okay, guys, let's go," he said somberly.

9

Sunlight splashed through the window of Cleveland Clinic Hospital and illuminated the cheeks of Marilyn Stone. She'd once had one of the most beautiful faces in the entire city of Cleveland but lying motionless for the last twenty-two months had robbed her of her once stunning beauty. The angelic face Frank looked forward to waking up to every morning to was now ashen and dry. Her eyes were sunken into her head. Her lips were now cracked and dehydrated. But none of that mattered to Frank. Not in the least. In his eyes, she was still the same beautiful woman that had walked down the aisle to join him in holy matrimony all those years ago.

Unbeknownst to anyone but God, coming to visit his wife had always been bittersweet to Frank. Although it wasn't his fault, he still harbored guilt over asking her to pick up Frank Jr. from his boxing lesson that night. Frank and a few of his coworkers had stopped off at a bar to have a few beers, so he called his wife to see if she wouldn't mind doing so.

"No problem at all, dear," she'd told him.

"Thanks babe. And don't worry about cooking tonight. I'll pick up a couple of pizzas after I leave here."

"The kids will be happy to hear that. You know how they love pizza."

"Is that right? Seems to me like their mother loves it just as much as they do."

"Whatever, jerk," Marilyn said, laughing. "Hey, I was thinking about leaving Rhonda here while I go pick up Jr. What do you think?"

"I think it'll be okay. She's thirteen years old, so she's not a baby anymore. But to be on the safe side, ask Sadie to keep an eye on things while your gone."

"Okay. See you when you get home, honey. I love you."

"I lava you too, honey," Frank said, changing the pronunciation of the word like he always did when he told his wife he loved her.

It always caused Marilyn to smile when he said it, and that time was no exception. Frank had no idea that it would be the last time that exchange between the two of them would be made.

After grabbing her keys, Marilyn walked out of her house and went next door to ask Sadie to keep tabs on her daughter while she was gone. She then jumped in her car and headed toward I-90 West. She hated driving on the freeway and for one brief second, she contemplated driving through the city. But it was quickly getting dark, and she didn't want Frank Jr. waiting outside. The gym closed in fifteen minutes and the only way she would get there in time was to take the freeway. She was halfway there when her back tire blew out and she lost control of the car, causing it to slam into a concrete median. Marilyn suffered extensive head trauma and had been in a coma ever since. It was a burden that continuously weighed down Frank's soul every second of every day. He'd tried to convince himself that it was an act of God, but in the end, he just couldn't shake the feeling that he and he alone was responsible. The only thing that kept Frank going was his children.

The longest walk that Frank ever had to make in his life was the one he was making now. Rhonda had a tight grip on her father's hand as they walked across the parking lot and made their way toward the hospital's entrance. Once inside, they made a quick right and got on the elevator.

"You guys all right?" He asked his kids.

Neither of them spoke, opting instead to nod their heads. Their expressions were total contrasts of each other. While Frank Jr. was stone-faced, Rhonda had already begun to tear up. It broke Frank's heart to see his little girl so sad. Although he felt guilty about what had happened to his wife, Frank often thanked the good Lord above that he and Marilyn had decided to leave Rhonda at home that fateful night. Small sniffles could be heard coming from Rhonda the closer they got to her mother's room. Frank released her hand and wrapped his arm around her shoulders. Just as they got to the entrance to her room, he stopped.

Black Viper

"You guys ready?" he asked. Once again, they both just nodded.

As soon as they entered the room, Frank Jr. and Rhonda quickly made their way over to their mother's bedside. It was a routine that Frank had now gotten used to. He would stand back and allow his kids to have their time with their mother before taking his turn. As he stood there in the doorway, a nurse appeared next to him. She was an older woman who looked to be in her mid-fifties. She had short black hair that held a hint of gray around both edges. Black-framed glasses sat on the bridge of her nose. After staring at his kids for a few seconds, she looked at Frank and gave him a warm, sympathetic smile.

"Good morning Mr. Stone. How are you today?"

"I'm okay, I guess," Frank said, his eyes still trained on his children. He was trying very hard to keep the tears from falling. He wanted to remain strong for his children, but he struggled to do so each time they visited his wife. When he was finally able to tear his gaze away from Frank Jr. and Rhonda, he turned to the nurse and asked the same question that he'd been asking for nearly two years.

"Has there been any change?"

"I'm afraid not, Mr. Stone. I'm sorry."

"Thank you," Frank said. He looked at all the machinery his wife was hooked up to and shook his head. Although he knew that it was the machines keeping her alive, Frank just couldn't bring himself to permit them to disconnect them. When a doctor told him that Marilyn would probably never recover, his heart sank. He had a meeting with his kids after that and they'd all unanimously decided that they would not give up on her recovery.

After spending time with their mother, Frank Jr. and Rhonda went and sat down. This was Frank's cue to go over and spend time with the love of his life. Slowly he walked over to her bedside and looked down. In his eyes, she was still the most beautiful woman he'd ever seen in his life. Frank then reached down and grabbed Marilyn's hand. A feeling of love quickly washed over him.

"Hey honey. I'm sorry I couldn't come up here yesterday, but my boss ordered me to go check out a crime scene," he said, smiling down at her. He continued looking down at her for a few more seconds before motioning for his daughter to join him.

"Honey, did you know that we may have a star on our hands? Did your daughter tell you how impressed her drama teacher was with her acting skills the other day? I think we may be looking at the next Angela Bassett."

Rhonda smiled as tears leaked from the corners of her eyes.

"Come on over here, Floyd Mayweather," he said, waving his son over. Jr. pushed himself up from the chair and made his way over to his father's side. "And this boy here? Now I know that you were skeptical when he first started boxing, but I think we have the next world champ on our hands. Of course, he ain't got nothing on his old pop here," Frank said, as he planted a soft jab on his shoulder. Frank and his kids stayed there for another hour before Frank leaned down and kissed his wife on the forehead with the promise that he'd be back next Saturday. As always, his car was silent for most of the ride back home.

"Daddy, do you think Momma will ever wake up?" Rhonda asked.

"I don't know baby. That's up to the man above."

"Yeah, right," Frank Jr. said, frowning.

"What's that supposed to mean, Jr.?" Rhonda said with an attitude.

"Nothing baby. He didn't mean nothing," Frank said, cutting his eyes at his son.

Although Frank was a God-fearing man, he had never tried to force his beliefs on his children. The day his mother was nearly taken away from him was the day Jr. had stopped believing in God. Frank tried to talk to his son, but it was no use, so he let it go. However, Rhonda still believed that her mother was going to pull through and Frank wasn't going to tolerate Jr. destroying her faith.

Once they were inside the house, Rhonda ran into her room and closed the door. Frank Jr. had the same idea. He was on his way up the stairs until his father stopped him in his tracks.

"Jr., come back down here and sit down, son. I want to talk to you," Frank said sternly. Reluctantly, Jr. turned and started back down the stairs. He stopped at the bottom of the steps sat down on the last one. He remained quiet as his father slowly walked over to him and stood in front of him. Frank stared at his son for a few seconds before saying anything.

"You know, if you don't believe in God, okay. I've never tried to force my religious beliefs on you before and I'm not about to do it now. But do me a favor son. Don't try to destroy your sister's faith because you don't have any."

"I'm not trying to do that, Dad."

"Regardless of whether you're *trying* to do it or not, that's what the hell you *are* doing! And I want it stopped!"

"Dad, you said that you're not going to try to force your religious beliefs on me, but it seems like you're getting mad at me because I'm not a believer."

Frank took a deep breath. He needed his son to understand that that wasn't the case. He placed his hand on Jr.'s shoulder.

"Son, I'm not mad at you because you don't believe. That's your choice. But if you sister wants to believe then let her. Stop with the snide remarks and grunts whenever she asks me something about God. Got it?"

"Yeah Dad, I got it," Jr said, as he got up and jogged up the stairs.

Frank watched as his namesake walked into his bedroom and closed his door. He then went to the couch, sat down, and grabbed the remote. He had to be at work in a few hours so he wanted to relax and enjoy his downtime while he could. He had just turned on the television and started channel surfing when his cell phone vibrated next to him on the coffee table.

"Hello?" he answered without looking at the screen.

"Hey, what's going on?"

"Not much. Just about to kick back and watch a little *Shark Tank* before I come in. You there already?"

"Not yet, but I'm on my way in. Has your cell phone been turned off?"

"Actually, it has. I always turn it off when I go see my wife."

"Oh, no wonder she called me then."

"She who? What the hell are you talking about Amber?"

"Officer Brady. She said she was walking by your desk and your phone started ringing."

"And she answered it?"

"Of course her nosy ass did," Amber said laughing.

"I'm going to have to have a talk with her. I don't need her to answer my desk phone. I have voicemail for that."

"Well, anyway, when she couldn't get a hold of you, she called me."

"Since she called you, I assume she took a message?"

"Yep. Apparently, Veronica Baker wasn't one hundred percent truthful with us when we asked her if she knew of anyone who would want to harm her fiancé."

Frank's expression remained the same. Her hesitation when he asked the question insinuated that Veronica was holding out on them about that.

"Tell me something I don't know, Amber."

"Okay. Guess who spilled the beans on who it is?"

"If I had to guess, I would say that it was probably her employee, Wendy."

"Good guess. Now let's see if you can guess who hated Kevin Broadnax enough to want to kill him."

"Beats the hell out of me."

"Me too. I guess we'll find out when we meet her. She didn't want to discuss it over the phone and she definitely didn't want to come down to the station, so she agreed to meet us at Columbo's bar and grill."

"What time?" he asked.

"In two hours."

"Okay. I'll meet you there in an hour and a half."

10

Columbo's Bar and Grill in East Cleveland was located on the corner of Noble Road and Nelamere. It was a small, cozy establishment that had been there for over thirty years. Most of the people who frequented the place were blue-collar workers who often enjoyed good food and even better conversation. Unlike many of the other eateries in the area, Columbo's only played respectable music. They rarely played rap, but whenever they did, they made sure that it was respectable with absolutely no profanity whatsoever.

The outside of the bar consisted of brown brick from front to back. The inside was not particularly large, but the place never seemed to be crowded despite that fact. On one side was nothing but rectangular tables and booth like chairs. On the other side was the bar, and twenty feet down from that was the small kitchen where the all the food was prepared. The lighting was low, giving the entire place a romantic feel to it. The marble floor had a black and white checkered design. The bathrooms were located in the back of the place, near the rear entrance. Given the small proximity of the area, it wasn't exactly ideal for the detectives to be meeting Wendy there. If anyone wanted to eavesdrop, they would be able to do so with no problem. But since she was unwilling to meet them at the police station, they had very little choice in the matter. If they wanted to hear what she had to say, it would have to be on her terms.

Frank and Amber had planned to be there before Wendy, but when they arrived and entered the building, they spotted her sitting in a booth eating a plate of French Fries. When she looked up and saw them walking toward her, she picked up her glass and took a sip of her beverage. Amber couldn't see inside the glass, but she would bet her last dollar that there was alcohol in it.

The two detectives slowly made their way over to where Wendy was sitting. When Wendy looked up and saw that Amber had tagged along, she rolled her eyes. She didn't like the woman and didn't try to hide it. Detective Stone couldn't help but notice the nervous look on Wendy's face.

"Good evening Miss Lomax. I understand you have some information for us," Detective Stone said to her.

"Yeah, something like that."

The two detectives shot a quick glance at each other. They could tell by Wendy's mannerisms that she was having second thoughts about meeting with them.

"Are you okay?" Amber asked. Wendy looked at her and smirked.

"Oh, now you wanna be nice to me, huh? Yesterday, you treated me like shit, but since you think I've got something that can help you, you wanna be nice."

Amber glared at Wendy before turning her head to Frank. The look he gave her told her all she needed to know. The two partners had been doing this for a long time, so they both knew that Frank would get more out of her if he questioned her alone.

"You know what? I'm going outside to take a smoke break. I'll be back in a few minutes," Amber said. Shaking her head, she quickly slid from the booth and made her way toward the back exit.

"I thought you quit," Frank said to her as she walked away.

"I did. But the way this woman is getting on my nerves, I need something to calm them."

"Whatever," Wendy said, waving her hand in a dismissive gesture.

"Okay, Miss Lomax—"

"What the hell is her problem?" she asked, cutting Frank off.

"Amber? Nothing. She just wants to catch the person or persons responsible for your friend's boyfriend's death yesterday."

"Well, I don't like her attitude."

Frank took a deep breath. He needed to find a way to get Wendy to concentrate on the murder of her friend's boyfriend and not on her dislike for Wendy.

"Miss. Lomax, I know that Detective Davis can be a bit brash at times, but let's remember that we're all on the same team here. She wants to apprehend the killer just as bad as you do. You *do* want to find out who killed your friend's boyfriend, don't you?"

"Yes Detective, I do."

"Okay. Then let's get down to business so we can do our jobs. The longer the killer is out there, the more the odds favor him or her getting away."

"You're right, Detective. I apologize."

"It's quite all right. Now, what do you have to tell me?"

"First, I need your word that this isn't going to go any further."

"What do you mean?" Frank asked, playing dumb.

"I mean, I don't want anyone to know that I gave you this information, especially Victoria. If she finds out that I told you what I'm about to tell you, then not only will I probably lose my job, but my best friend as well."

The detective's eyebrows shot up. The fact that she didn't want Victoria to know about this conversation put an entirely different spin on the situation. Could Amber have been right all along?

Was Victoria playing the grieving lover when she was responsible for her boyfriend's death all along? Frank didn't believe so, but it did give him another angle to consider.

"Let me get this straight. You don't want your friend to know about this conversation? May I ask why not?"

Wendy smiled. She wasn't about to fall into that trap.

"Your word, Detective. I need your word."

With a deep sigh, Frank conceded. But even though he was about to give her his word, Frank knew that he might not be able to keep it. If what she said had anything to do with Victoria being guilty, him keeping his word would go straight out the window.

"Okay, you have my word. Now, tell me who it is who has a big enough grudge against Mr. Broadnax that they would want to see him dead."

Wendy took another deep breath, lifted her glass, and took a large gulp. Just before she began to speak, she leaned across the table so that only Frank could hear what she was saying.

"Look, Victoria wasn't being completely honest with you when she said that she didn't know of anyone who would want to harm her boyfriend."

"Oh really? Now, technically, you know that we could pick her up for obstruction of justice, right?"

"No Detective. You gave me your word, remember?"

"I know I did, Miss Lomax. But you need to give me something more to go on, because the way it looks now, either your friend knows who did this and she's protecting him, or maybe she did it and is trying to put us on the wrong trail," he said, shrugging.

Wendy shook her head vigorously.

"Detective, I can vouch for Victoria. She is not a murderer," Wendy said, struggling to keep her voice down. "And she definitely wouldn't protect that asshole if she thought he was involved."

"Who, Miss. Lomax? Who are you talking about?"

"If I were you detective, the next person I would question would be Victoria's brother, Saffold."

"Victoria's brother?" Frank asked, mildly surprised. "Why would he want to kill his future brother-in-law?"

"Because he's a racist asshole! He's hated Kevin from the moment he laid eyes on him, just because he's African American."

Frank took out his note pad and jotted down Saffold's name.

"Is his last name the same as his sister's?"

"Yes."

"Do you know his address?"

"He lives in Cleveland Heights. A few blocks from her actually, on Noble Road."

Frank pushed the pen and pad across the table.

"Write down his complete address." After receiving the information, Frank left the bar and gave Amber a brief synopsis of what he'd learned.

"When do you want to question him?" she asked.

"No time like the present. I'll follow you home. We can take my car to go question that asshole."

11

Noble Road in Cleveland Heights was a nice, clean street that was always busy. This was especially true in the summertime, as young kids frequently played on the sidewalk, while the older teenage boys played football in the street. Young ladies sat on the porch with the friends talking about the boys they had crushes on. The houses were some of the nicest in the neighborhood. Most of them were single-family homes with manicured lawns and huge back yards. Nearly every house on the street had a two-car garage. The city of Cleveland Heights routinely sent housing inspectors around to ensure that the occupants maintained the upkeep of the properties.

Ninety-nine percent of the people living on the street were friendly and cordial. It wasn't uncommon to see neighbors visit each other and take each other food or gifts. The one house that didn't participate in the friendliness was the one on the corner at the far end of the street. It was the residence occupied by Saffold Baker. It was common knowledge around the neighborhood that Saffold was racist. Since the street was littered with African Americans and Caucasians, with a few Asians sprinkled in, Saffold pretty much kept to himself. He wanted nothing to do with anyone living on the street, and in turn they wanted nothing to do with him. Today was no different as Saffold sat on his porch and watched the various races of kids and young adults interact with one another.

With one leg resting on his banister and a glass of Jack Daniel's mixed with Coke in his hand, Saffold just shook his head in disgust. For no less than the fifth time since he'd awoke, his cell phone rang. He gazed at it for a few seconds before giving it the finger. There was no need for him to check the caller ID because he already knew the caller's identity. Saffold had been in a dark mood ever since his sister had flaunted in his face that she was going to bear a child by a Black man. Victoria had been calling him since he'd left the bar the previous day, but he was so pissed that he ignored every single one of them. An evil scowl had been plastered on his face ever since.

The only thing that caused him to smile was seeing the black Crown Victoria turn onto his street and slowly cruise down it. His smile got even larger when the car stopped in front of a group of African American teenage boys standing on the sidewalk. He was hoping to experience the pleasure of seeing one or all of them get slammed on the hood of the car. Disappointment set in as it continued on its way down the street. A surprised expression popped onto Saffold's face when the unmarked vehicle stopped in front of his house. That expression turned to worry when the two detectives got out of the car and made their way up the concrete steps and onto his porch. He knew that it was never a good sign when two detectives came to your home to pay you a visit.

"Good evening sir. My name is Detective Stone. This is my partner, Detective Davis. We'd like to have a word with you if you don't mind."

Saffold looked from one detective to the other as they flashed their badges.

"Uh . . . sure, Detectives. What can I help you with?"

"Do you know a man named Kevin Broadnax?"

"Yeah, I know him. Can't say that I like him though."

The two detectives glanced at each other.

"Really? Why not?" Amber asked.

For the same reason I don't like you, darkie, Saffold thought to himself.

"No particular reason. I just don't like the guy."

"Would it have anything to do with the fact that he's dating your sister?" Frank asked.

Saffold's jaw tensed. Being reminded that his sister was dating someone out of her race was something that he didn't like to be reminded of.

"Something wrong?" Amber asked, noticing the change in his expression.

"No."

"Are you sure? You seemed to get a little tense when my partner asked you about your sister dating the victim."

Saffold's face twisted. He had no idea what was going on.

"Victim? What the hell are you talking about?" he asked.

The two detectives shared another look before turning their attention back to Saffold.

"So, are you trying to tell us that you didn't know that your future brother-in-law had been murdered?"

"Murdered? You mean to tell me that he's dead?"

Saffold had to fight hard to suppress a smile. Being the bigot that he was, this was the best news he could have received. Now he knew why his sister had been ringing his phone off the hook for the last day and a half. She wanted to cry on his shoulder about her coon of a boyfriend being killed. Amber cocked her head and stared at Saffold.

"You don't seem too choked up about it."

"Why would I be? I told you that I didn't like him," Saffold said with a shrug.

"But you didn't say why."

"Like I told you Detective, I didn't have a particular reason. I just didn't like the guy."

"Oh, come on Mr. Baker. No one dislikes anyone 'just because.' There must be a reason. Maybe he did something to you to piss you off. Maybe he got into it with your sister and you stepped in as the big brother. Maybe one thing led to another and you two got into a physical altercation," Frank said.

"What are you trying to say?" Saffold asked. It had finally dawned on him why they had come to pay him a visit.

"We're not trying to say anything. We're just giving you a scenario of what we think could have happened."

"Could've but didn't! Look, I don't know who did the world a favor and got rid of that asshole, but it damn sure wasn't me! Now if there's nothing else-"

"You know, it is illegal to have an open container outside of your home," Frank said through gritted teeth. Saffold was seriously beginning to piss him off. It was bad enough that a man was dead, but to hear Saffold gloating about it caused his blood to boil.

"What?"

"I think you heard the detective," Amber said. "So, either pour out what's in that glass or go in the damn house."

Saffold smirked as he poured the remaining liquor over the railing and onto the ground below. As soon as his comment about someone doing the world a favor left his mouth, he knew it would get under their skin. Now they were screwing with him just because they could. After emptying his glass, Saffold turned and headed for his front door.

"Like I said, Detectives. If there's nothing else-"

"Actually, there is just one more thing. Where were you yesterday between the hours of two and four?"

"Excuse me?"

"Are you hard of hearing Mr. Baker? He asked you about your whereabouts between the hours of two and four pm yesterday."

Saffold smiled at the two detectives before giving them his answer.

"I left my sister's bar at about 1:45. If you don't believe me, ask my sister. She saw me leave, and her cocksucker of a boyfriend was alive when I left so you're barking up the wrong tree, Detectives."

"You know what's funny though, Mr. Saffold? Not one time have you asked how he died," Frank said.

"Maybe he already knows," Amber chimed in.

"Wow, you people just won't quit, will you? Okay, I'll bite. How did he die?"

" 'You' people huh?" Frank said with an edge to his voice.

"Yep, 'you people,' " Saffold said smiling.

Frank ignored the obvious racial connotation and continued.

"Someone sliced his neck pretty good. Cut his throat from ear to ear."

"Good for them," Saffold said, grinning wickedly.

Before the detectives could say anything else, Saffold walked into his house and slammed the door behind him. Frank stood there for a few seconds before Amber grabbed his arm and tried gently to pull him away.

"Come on Frank. Let's go."

It took Frank a few more seconds to relent, but he finally turned and followed Amber down the stairs. Once they got in the car, Amber looked at Frank and smiled.

"You do know it's not illegal for him to drink alcohol on his own porch, right?"

Frank smirked and nodded his head.

"Of course, I know that. But he doesn't."

"Franklin Stone, you are something else," Amber said as she pulled her seat belt across her chest. "So, should we keep an eye on him?"

"Not at all."

"Why not?"

"Because he didn't do it."

Christopher Speight

12

Captain Marie Snyder paced back and forth in her office with her phone pressed against her ear. Every now and then she would run her hand through her short blond hair. She'd been captain of the force for the last fifteen years and had earned the respect of not only her peers but also the chief, deputy chief and the mayor. She was no-nonsense and tough as nails. With two kids and a husband who believed that chores around the house were women's work, she had no choice but to have an iron backbone.

Marie Snyder wasn't a very big woman. She stood at a shade under five feet five inches tall and weighed one hundred twenty-eight pounds. But what she lacked in stature, she more than made up for in grit and determination. It wasn't easy to tell when she was upset because she played her feelings so close to the vest. Although Frank and Amber had both seen that side of their boss before, she never let it show regarding personal matters. Captain Snyder had a great poker face and usually kept her personal life separate from her private life. None of her coworkers ever knew what was going on with her outside of work because she never brought her home life to the job. Unfortunately for her, the situation with her husband had become toxic and it was taking a lot more effort for her to keep the two entities apart.

"I don't give damn! Do what you have to do," she screamed into the phone before pressing the end button. Frank and Amber remained quiet as their boss plopped down in her chair and crossed her legs. Ten seconds later, she took a deep breath and looked from Frank to Amber.

"Okay, what have you got for me on the Kevin Broadnax murder?"

Amber looked at Frank and nodded in his direction. In light of Captain Snyder's mood and the fact that Frank was the senior detective, she was more than willing to let him give her the details. She watched as Frank pulled out his note pad and flipped through a few pages.

"Well, ma'am, after interviewing the victim's girlfriend, a Miss Victoria Baker, we later received a call from her friend and employee, a Miss. Wendy Lomax, who informed me that she wanted to meet with us. We met with her roughly an hour ago and she had something very interesting to say about who she thought should be the prime suspect, a Mr. Saffold Baker."

The captain's eyebrows shot up. "Same last name, huh? So, who is he? Victoria's ex-husband?" she asked.

"Nope. Saffold is Victoria's brother. Apparently, he's a racist piece of crap who despises African Americans."

"Interesting. Well, tell me, Detective. You've met this clown. Does the shoe fit?"

"Not to me. I think he just likes being a racist prick."

Snyder looked at Amber. "What do you think, Detective Davis? You've been pretty quiet during this meeting."

"I agree with Detective Stone. He's definitely an asshole, but I don't think he's a killer."

"Damn! Okay, keep working on the case and let me know if anything shakes out. As a matter of fact, maybe you should pay the victim's girlfriend another visit. I don't like the fact that she knew her brother hated her man and didn't say anything about it. If she failed to mention him, there could be someone else she purposely left out of the conversation."

"Got you, Captain," Frank said. "You want us to——"

Frank couldn't get his question out fully before the ringtone on Captain Snyder's cell phone blared out. His eyebrow's shot up when he recognized the song.

"Independent Women?" Amber mumbled.

"Don't judge me! Just get the hell out of my office and find out who killed Kevin Broadnax! And close the door on your way out!"

"You just had to say something didn't you?" Frank said, shaking his head.

"My bad. Are we going to question Victoria Baker today, or do you want to wait until tomorrow to hear what kind of lie she has in store?"

"What makes you think she's going to lie?"

"Why wouldn't she? She already left out an important detail."

"That's only because she was trying to protect her brother. I can guarantee that when we talk to her, she won't be able to name anyone else."

"Then it can wait until tomorrow?"

Frank thought for a minute. Although he was ready to call it a day, he, much like his captain, also didn't like the fact that Victoria had failed to mention her brother.

"Tell you what. Let's head over to Victoria's bar. If she's there, we'll talk to her. If she's not, we'll just call it a night."

"Sounds like a plan. Let's roll."

The two detectives then headed out of the precinct, hopped in the unmarked car, and headed to *Vicky's*.

Christopher Speight

13

Victoria's right hand shook slightly as she stared into a glass of white wine. She'd been sitting in the back of her bar for the last hour crying. Her chest heaved in and out as her tears dripped into the glass. Every few seconds, she would raise the glass to her lips and prepare to take a sip. But as soon as she did, the thought of her unborn child popped into her head and quickly caused her to lower the glass back down. Thoughts of her murdered boyfriend continued to spiral through her mind. The shock of him being killed was beginning to set in, and the reality of the situation was hitting her like a freight train. Through tear-soaked eyes, she looked up to see Wendy walking toward her. With a warm, reassuring smile on her face, Wendy walked over and placed a hand on Victoria's shoulder.

"How are you holding up?" Wendy asked.

All Victoria could do was shrug weakly. A faint smile was on her face as she tried to be strong during what was one of the hardest periods of her life.

"I would say that I'm okay, but that would be a lie."

"I know sweetie, I know."

Wendy placed her hand on the side of Victoria's head and pulled it onto her shoulder. She used her other hand to wipe Victoria's tears from her face. After doing that, she slowly reached down and took the glass of wine out of her hand.

"You don't need this, my friend."

"I know," Victoria said, nodding her head in agreement. "I just don't understand this, Wendy. Who could have done such a thing? As far as I know, Kevin didn't have any enemies."

"Are you sure, Vicky? I mean, everyone has someone who doesn't like them. Haters are everywhere."

"Well, I've never met any of his. The only person who I can think of who doesn't like him is Saffold, and I know damn well he didn't do this."

Wendy took a deep breath. A tug-of-war ensued in her mind as to whether she should convey her concerns to her friend. On several occasions, Wendy had noticed the hatred in Saffold's eyes whenever Kevin was around. She didn't know if Saffold was the murderer, but she did know that he hated Kevin with a passion. Deciding that she didn't want to offend her friend, Wendy remained silent. Victoria must've felt the vibe because she turned her head and looked up to face her friend.

"What?"

"I didn't say anything."

"Exactly. You didn't say anything. You're never quiet, so I know something is on your mind when you don't talk. What is it?"

"Vicky, I really don't know if I should say what I'm thinking."

"Wendy, you're not only an employee here. I consider you my friend. No matter what you say, that's not going to change."

Wendy blew out a slow deep breath.

"Okay. . . I mean . . . and I'm just asking Vicky. How sure are you that Saffold didn't do it? It was no secret that he hated Kevin."

Victoria closed her eyes as, once again, tears began to run down her face. She'd been trying to block out the possibility that her brother was responsible for her boyfriend's death. Hearing it from someone else however, was now forcing her to at least consider it.

"Not very, Wendy, I'm not," Victoria said, crying harder now. "But I didn't want to tell the police that. If I had done that, and my brother found out, he would never forgive me."

"I understand that. But you owe it to Kevin, as well as his baby growing in your belly to find out who did this to him. Now, I hope Saffold is innocent, I honestly do but keeping things from the police isn't going to help anything."

"No, it isn't," a voice sounded out. When Victoria and Wendy turned their heads, they found Detectives Stone and Davis standing there. Lingering behind them was her manager Greg. Victoria instantly got angry. She didn't appreciate her privacy being violated.

"Detectives, is there a reason that you're standing there eavesdropping on our conversation?"

Both detectives walked over to where she sat and stood in front of her. Even though they both felt compassion for her loss, they were a little ticked off that she didn't inform them of her brother's dislike for her boyfriend.

"Miss Baker, the last time we talked to you, we asked you if there were anyone you could think of that would want to see your boyfriend harmed and you told us no. Now we find out that your brother hated him. Why did you lie?" Detective Stone asked.

"I didn't lie."

"You omitted the truth. In a murder investigation, that's the same as lying."

"Look, my brother had nothing to do with this, okay?" Even as the words left her mouth, Victoria herself was beginning to wonder. She'd tried to call her brother a number of times since the murder and he had yet to pick up his cell phone.

"And you know this how?" Amber chimed in.

"I just know!" Victoria yelled.

"First of all, Miss Baker, calm down. And second, that's not a good enough answer. If you know something you need to tell us."

Frank was starting to get aggravated. He couldn't understand why Victoria was keeping things from him.

"Okay, look, Detectives. The last time I saw my brother was the day Kevin was killed. He was leaving the bar while I was going back in, and Kevin was alive."

"How long were you in the bar?" Amber asked.

"I don't remember. Five, ten minutes maybe."

"Well, it takes less time than that to kill someone," Amber said.

Although Frank had voiced his disbelief that Saffold was the killer, she still had her doubts.

"Look, the longer you withhold information from us, the longer it's going to take for us to find your boyfriend's killer. And like Wendy said, you owe it to your murdered boyfriend as well as your unborn child to help us find the killer. Now, is there anything else that you're not telling us?"

"No," Victoria said softly. The two detectives stared at her for a few more seconds before turning and heading for the exit.

"We'll be in touch," Frank said as they disappeared through the door.

14

Although he knew that his father and sister were going to be upset about him bailing out on their family game night, Frank Jr. felt that they would just have to get over it. There would be other game nights, but if he declined Kisha's invitation to go to the movies with him, he might not get another chance. Frank Jr. liked Kisha. A lot. He'd been trying to figure out a way to ask her out for a couple of weeks but every time he got ready to do it, he got cold feet. It was just his good fortune that she liked him just as much as he liked her. He lay on his bed, with a large smile plastered on his face as he talked to Kisha on his cell phone.

"Now, I know you're going to buy me some popcorn when we get there, right?" Kisha asked.

"Of course. You know I got you," Frank Jr. said smoothly.

"Okay, I was just asking. I've heard about your cheapskate behind," Kisha said laughing.

"Cheapskate? Who in the heck told you that I was a cheapskate?"

"Don't worry about all that. I just wanted to make sure that I wasn't dating someone who didn't want to spend any money on me."

"Whatever. Don't believe everything you hear. . . Wait, did you just say that we were dating?"

"Uh, yeah, I did. You got a problem with me saying that?"

"Not at all." The smile that was already on Frank Jr.'s face got so wide that his cheeks threatened to crack. It temporarily disappeared when his bedroom door flew open, and Rhonda burst in.

"Rhonda! What the heck is wrong with you bursting in my room like that?" he yelled.

"Daddy wants to know what kind of snacks you want for the monopoly game later. It's your turn to choose."

Frank Jr. stared at his sister in anger. He wanted to get up and strangle her. The smirk on her face caused his nostrils to flare.

"Rhonda, get your nosy behind out of my room!"

"I ain't nosy," Rhonda said, right before asking her brother who he was talking to.

"None of your business! Get out of my room!"

"Not until you answer my question."

"Like I said, it's none of your business."

"Not that question, dummy. The other question. Daddy wants to know what snacks you want for game night."

"Let me call you back, Kisha."

"Is everything okay?" Kisha asked.

"Yeah. I just have to handle something with my sister right quick."

"Okay. We're still going to the movies tonight, right?"

"You doggone right, we're still going."

"Okay. I'll meet you at Richmond Mall around five thirty."

"Okay. Talk to you later." After disconnecting the call, Frank Jr. noticed the twisted expression on his sister's face.

"What the heck is wrong with you?"

"Did you say Kisha? As in Kisha Montgomery?"

"Yeah, why?"

"You talking to her now?"

"None of your business!"

"Ughhh! I can't stand that broad!"

"So what? Knowing you, she probably can't stand you either." Frank Jr. got off his bed and headed for the door.

"Like I care! And you still ain't answered my question about the snacks yet."

"And I'm not going to answer it either. Where's Dad?"

"Find him yourself, butt head," Rhonda spat as she stormed down the hallway to her room.

Waving his hand in her direction, Jr. turned to head in the opposite direction but stopped when he saw his father coming up the stairs.

"What in the world is wrong with you two? What's all this shouting about?"

"Dad, I need to talk to you about something," Jr. told his father.

"Talk to me about what?" Frank asked. His son looked back toward his sister's room and then back at his father.

"It's private."

Frank's entire expression changed. He prayed to God that his son didn't want to talk about sex. Even though he'd given him 'the talk', Frank had told his son during the talk that if he ever felt like he was ready to have sex to come and talk to him. He thought back to Sadie telling him that she'd overheard him talking on the phone and immediately started to sweat.

"Dad? Did you hear me? I need to talk to you."

"Okay, son. Let's go in the basement then."

Frank Jr. followed his father down the stairs, through the kitchen, and down into the basement. Detective Stone's basement was the typical man cave. Being that he was a lifetime Cleveland Browns fan, football paraphernalia was littered throughout. While one wall held multiple posters of Browns' legends of yesteryear, including Jim Brown, Brian Sipe, and Bernie Kosar, the one directly across from it held posters of newer heroes like Myles Garrett, Nick Chubb, and Baker Mayfield. In the middle of those two walls hung a sixty-inch big screen television. The carpet was brown, with a large orange helmet in the middle. Underneath the television hung three jerseys encased in glass. All three of them were signed by the players to whom the numbers belonged. One jersey belonged to Greg Pruitt. One belonged to Bernie Kosar. One belonged to Jim Brown. Even the furniture was brown. The place was a Browns' fan's dream. Frank Jr. had always thought that his father had gone overboard while constructing the place, but out of respect for his father's love for the team, he kept his opinion to himself.

"Have a seat son," Frank said, as he reached into the minifridge and took out a beer.

"Let me get one of those, Pop."

Shrugging his shoulders, Frank took out a second beer and extended it to his son. A surprised look dropped across his face as he reached for the bottle. His hand had almost reached it when his father snatched it back.

"Oh, I'm gonna need to see your ID first."

"Huh?"

"Your ID. What? You don't have ID?"

"Dad, you know I don't."

"Oh well. No beer for you then," Frank Sr. said, laughing.

"Man."

"Okay son. What do you want to talk to me about?" he asked nervously.

"Well, it's about game night later on."

Frank breathed a sigh of relief. For once he was relieved to be wrong.

"Oh yeah? What about it? Did your sister tell you what I said? It's your turn to pick what snacks we're having."

"I know, Dad. But the thing about it is that I'm not going to be able to play tonight."

Frank Jr. stared at his son. The three of them had been having a game night on Sunday evenings for the last six months. Frank felt that it was important for them to come together as a family and heal together after visiting his wife on Saturday, so Frank Jr. had better have a damn good reason for blowing them off.

"Son, you know how I feel about game night," Frank said, a frown on his face. "Game night is a way for us to heal after seeing your mother on Saturdays."

"I know, Dad, and I wouldn't ask to be excused if it wasn't important to me."

"Okay. So, did you make other plans or something?"

"Something like that," Jr. said, trying to contain his smile from breaking through. Frank Sr. cocked his head. It only took him a fraction of a second to realize what was going on.

"What's her name?"

"Huh?"

"You heard me. What's her name? I can't think of any other reason that you would blow off game night other than a girl."

Black Viper

Frank Jr. blushed. He didn't think that his father was going to figure it out before he'd had a chance to tell him, but he was wrong. He could no longer hold his emotions as a large grin pushed through.

"Kisha."

"Kisha, huh?"

"Yep."

"Well, you must like her a lot to let her come on between the family."

"What? Oh come on Dad. I'm not letting anyone come—"

"I'm just teasing with you son," Frank said laughing. "I guess you're gonna need some money, huh?"

"Well, now that you mention it, I could use a few bucks."

"I'm sure you can," Frank said, reaching into his back pocket for his wallet. After taking it out, he opened it up and took out two crispy twenty-dollar bills.

"Here you go son. Have a good time." Frank Jr. smiled as he reached for the money. Just as he grabbed it, his father tightened his grip on the cash.

"Don't make this a habit. From now on, you and this Kisha girl will have to go to the movies on Saturday. Sunday's are reserved for me, you, and your sister. Got it?" Frank asked with a serious look on his face.

"I got it Dad. And thanks for the money."

"No problem. What theatre are y'all going to?"

"The one at Richmond Mall."

"What time?"

"I'm supposed to meet her at five thirty."

"And just how do you plan on getting there."

"I was planning on catching the bus."

Frank rubbed his chin.

"The bus, huh? You know what? I'll run you up there."

"Cool Dad! Thanks!"

"No problem," Frank said, checking the time on his watch. "You'd better go get ready. You only have an hour."

Frank Jr. gave his father a tight hug and headed back up the stairs. His right foot had just touched the bottom step when a thought he'd had for the last six months crossed his mind. He hadn't brought it to his father yet, but in light of what they had just discussed, he felt that it was the right time to do so.

"You know Dad. I was just thinking. Maybe it's time you found someone to start going out with."

The comment nearly knocked Frank Sr. to the floor. "What did you just say??"

"No disrespect to Mom, but maybe it's time you started living your life again. I know that you and Rhonda have all this faith that a higher power will miraculously heal Mom, but I just don't believe it. Maybe it's time for you to move on."

Since he never turned back around, Frank couldn't see his son's face. The way his voice had broken, however, he had no doubt that his son had shed a few tears. Frank was speechless. Neither of his kids had ever expressed any interest in him moving on. Apparently, his son had noticed something that he himself hadn't. Frank appreciated his son's concern for him. But there was just one problem.

He wasn't ready to move on.

15

The car had barely come to a stop before Frank Jr. was reaching for the door.

"Boy what in the world is wrong with you? You can't wait until the car comes to a stop first?" his father asked.

"Oh, sorry Dad."

"How long is this movie?"

"About two hours."

"Okay. I'll be back up here to pick you up at eight o'clock. See if your girlfriend has a ride home. If she doesn't, tell her that I'll be happy to give her one."

"Girlfriend? Yeah, right. That ain't none of his girlfriend," Rhonda spat.

"You don't know that. Mind your own business, heifer!" Frank Jr. insulted his sister.

"Hey! Cut that out!" Frank yelled.

"Heifer? The heifer's the one standing out there waiting on you?" Rhonda shot back.

"Hey!! That's enough!" Frank screamed. "Jr., get your ass out of this car and go on your date!"

Frank Jr. shot Rhonda a nasty look before getting out of the car. When Frank looked back at his daughter to chastise her, he noticed that she was staring out the window. He followed her line of sight and saw that she and the young lady he assumed to be Frank Jr.'s date staring daggers at each other. Before Rhonda could even think about rolling down the window and embarrassing them, he pulled off.

"You want to tell me what that was all about?" he asked her.

"I can't stand that tramp."

"Why not?"

"I just can't."

"Teenagers," Frank mumbled to himself.

Frank Jr. watched as his father pulled out of the mall's parking lot. Slowly he turned to Kisha and looked into her eyes.

"Okay, what's going on with you and my sister?"

"What do you mean?"

"I saw the way you two looked at each other when I got out of the car. Plus, when we were on the phone earlier, and I mentioned your name, she flipped out. So like I said, what's up with you and my sister?"

Kisha took a deep breath and smiled. She liked Frank Jr. and was not about to let the prior disagreement with Rhonda mess that up.

"Look, Frank, nothing is going on with me and your sister. Just a little disagreement we had a few months ago. Now, let's go in here and enjoy this movie."

Kisha then did something that Frank Jr. never expected. She leaned forward and kissed him on the cheek. He was so shocked that he was speechless. He didn't know what the disagreement between Kisha and Rhonda was about, but whatever his sister's problem was, she was just going to have to get over it because he wasn't about to stop seeing Kisha. The two of them walked hand in hand as they entered the movie theatre. Occasionally, one would glance at the other. They continued to make goo-goo eyes at each other as they walked to the concession stand.

"Are you still going to buy me some popcorn?" Kisha asked, batting her eye lashes.

"Stop trying to butter me up."

"Butter you up?"

"Yeah, butter me up."

"Whatever. Ain't nobody trying to butter you up. But, hey, if you don't want to stick to your word—"

"Hey, I promised you popcorn, so I'm going to buy you popcorn."

After reaching into his pocket and taking out the money his father had given him, Frank Jr. paid for a large tub of popcorn and two large sodas. Being the chivalrous young man that his father taught him to be, he carried the popcorn and the drinks.

Black Viper

"Open wide," Kisha said as she grabbed a few of the kernels and popped them into his mouth. The two of them were just getting ready to go into the movie when someone spoke to them from behind.

"Ah, ain't that sweet."

When Frank Jr. and Kisha turned around, they came face to face with Kisha's ex-boyfriend, Harold. Harold was a first-class jerk who'd gotten mad at Kisha because she'd refused to put out. He was known around the school as a lady's man, so when he struck out with Kisha, it hurt his pride. Instead of sucking it up like a man and moving on, Harold decided to tarnish Kisha's reputation by claiming that the two of them had been intimate. When Kisha found out, she went ballistic and dumped him. He'd been bitter ever since.

"Oh my God! Harold, are you following me?"

"Now why in the hell would I be following you? You're old news."

"Excuse me?"

"You heard me. Old . . . news!"

Frank Jr. looked at Harold and then at Kisha. "Look here, my dude. I don't know how you two know each other, and I really don't care. But if you want to have a conversation with her, I suggest you do it on your time because right now, you're infringing on mine."

"What you say bro?" Harold said, taking a step toward Jr. Not one to back down, Frank Jr. stepped forward to meet him.

"You heard what I said."

"Okay, hold up," Kisha said, stepping between them. "Look Harold, you can call me whatever you want to call me. The fact of the matter is that you and I are over, and I'd appreciate it if you'd stop stalking me."

"Stalking you? Girl, please! Ain't nobody stalking your ass."

"Yo', man. You'd better stop talking to her like that," Frank Jr. said, balling up his fists.

"And what if I don't, punk? What are you going to do about it?"

"Hey, is there a problem over here?" a large security guard asked walking over to them. Frank Jr. and Harold continued to stare at each other, neither one willing to back down.

"Yes sir, there is a problem. Me and my friend are trying to go see a movie, but this clown here keeps bothering us," Kisha said.

The guard looked at Harold and could tell right off the bat that he was a troublemaker. His shifty eyes and sinister smirk all but said so.

"You two. Go on in and see your movie," he said to Frank Jr. and Kisha. He then turned to Harold.

"Do you have a ticket to see the movie, young man?"

Harold thought about lying but knew if he did, the guard would probably ask him to produce a ticket, which he didn't have. He'd come into the theatre for the sole purpose of causing trouble.

"Nah, I don't."

"Then you have no business being in here. Let's go," the guard said, ushering Harold out of the theatre.

16

The morning light was just starting to break through. Except for two people engaged in a fierce foot race, Euclid Creek was completely empty at this time of the day. It was the perfect scenario for the couple to settle this debate once and for all. No one would be in the way. They themselves weren't even supposed to be there. Because of construction work being done, Euclid Creek, which normally opened at eight o'clock in the morning, was now opening at nine. Since the two of them had thrown caution to the wind and went there at eight anyway, there would be no other distractions.

Serena's legs pumped up and down as she struggled to keep up with her boyfriend Mark. Sweat ran down the middle of her forehead. She inhaled and exhaled sharply, simply refusing to allow him to defeat her. It started out as an innocent challenge. Both of them had run track in high school, so naturally, they both thought they could still compete at a high level. Since they were only competing against each other and not an athlete in their prime, it was a match made in heaven. The stakes were simple. The loser had to cook dinner for the next two weeks. Usually, they shared the cooking duties, alternating every two days and although they both enjoyed doing so, neither one of them was looking forward to doing for fourteen straight days.

Mark cut his eyes at Serena and smiled. He could see the large oak tree that they'd agreed would be the finish line. He grunted and picked up the pace, causing her to match his stride.

"You good over there?" he asked Serena.

"I'm more than good," she said huffing and puffing.

"You sure? You look like you're about to pass out."

"Whatever. I'm just as fresh now as when we started this little race."

"Whatever you say. The finish line's coming up. What I want you to cook for the next two weeks is already in an email draft ready to be sent," he bragged.

"Is that right?

"Thaaattt's riiighttt."

"I hear you babe. There's just one problem with that."

"Oh yeah? And just what would that be?" he asked, breathing heavily.

"You're tired, and I'm not," she said, as she accelerated and sped away from him.

Mark uttered a curse and tried his best to catch up with Serena. She was so far ahead of him that she was able to turn around and jog backward the last ten yards of the race and still emerge victorious. After passing the oak tree, Serena continued to jog backward until she got to a wooden bench. She sat down, folded her arms, and smirked. Stunned, Mark stood in front of her with a bewildered look on his face.

"You tricked me, dammit," he said, still breathing heavily. Thirty seconds ago, he was all ready to let her know how he wanted her to cook the succulent steak he was going to demand. Now, he had to stand there and listen to her gloat.

"Tricked you? Come on babe. You know I wouldn't do a thing like that," Serena said, grinning. Although they were both slightly out of breath, Mark was by far the more exhausted of the two.

"I thought I had you," he said, sitting down next to her.

"I know you did," she said.

Mark threw his arm around Serena's shoulder and pulled her close to him. Planting a soft kiss on her temple, he gently stroked her hair. Using his thumb and forefinger, he turned her head so that they were facing each other and kissed her passionately.

"Do you know how much I love you?"

"No. How much do you love me?" she asked.

"I love you to Mars and back."

Serena laughed out loud. She loved when her man professed his love for her, even if it made him sound like the corniest man in the world.

Black Viper

"To Mars and back? Oh God, why did I even ask? Babe, I'm sorry, but you have got to be the corniest man who ever lived."

"Oh really? Just for that, I'm not going to. . .What the hell?"

"What's wrong, baby?"

Before Mark could tell Serena about the red dot he noticed when he looked down, his chest exploded. The small red dot quickly expanded into a large hole. Blood began to pour out of Mark's chest as he slumped forward. Serena screamed in terror as she watched her lover keel over. Mark collapsed to the ground and rolled over on his back. Serena slid off the bench and dropped to her knees.

"Oh my God, no!!" she screamed. "Mark! Mark, please say something!"

But Mark could no longer speak. His eyes were open, but he was no longer able to see. The bullet that entered the left side of his chest had ripped through his heart. Mark never had a chance. Serena grabbed his hand and squeezed it. She was praying for a miracle, but unfortunately, her prayers would go unanswered.

"Somebody, help me, please," Serena screamed, forgetting that they were the only two people in the park. She and Mark had both agreed to leave their cell phones at home. They wanted zero distractions. That decision was now coming back to haunt them. A sliver of hope arose when Serena looked up and saw through tear-soaked eyes a figure coming toward her.

"Please, help me," she begged.

"Oh my God, what happened?"

"I don't know. We were sitting here talking and he just fell over! I think he's been shot!"

"Who is he? Is this your husband?"

"Not yet. He's my fiancé. We're supposed to get married next year."

"I see. Well, don't worry. You two can continue your courtship in hell."

With no remorse whatsoever, the stranger then pulled out a silencer attached, semi-automatic pistol and shot Serena point blank in the face.

Christopher Speight

Black Viper

17

As he got ready for school the next day, Frank Jr. was still on cloud nine. Aside from her ex-boyfriend almost ruining their date, he'd had a fantastic time at the movies with Kisha. He still couldn't believe that she'd approached him first. But as his father had told him time and time again, he was a handsome young man. It was only natural for young ladies to be attracted to him. Over the last year, he'd grown a full two inches and now stood six feet tall. Frank Jr. had smooth brown skin and a muscular frame. He had light brown, oval-shaped eyes. His smile was very bright and charming. A light moustache was beginning to form on top of his upper lip.

After showering and getting dressed, Frank Jr. went downstairs to eat breakfast. He couldn't wait to get to school so he could brag to his friends. He wasn't the only young man in the school who had their sights set on Kisha. Even though she wasted a few weeks dealing with Harold, she was still the most sought-after young lady in the school.

"I take it you had a good time at the movies yesterday?" Frank Sr. asked, seeing the smile on his son's face.

Frank Jr. blushed. His father's question caught him off guard.

"Why are you looking all stupid?" Rhonda asked.

"Rhonda, be quiet and eat your food."

Rhonda smacked her lips, causing her father to give her a hard look.

"Sorry, Dad."

Frank Sr. stared at her for a few extra seconds before turning his attention back to his son. He'd never tolerated disrespect from either of his children and he wasn't about to start now.

"Well, did you?" he asked Frank Jr.

Frank Jr. cut his eyes at his sister. He really didn't want to talk about anything in front of her. His father caught the hint and changed the subject.

"Rhonda, when is your next play?"

"I don't know, Daddy. I'll have to ask Mrs. Turner today."

"Okay. Just let me know. And by the way, after school today, I want you to go next door and thank Sadie for coming to your play. She told me to tell you that she was really proud of you."

"For real?" Rhonda said, beaming.

"Yep. She thinks that you're the next Angela Bassett."

"Oh please," Frank Jr. said, laughing.

"Whatever, hater. You're just mad that you don't have any talent."

"Hey, I got talent. I'm going to be the next Floyd Mayweather, ain't that right Dad?"

"Yeah, right," Rhonda said, rolling her eyes.

"I bet you I'll be a champion boxer before you become an actress."

"I bet you won't."

"Bet!"

"Bet!"

"Okay, you two, that's enough. Hurry up and finish eating. It's almost time to go."

Frank got up from the table and left his two bickering children sitting there. Although he would never admit it to them, he loved to see his kids competing with each other. Whether it be in cards, boardgames, or talking about how successful they would be when they became adults, they were always trying to outdo each other. Frank felt that it brought out the best in them so instead of discouraging it, he encouraged it.

Ten minutes after leaving their house, Frank was dropping his kids off at school. He gave each of them five dollars apiece for lunch money and sent them on their way. He watched closely as they walked up the sidewalk and made their way toward the school's entrance. When they were halfway there, he pulled off.

From the time they got out of their father's car, Frank Jr. and Rhonda both remained quiet. They continued to do so until they got to Rhonda's locker. Neither of them cared for their father's demand that Frank Jr. walk his sister to her locker every day. But Frank Sr. wanted to make sure that Rhonda was going to be protected, so he gave his son the task of escorting her to her locker daily.

"Rhonda, what is your problem?"

"Frank, what are you talking about?"

"You've been acting crappy ever since yesterday. Did I do something to you?"

"You're imagining things, big brother."

"No, I'm not."

Frank Jr. thought back to the day before and it suddenly dawned on him exactly when his sister started acting like a jerk.

"Ooooh, now I know what it is. For some reason, you're mad because I went to the movies with Kisha. What have you got against her?"

"I just don't like her, bro."

"Why?"

"I just don't. Do I have to have a reason? Dang!"

"Uh, yeah, you kinda do."

"Well, I don't."

"Bull crap! No one dislikes someone for no reason at all. There has to be a reason."

Rhonda took a deep breath and slammed her locker shut. With fire in her eyes, she turned to face her brother. "Okay, I do have a reason. I'm just not going to tell you," she said and stormed off.

All Frank Jr. could do was stand there and shake his head. By arguing with his sister, he'd cut down the time he had left to get to his homeroom. As he turned to leave, he spotted Harold and a couple of his friends walking on the opposite side of the hallway. The two of them eyed each other. Harold cupped his hand and whispered into one of his friend's ear. The friend responded by slamming his fist into his palm a couple of times. The gesture caused Frank Jr. to burst into laughter.

"What's so funny, punk?"

"You and that clown you're walking with."

"Oh, I see you want some smoke, huh?" Harold said.

Every kid in the hallway stopped as he started a slow walk toward Frank Jr.

"You ain't said nothing but a word." Frank took off his backpack and was about to lay it on the floor.

"I'll hold that for you, man," someone standing behind Frank said. When Frank turned to look, the right corner of his lip twisted into a smile. Reaching for his bag was his best friend Wallace. Other than Rhonda, Wallace was the only person in the entire school that knew Frank was taking boxing lessons. This fight was going to be a mismatch, and he was the only one, aside from Frank Jr. himself, who knew it.

"Looks like I arrived just in time. Now it can be a fair one," Wallace said when he saw Harold's friend.

"Hey, you ain't got nothing to do with this, man," Harold said.

"Neither does your boy, but from the look on his face, he can't wait to get involved. That two on one stuff ain't happening. If they throw down, it's going to be a fair fight."

"Man, please! I don't need nobody to put the beatdown on this chump," Harold bragged.

"Let's do this then, fool! Don't talk me to death!"

Frank Jr. knew that he would have to face his father's wrath if he got suspended. He also knew that his father wouldn't be happy if he backed down. Frank Sr. had always told him not to start a fight, but never back down from one. A half second after the two of them threw up their hands, the assistant principal made his way through the crowd.

"Hey, what's going on here? Does someone want to get suspended today?"

Frank Jr. and Harold dropped their hands and walked away from each other, but they continued to eye each other until they were no longer visible to each other.

18

Because they had to hurry and get to their respective homerooms, Frank Jr. didn't have time to explain to his buddy why he and Harold were about to throw down. But now that they were in gym class, Wallace was putting pressure on him to reveal what was going on.

"Man, what was all that about?"

"Man, that clown was just salty because he saw me at the movies with Kisha. You know they went out a couple of times."

"Wait. . .What? Man, you didn't tell me you had a date with fine ass Kisha."

"I hadn't seen you yet. I didn't want to talk about it on the phone, so I figured that I would tell you in school today."

"Damn, man. How in the hell did you pull that off?"

"Man, she came after me."

"What? Man, get the hell outta here."

"Nah, for real, man, I ain't lying. She slipped me her number in English class and asked me to call her."

"Man, you lucky! Kisha is the finest broad in this school!"

"I know, right?"

"Stone! Grant! Get up and join the group! It's time to run the mile!" the gym teacher, Maurice Howard yelled out. He was also the track coach and was always on the lookout for a potential track star in one of his classes. Frank Jr. knew this, and because he absolutely hated running, he always did less than his best for fear of being recruited. In his opinion, he ran enough while learning how to box. Eight laps around the track equaled one mile. Frank Jr. purposely slowed up the last two laps. He didn't want to take the chance that his gym teacher was going to pester him about joining the track team. Thinking that his ploy had worked, Frank Jr. headed for the locker room after class. His lunch period was next, and he couldn't wait. Running that mile had built up his appetite. Just before he walked through the locker room doors, his gym teacher called out to him.

"Hey, Stone, come here for a second!"

Frank Jr. and Wallace frowned as they headed back toward Mr. Howard.

"What the hell does he want?" Wallace mumbled. As soon as they were within normal talking range, Howard addressed both young men.

"Grant, why are you here? I didn't call you. I called Stone."

"Oh, my bad. Peace out dawg. I'll see you at lunch." Wallace quickly scampered away, grateful that he didn't have to stand there and listen to his gym teacher.

"What's going on, Mr. Howard?"

"Stone, how long are we going to play this little game?"

"Huh? What are you talking about, sir?"

"I'm talking about you slowing up on purpose with two laps left to go in the mile."

Frank Jr.'s mouth fell open. He had no idea that his gym teacher was even paying attention to him, let alone figured out that he was slacking off.

"Don't look so surprised Stone. You think I just started teaching yesterday? You're not the first person to get bad times in the mile because they don't want to run track."

"I'm sorry Mr. Howard. I just don't like running."

"How do you know? Have you ever run track before?"

"No sir."

"Then how in the world do you know that you don't like it?"

"Mr. Howard, I just don't like running far like that."

"Who said you had to run far? Son, track is more than running the mile. There's the one-hundred-meter dash. The two-hundred-meter dash. The discus throw. The four-hundred-meter relay. It's not just the mile run. You have several options to chose from."

Mr. Howard placed a gentle hand on Frank Jr.'s shoulder. "Just think about it, okay?"

"Okay sir. I'll think about it."

Black Viper

Mr. Howard smiled and walked away. As soon as he did, Frank Jr. hurried into the locker room to change back into his regular school clothes. Thanks to his gym teacher, his stomach had begun to rumble. He got dressed as fast as he could and ran out of the gym. On his way to the lunchroom, his cell phone vibrated. He took it out of his pocket and checked the text message. Rage overcame him as he silently read Wallace's message.

Hey, man. You need to get here. This clown Harold just dumped a carton of milk on your sister's head.

Christopher Speight

19

After dropping his kids off at school, Frank decided to call his partner and see if she wanted to get some breakfast before they went to work. The call went directly to her voicemail. Although he thought that was unusual, Frank just shrugged his shoulders and ended the call.

"Oh well, I guess I'm going solo today," he mumbled.

Frank drove half a mile up the street and made a right into the parking lot of The Sidewalk Café. It was a small, cozy restaurant just off the freeway. Frank and Amber would occasionally meet there before their shifts and fill their bellies. It was their favorite place to get food before they went out into the world to fight crime. The thing Frank liked most about the place, however, was that they sold the kind of food that he would cook in his own kitchen. Grits, oatmeal, ham, biscuits, pancakes, and things of the like were all sold at The Sidewalk Café. It wasn't that he couldn't get that type of food anywhere else in the area. But at The Sidewalk Café, he could get them all in one place. He also liked their prompt service when he ordered food to go.

As Frank entered the restaurant, he thought about ordering his food to go. The place was a little more crowded than it usually was, which made it louder. That, in itself, was enough to get on Frank's nerves. He didn't like a lot of excessive noise. Against his better judgment, he sat down at one of the tables. Two minutes later, a young, attractive waitress walked over to him and offered him a menu. Since he'd never seen her in the restaurant before, Frank assumed that she was a new employee.

"Good morning. Do you need a menu?"

"Nah, I know what I want."

It was an innocent enough statement, but the way it came out, combined with Frank's baritone voice, made it sound sensual.

"Is that right?" the waitress asked, lifting her right eyebrow.

She was very attractive with honey-colored skin, a thin waist, chestnut eyes, and a very ample bosom. Her jet-black hair was pulled back into a ponytail. The only flaw to be seen in her was a chipped upper front tooth, but her other attributes more than made up for her broken bicuspid.

"Uh, yes," Frank said, purposely twisting the wedding ring on his finger. He'd been around long enough to know when a female was flirting with him. Although he was a middle-aged man with two kids and a wife, his physical stature still made him desirable to most females. Frank was a shade over six foot one with a short Afro that carried a hint of gray on both sides. His muscular frame carried a weight of two hundred fifteen pounds. His thick mustache was always kept neatly trimmed. Before he could inform the waitress of his order, his cell phone vibrated. Frank raised his index finger, indicating to the waitress that he needed a second.

"Hello?"

"Yeah, it's me," Amber said.

"You okay?" Frank asked. He thought he heard a quiver in her voice.

"Yeah, I'm fine."

It was fairly evident that something was bothering her, but Frank wasn't about to pry.

"Okay. Where are you?"

"On my way to work. What's up?"

"Well, I was wondering if you wanted to stop at The Sidewalk Café before work."

"Sounds like a plan. I'll see you in a few minutes. Order for me. You know what I like."

Amber hung up and wiped her eyes. She was an emotional wreck. She knew that she had no business going to work, but in her line of employment, she had to keep her game face on at all times. Shortly after leaving Vicky's the previous day, she'd received a call from her ex-husband.

"Amber, we need to talk," he said.

Black Viper

Thinking that it was his sneaky way of trying to get into her pants, she blew him off. "Roger, I don't have time to come over there for your BS. Whatever you want, tell me on the phone."

"No, I can't. We need to talk about this face to face."

"Well, that's just too bad. I'm tired, and I'm going home. Whatever you want is going to have to wait until tomorrow."

"Amber, it's important."

"So is getting my damn rest. So, you can just——"

"Amber, it's about our son," he said, cutting her off.

"What? What's going on, Roger? Is there something wrong with my son?"

"I had to take him to emergency earlier today."

"Emergency? What happened?"

"His migraines returned," Roger informed her.

"What? I thought the doctor said he was cured from having them. And why in the hell didn't you call me?"

"First of all, I did call you! Your voicemail was full! I tried to call you again this morning when I took him to see his primary doctor and your voicemail was still full, so if you want to get mad at someone, then get mad at yourself," he'd told her.

Amber had tried to call her son, but he wasn't picking up. She'd left him a message begging him to call her and it was killing her that he hadn't.

Ten minutes after hanging up from Frank, Amber pulled into the restaurant and parked. She made sure to wipe her tears away before getting out of the car. The last thing she wanted was for Frank to see her in an emotional state, and she definitely needed to get herself together before they got to work.

Amber got out of the car and made her way into The Sidewalk Café. Her growling stomach reminded her that she hadn't had anything to eat for the last sixteen hours. As soon as she entered the place, the intoxicating aroma of food seized her sense of smell. She walked over to where her partner was sitting, dropped into the chair, and quickly dug into her food.

"Well good morning to you too," Frank said when she didn't speak.

"Oh, I'm sorry partner. Good morning."

"Hungry?"

"Starving. I haven't had anything to eat since before we went to interview Victoria Baker yesterday."

"Wow. I guess you are hungry then," Frank said, laughing.

"Excuse me, sir. Would you like some more coffee?" the waitress asked.

"Uh yes, thank you."

The waitress alternated her gaze between Frank and the coffee cup as she poured. While she was doing that, Amber's eyes were locked on her. The waitress, however, never gave Amber a second look. As soon as she refilled Frank's cup, she smiled at him before turning to walk away. When Amber looked back at Frank, she saw that he was busy looking at his cell phone. Shaking her head, she snorted out a laugh.

"What's so funny?" Frank asked her when he noticed her gaze.

"The male species."

"Excuse me?"

"You heard me. You men are funny as hell."

"Amber, what the hell are you talking about?"

"Can't you tell when a woman is interested in you? That heifer was flirting with you."

"Wow. You think so?" he said sarcastically.

Immediately, Amber picked up on his tone.

"Don't be a smart ass, Frank."

Now it was Frank's turn to laugh. "I'm not being a smart ass, but don't you think I know that? I wasn't born yesterday, Amber. I definitely know when a woman is flirting with me."

"Oh, okay. I mean, you didn't react to her."

"That's because I'm not interested in her. Did you forget that I was still married?"

"Not at all."

An awkward silence hung in the air before either of them said anything else. Although they were partners, they rarely discussed Frank's marital situation. Amber knew that it was still very painful for

Frank to talk about the accident that left his wife in a coma, but she did wonder if Marilyn was progressing.

"How is she?"

"About the same."

"Sorry to hear that."

"Me too. So have you thought anymore about the case?" Frank asked, purposely changing the subject.

"Actually, I do have another theory about the murder. What if Wendy is the guilty party?"

Frank gave Amber a strange look.

"Hear me out," she said, seeing his expression. "Wendy not only works for Victoria, but the women also seem to be pretty good friends. And what do female friends talk about the most? Men! What if Victoria had a habit of bragging about how wonderful her man was, and Wendy got curious. Maybe Victoria bragged to her about how good he was in the sack and Wendy decided to find out for herself."

"What? You mean to tell me that you women actually sit around and talk about how good men are in the sack?"

"You mean to tell me that you didn't know that?" Amber said, twisting the right side of her lip.

"Of course I did. I'm just being funny because most women say they don't do that."

"Well, they're lying. Anyway, after hearing about how good her friend's man is in the sack, Wendy puts the pressure on him to give her a roll in the hay. He sees this as an opportunity to screw his girlfriend's best friend. What man can turn that down, right?"

Amber paused for a few seconds. Purely out of curiosity, she wanted to see how Frank felt about such a thing. When Frank didn't respond, she continued.

"So, Wendy and the boyfriend agree to meet a few times to scratch their itch. But then something happens that Wendy never expected. Her feelings get involved and she falls in love with him, but he doesn't feel the same way. What started out to both of them as having a little fun changed when her feelings for him did, but she can't bear to watch another woman, especially her best friend, have the man she wants. And remember, she would have to sit back for the rest of her life and stew over the fact that her best friend is screwing a man she wants on a nightly basis. What do you think?"

Frank leaned back in his chair and thought for a moment. He ran his hand across his face and looked up toward the ceiling.

"Well, it is an interesting theory, but I didn't get the feeling that Wendy had any romantic interest in the victim. From what I could see, she really wants to be there for her friend."

"She could be faking it. It wouldn't be the first time we've run across a vengeful woman trying to gain revenge on a man that has done her wrong."

"True." Frank continued to think about his partner's theory as he used the knife and fork to cut his pancakes into pieces. He picked up the bottle of maple syrup and watched as it slowly came out of the bottle and streamed down onto his plate.

"Well?" Amber asked, anxious to know his thoughts.

"Okay, let's say that your theory is somewhat correct. Hell, let's say that it's all the way correct. There's just one problem with your it. There is no way to prove anything you just said."

"Yeah, I know. That's the frustrating part," Amber acknowledged. "What the hell is that?" Amber asked, looking past Frank and out of the window. When Frank turned around to see what she was referring to, she stuck her fork into a piece of his turkey sausage resting on his plate and popped it into her mouth.

"Oh, never mind. I thought I saw a deer run through the parking lot."

Frank looked at her and cocked his head. "A deer?"

With a smile and nod, Amber quickly chewed up the food and swallowed it. Frank stared at her for a few seconds before breaking into a wide smile.

"Detective Davis, why are you trying to play me?"

"What are you talking about, Detective Stone?"

"You think I don't know how many pieces of sausage I had on my plate?"

Amber broke into laughter. "Hey, I was trying to save you."

"Is that right? And just how were you trying to do that?"

"By lowering your cholesterol. Do you know how much grease was in that one piece of sausage I snatched off your plate?"

"I can't say that I do, but I do know how full of shit you are!"

Frank got up from the table laughing out loud. He walked toward the back of the restaurant and headed toward the restroom. While he was gone, the waitress came back over.

"Do you know if the gentleman wanted more coffee or not?" she asked Amber.

"No, he's good. Hubby never drinks more than two cups of coffee in a day."

"Hubby?" the waitress asked, disappointedly.

Amber smiled wickedly.

By this time, Frank was making his way back to the table. The moment he got there, he could tell the vibe had changed. A small degree of tension floated in the air as he sat back down.

"Something wrong, ladies?"

"Not at all sir. I was just about to pour you another cup of coffee, but your wife told me that you never drank more than two cups a day."

Frank's eyebrows shot up. "Is that right?"

"Yes honey. You know how your acid reflux acts up when you have too much caffeine."

Amber batted her eyes at Frank, who just shook his head.

"You heard the wife. No more coffee."

"Yes sir."

The waitress quickly removed the dishes from the table and left. As soon as she was out of earshot, Amber doubled over in laughter.

"Amber, why did you do that?"

"Do what?"

"You know what. Why in the world did you tell that young lady I was your husband?"

"I didn't tell her that. I said *hubby* never has more than two cups. I didn't say *my hubby* never has more than two cups. Besides, if she thinks you're married, you don't have to worry about her bothering you again."

"Maybe, maybe not."

The change in the waitress's mood was evident when she came back over and placed the bill on the table. After giving Frank a light smile, she rolled her eyes at Amber and walked away.

"Wow, somebody looks upset," Amber said.

After examining the bill, Frank took his wallet out of his pocket and pulled out two twenty-dollar bills. The price of the meal was only twenty-three dollars but because the waitress made Frank feel good by flirting with him, he decided to leave a very generous tip. Frank loved his wife very much, but like any other man, having his ego stroked appealed to him. As he and his partner headed for the exit, Frank glanced over his shoulder. It wasn't a surprise to him to see the waitress staring at him. Frank didn't want to give the young lady a false sense of hope, so he quickly turned and hurried out the door.

20

"I still can't believe you allowed that waitress to think we were married," Frank said as he held the door open for Amber.

"I can't believe you're still on that. What? You trying to get with her or something?" Amber asked. Her voice was a little sharper than she intended it to be, and Frank picked up on it.

"What the heck is wrong with you?" he asked.

Realizing that she may have sounded a bit harsh, she softened her stance. "Nothing, partner. I'm just saying."

Amber forced a smile. She had to be very careful not to let her personal feelings for her partner show. Ever since she'd been transferred to Frank's precinct, Amber had secretly had a crush on him. Although she did feel bad for Frank after his wife suffered that terrible accident, she had pretty much made up her mind that she would go after him when the time was right.

"Well, you can stop just saying. That young lady is young enough to be my daughter."

"Oh, I'm sure she doesn't give a damn about that."

The two detectives made their way to their respective desks. They were just about to sit down and get to work on the Kevin Broadnax case when Captain Snyder's door flew open.

"Stone! Davis! Get in here!"

Frank and Amber looked at each other, confused. Judging from her tone, Frank could tell that whatever his boss had to say was important.

"Close the door," she said when they entered her office. Frank noticed an exasperated look on his boss's face. Whatever she was about to tell them wasn't going to be good news.

"What's up Captain?" Amber anxiously asked.

"I'm going to need the two of you to get out to Euclid Creek."

Snyder opened her mouth to continue but Amber cut her off. "Euclid Creek? What's going on there?"

"Davis, if you give me a damn second, I'll tell you."

"Sorry, ma'am."

"Now, like I was saying. I'm going to need you two to get out to Euclid Creek. Someone jogging in the area stumbled upon two bodies. A man and a woman. Both deceased."

"Uh, okay," Frank said.

"Something wrong, Bama?" Captain Snyder asked. It was a name that she often called him in reference to his being born in Alabama.

"No ma'am. I just thought that you would want us to concentrate on the Kevin Broadnax murder."

"I do. But I also want you to check this one out. Since both murders happened within a couple of days of each other, maybe there's a correlation between the two. If there isn't, I'll put someone else on it. If there is, it's in your laps."

"Okay Cap. We're on it. Let's roll Amber."

"Oh, and Detectives? The next time you two stop off to get breakfast, I expect to be digging into a stack of pancakes five minutes after you arrive at work."

"How in the hell did you know we stopped to get breakfast?" Frank asked.

The captain simply smiled and pointed to his shirt. Frank reached down with two fingers and pulled his shirt out far enough to look down at it. He frowned when he saw the small drop of syrup lying on it.

"You got it Captain. Pancakes on us next time. Now I know what to get you for Christmas, Frank," Amber said, laughing.

"Oh yeah? And just what would that be?"

"A bib," she said, as she headed out of the captain's office ahead of him.

Euclid Creek was roughly two miles from the precinct, so it didn't take them long to get there. After parking, the detectives got out of their car and surveyed the area. As they expected, a plethora of police officers was doing their best to contain the scene. At least twenty spectators were gathered around trying to figure out what happened, and nearly all of them were trying to get a look at the bodies.

"Look at all these damn people. I'll bet you twenty dollars to a doughnut that not one of them saw anything," Amber said.

"Hell, you could make it a thousand dollars to a bucket of piss and I wouldn't take that bet," Frank said.

The two detectives carefully walked across the dewed grass. Their seasoned eyes scanned the area for clues. Their faces were solemn as they walked under the yellow tape and focused on the two bodies.

"Good afternoon Detectives. We gotta stop meeting like this," Timothy Jordan joked. He was hoping to ease the tension in the situation but the only thing his comment garnered were hard stares from the two detectives.

"Sorry. Just trying to lighten the mood."

"Lighten the mood? If it were one of your loved ones lying there dead, would you want the officer's working on the case to 'lighten the mood'?" Amber asked.

Officer Jordan looked from one detective to the other. His mouth suddenly got dry. He was practically a rookie and here he was getting on the wrong side of two detectives because he was trying to lighten the mood. The detectives continued to stare at him for a few more seconds before they both broke into a sly grin.

"We're just messing with you Tim," Frank said, placing his hand on his shoulder. "But remember, it's much different when you have to deliver this devastating news to the victim's families.

"That is not a fun conversation at all," Amber chimed in.

"Does it get any easier?" Jordan asked.

"Telling someone that their loved one is gone forever? No. It never gets easier doing that. As a cop, you just get used to it. What's the deal here?"

"One GSW to the chest for him. One GSW to the forehead for her. Neither of them ever had a chance."

Frank bent down and examined the bodies. While he was doing that, Amber pulled on a pair of gloves and took a plastic bag out of her pocket. Her eyes scanned the ground and after several minutes, she found what she was looking for. Using the end of an ink pen, she scooped a spent cartridge off the ground and placed it in the bag. She looked around for a while longer but was only able to find one shell.

"Just from the shape of the wound, I have to say that they were shot with two different guns. The hole in his chest is much larger than the one in her forehead, even though she was shot at close range and he wasn't."

"How do you know that?"

"Know what?" Frank asked.

"That he was shot from far away and she was shot at close range."

"Oh brother," Amber said as she rolled her eyes, just before shaking her head. "I keep forgetting that you're still a rookie."

"Take it easy Amber. The young man has to learn. To answer your question Tim, there are a couple of reasons I said that. One, Detective Davis found only one shell. Had both victims been shot at close range, she would have found both the shells. Also, I've seen enough gun shot wounds to know that the one this man suffered was inflicted by a rifle. Hers was inflicted by a simi-automatic pistol. A .9-millimeter Caliber."

"Oh, okay," Timothy said sheepishly.

"Don't worry about it, kid. You'll get the hang of this police thing," Amber told him.

While Amber engaged Timothy in light banter about police work, Frank's mind traveled back to the Kevin Broadnax murder scene. Captain Snyder had told him to see if the two cases were related, but he hadn't found anything to lead him in that direction so far.

"Did you check their ID?" Amber asked, breaking his train of thought.

"Yeah. The man's name is Mark Burton. The woman's name is Serena Carter. Their addresses are the same, but I don't think they are married. Neither one of them is wearing a wedding ring."

"So what do you think? Are we dealing with a serial killer here?"

"I think it's too early to tell. I can't find anything that connects these two murders to the one we investigated the other day. It looks like we'll be handing this off to someone else."

Frank watched the coroner's truck pull into Euclid Creek's entrance. Although nothing was connecting the two cases, a nagging feeling burned in the pit of his stomach. The connection was there. He felt it. Now all he had to do was figure it out. His cell phone vibrated in his pocket, interrupting his thoughts.

"Hello?"

"Yes, is this Mr. Stone?"

Frank instantly became irritated. He could never understand why someone would call a particular person's phone and then ask if they were that person. He thought it was stupid.

"Yes, this is Mr. Stone," he said, annoyed.

"Mr. Stone, this is Grace Ponder, principal of St. Joseph's High School. I'm calling to inform you that Frank Jr. got into a fistfight today and I need you to come down here so we can sort this mess out."

"A fistfight?"

"Yes, and apparently your daughter was involved."

"I'm on my way."

Christopher Speight

21

Frank Jr. sat in a chair in the office fuming. He and his sister were constantly at each other's throats, but when it came to anyone else harming or disrespecting her, that's where he drew the line. His fists were balled up tightly. His eyes were narrowed into slits. His heated gaze was aimed directly at Harold, who sat approximately twenty-five feet across from him.

Harold's face was a bloody mess. A large horizontal cut was visible over his right eye. A blood splattered cloth was pressed against it, restricting the flow of blood. His lip was split down the middle, and although it wasn't bleeding his nose was slightly swollen. Frank Jr. had beaten the stuffing out of him. Had it not been for the three-hundred-pound security guard standing between them, Frank Jr. would have gone after him again. He hadn't planned on getting into a fight but the moment he saw his sister sitting there with tears in her eyes and Harold laughing, he lost it.

According to his friend Wallace, Harold had tried to strike up a conversation with Rhonda. He knew that she and Frank Jr. were siblings and planned to get even with him because he was dating Kisha. His intentions weren't pure, and Rhonda saw right through him. She'd told him in no uncertain terms to get lost. It angered him when his friends laughed at him, prompting him to pour milk on top of her head. That was when Wallace texted Frank Jr. When Wallace finally pulled Frank Jr. off Harold, he was a thoroughly beaten young man.

Frank Jr. rocked in his chair. More than anything, he wanted to give Harold another beating. He knew that he would to have to incur the wrath of his father, but once he told him he did it to protect his sister, he was sure that his father would understand. At least he hoped he would. He was still glaring at Harold when Frank Sr. walked into the office. After looking at his son and the other young man, Frank had to work hard to suppress the smile that threatened to break through. He gave his son a stern look as he walked up to the desk.

"May I help you?" the silver-haired secretary asked. She was an older Hispanic woman who was two years short of retirement and couldn't wait to get away from the headache of dealing with other people's kids.

"Yes, I'm Detective Franklin Stone. I received a call from Principal Ponder informing me that my son had gotten into some kind of fight."

Frank knew he didn't have to reveal the fact that he was in law enforcement. He only did it to put a measure of fear into the young man with whom Frank Jr. had gotten into the fight with. He knew it was petty, but he couldn't help himself. The receptionist picked up a phone and paged the principal to the office. While she was doing so, Frank walked over to Jr., leaned down, and whispered in his ear.

"You'd better have a good reason for fighting in this school and risking suspension."

"I do," Frank Jr. answered, still glaring at Harold.

"Stop staring at that young man like that. This is over, you understand?"

"Yes sir."

Five seconds later, the door opened, and Principal Ponder walked in. Since Frank Jr. had never gotten in any trouble at school before, the principal had never met Frank Sr. After noticing the resemblance, she assumed correctly that Frank Jr.'s father had arrived.

"Good afternoon, Mr. Stone. Please follow me into my office."

The principal lead Frank through a set of glass double doors and into a medium sized office. She closed the door and made her way behind a brown wooden desk. Although he was there to find out what had led up to the physical altercation between his son and the other young man and what punishment he would receive, Frank couldn't help but notice how attractive Grace Ponder was.

She was rather tall for a woman, standing six foot even and weighing a hundred eighty pounds. She was thick in all the right places and had naturally curly hair that usually hung down to her shoulders. On this particular day however, she had it pulled back into a ponytail.

Black Viper

Her charcoal-gray business suit fit her perfectly, hugging her every curve. Because she was insecure about her height, Principal Ponder often wore flat-soled shoes. She had a perfect set of teeth with full lips connected to a very beautiful face. Her bronze-colored skin was smooth and blemish free. The only flaw on her otherwise perfect appearance was a small scar behind her right ear. The scar stemmed from an altercation she had with her ex-husband, Myron. He was a raging alcoholic who got his kicks by beating on women. It only took Grace Ponder three months of marriage to discover what kind of monster he was, and she quickly divorced him.

Frank watched as Principal Ponder eased into her seat. She was by far the most attractive woman that he'd seen in a long time. She reminded him of Naomi Campbell. To contend with the fact that he was in the presence of a beautiful woman, Frank did what he always did in that situation. He used his thumb to rub his wedding band. It was his way of warding off the beauty and charms of any other woman. Although he would never admit it to anyone, Frank did get lonely at times, but he wasn't about to be unfaithful to his wife.

"Please, Mr. Stone, have a seat. "Normally, I would just suspend——"

Principal Ponder hesitated when she spotted Frank's firearm peeking from underneath his jacket. Frank smiled, reached into his jacket pocket, and pulled out his badge.

"Oh, you're a cop."

"Detective," he corrected her.

"I see. Well, like I was saying, normally, I have a zero tolerance policy for fighting and would suspend both parties for five days. Since your son had never been in any trouble in this school, I'm inclined to reduce his penalty to five days of alternative learning. The only problem with that is that I have to give Harold the same punishment."

Frank noticed the look on Principal Ponder's face as she said this. It was apparent to him that Harold was a thorn in her side.

"Well, I haven't had a chance to talk to my son, so I don't know what happened. Would you fill me in, please?"

Principal Ponder leaned back in her chair and steepled her hands together. Just as Frank had been checking her out earlier, she was now doing the same to him. A disappointed look washed over her face as she glanced down and noticed his wedding ring. It was also refreshing to her to hear a parent being so polite. She usually had to deal with parents swearing at her and blaming her for their kids' lack of discipline and inability to control their emotions.

"According to his friend, Wallace, Harold poured milk on top of your daughter's head and when your son found out about it, he beat Harold up."

"Wait. Are you telling me that asshole out there did something to my daughter? Where is she? Is she okay?"

"She's fine, Mr. Stone. Just a little embarrassed about having milk poured into her hair. I let her go to the restroom to get herself together, then sent her back to class."

Hearing that his daughter was fine took some of the tension out of Frank's voice. "Well, I apologize for my son's behavior, but I can't apologize for him taking up for his sister. I've always told him to look out for her."

Principal Ponder leaned forward. She wanted to be sure that no one other than her and Frank would be able to hear what she was about to say.

"Off the record, I'm glad your son beat the hell out of that boy. He has given me nothing but problems since he's been here. He and his mother. It's not my first go 'round with him, and I'm sure that it won't be my last."

Loud shouting coming from the office waiting area caught Frank's and Principal Ponder's attention.

"Here we go," she said, rising from her seat.

"What's going on out there?"

"If I had to guess, it's probably Harold's mother. Every time he gets in trouble, she comes up here and causes a scene. For some reason, she can't get it through her head that her son is a troublemaker."

Shaking her head, Principal Ponder walked out of her office, followed closely by Frank.

"What is going on out—Hello Ms. Green," Principal Ponder said when she saw Harold's mother. Yolonda Green was rail-thin with short cropped hair. The security guard was standing between her and

Frank Jr. Quickly realizing what was going on, Frank moved next to his son. He had no intentions of putting his hands on a female, but he wasn't going to let her assault his son either.

"Hello, Principal Ponder. Could you please tell me why my son is sitting over here all bloodied the hell up?"

"It's like I told you on the phone. He got into a fight and—"

"I can see he got into a fight! What I want to know is what you plan on doing about it."

"Both parties will be in an alternative learning environment for the next five days. I normally issue an out-of-school suspension but wanted to give them a break," the principal lied.

Ms. Green looked from her son to Frank Jr. and frowned. "Why is my son being punished? He seems to have gotten the worse end of this."

"He also started the whole thing, Ms. Green. If you want to go that route, then technically, your son should get the worse end of the punishment, but I believe in being fair. Both parties are guilty, so, like I said, starting tomorrow both parties will be in an alternative learning environment for the next five days."

"You know what? Fine! But I'm getting tired of this school blaming everything on my son. It's always something with this place."

Ms. Green then turned her gaze on Frank Sr. "And you, I'd appreciate it if you tell your son to keep his hands off mine."

"Then tell your son to keep his hands off my daughter," Frank responded.

"My son didn't touch your damn daughter!"

"The hell if he didn't!"

Yolonda Green turned and looked at her son.

"Harold, did you put your hands on this man's daughter?"

"No ma'am," he lied.

Frank Jr. took a step toward him but was restrained by his father.

"See! I told you my son didn't do what he's being accused of!"

"Is that right? I guess teenage kids don't lie, huh?" Frank said.

"Maybe your kid does! My son would never lie to me!"

All Frank could do was stare at the naïve woman. It was evident that her son had her wrapped around his little finger. Frank noticed the devious look in Harold's eyes and shook his head. From his experience, this young man was on a path to destruction and, unless his mother opened her eyes to his sneaky and mischievous ways, she would be visiting him in either the penitentiary or the graveyard.

"Ms. Green, we have several witnesses who saw Harold—"

"I don't care what those little snot-nosed bastards said! My son is not a liar! Harold, let's get the hell out of here."

Harold fell in step behind his mother. Just before turning the corner, he looked back at the principal and smiled.

22

"Boy don't you walk past me without giving me a hug," Sadie said to Frank Jr. He was still upset about what Harold had done to his sister, so much so that he never even saw Sadie sitting on the porch. She was stretched out in a lawn chair munching on a bowl of Butter Pecan Ice Cream.

"Oh, I'm sorry Ms. Sadie."

Frank Jr. walked back down the steps and jogged across Sadie's lawn. Taking the steps two at a time, he hopped on her porch and threw his arms around her.

"You okay?" she asked.

"Yes, ma'am."

"Where's your sister?"

"She had drama practice, so she won't be home until later. Ms. Sadie, did I do something wrong? I mean, I thought I was doing something good by protecting my sister."

"Sweetie, you did do good. You're supposed to protect your sister. Now and always."

"That's what I thought. But the way my dad looked at me when he left the school made me feel like I had messed up somehow."

Frank Sr. walked out onto his porch and looked around. When he spotted his son talking to Sadie, he walked over to the railing.

"Jr., get inside and take that garbage out. When you get done with that, wash the dishes."

"Wash the dishes? But it's Rhonda's turn to wash the dishes."

Frank Sr. stared at his son for a few seconds before speaking again. "Did you hear what I said?"

"Yes sir."

"Then get in there and do it."

With slumped shoulders and a frown on his face, Frank Jr. walked down Sadie's steps, up his own, and into his house.

"Meanie!" Sadie yelled in Frank's direction. When Frank was sure that his son was out of earshot, he broke into a smile.

"Now why would you call me that? And I hope that's sugar-free ice cream you're eating."

Sadie rolled her eyes and sighed. Had she known that Frank was coming back out onto the porch, she would have waited until later to enjoy her guilty pleasure. She began to rue the day that she revealed to him and his children that she had diabetes. They only stayed on her case about it because they loved her, and while she understood the method behind their madness, it sometimes grated her nerves.

"Frank, it ain't but a spoonful of ice cream left in this container. I'll be done in a minute."

"Is that right? Let me see."

Before Sadie could protest, Frank leaped off his porch and made his way toward her. Not wanting him to see how much was really inside the container, Sadie tried to hurry and eat the remaining contents. She was just sticking the last spoonful in her mouth when Frank reached down and tilted the container.

"See? I told you that there was only a spoonful left."

Frank looked inside the container, and then back at Sadie. "Whatever Sadie. You ate damn near a gallon before I got over here."

"Did not."

All Frank could do was laugh and shake his head.

"Your son thinks that you're mad at him."

"I know."

"Well, are you?"

"Not at all."

"Then why are you making him do Rhonda's chores?"

Frank looked around to make sure that his son wasn't coming out before addressing Sadie's question. "The only thing in that sink is a coffee cup and a fork. Hey, I had to punish him some kind of way. Plus, I'm teaching him something that will help him as he gets older."

"Yeah, well, maybe you should tell him that, Frank, because he thinks that he did something wrong by protecting his sister."

This news surprised Frank. Although he did give his son a hardened look when he left the school, he didn't want him to think that he'd done something wrong in protecting his sister.

"Really? Well, I guess I'd better talk to him about that. I'm never going to get mad at him for protecting his sister."

"I know. I told him that, but I think it would resonate more if he heard it from you."

Frank nodded his head in agreement. He talked with Sadie for a few more minutes before heading back into his own house. He was halfway inside when he heard loud yelling and cussing coming from across the street. When he turned to see what was causing all the commotion, he saw a woman fleeing from a huge man. She had a terrified look on her face and appeared to be running for her life. The brutish-looking man chasing her had an evil scowl plastered on his face. His bloodshot eyes told the tale of a man who looked to have had a little too much to drink.

"Help, my God, somebody, please help me!" the woman screamed. The look etched on her face confirmed that she was frightened beyond belief. Her blouse was torn halfway off, exposing her bra.

"Come back here, you whore!" the enraged man shouted, as he chased after her.

Sadie turned to alert Frank, but he was already in motion.

Christopher Speight

23

"Call the police," he said, leaping off the porch. In a flash he was across the street. He arrived just in time. The man was just getting ready to land a blow to the young woman's face when Frank tackled him to the ground. The man was larger than Frank, so it was a struggle to keep him subdued.

"Get off me! Get the hell off me! I'm gonna kill that no good-cheating slut!"

"Hey! Calm down! Take it easy!" Frank yelled.

If the man heard Frank, he didn't pay him any attention. The more Frank tried to calm him down, the more the man tried to break free. The two men began rolling around on the ground.

"Sir, I'm going to tell you one last time to calm down! I'm the police, and if you don't calm down, I will be forced to take you to jail!"

"I don't give a damn who you are! That slut cheated on me with my brother, and I'm going to break her damn neck!"

The man finally broke free of Frank's grip. He stood up and looked around. When he didn't see the woman he'd been chasing, he turned his rage on Frank.

"Since you wanna come to her defense, I'm gonna give you some of what I was about to give her ass!"

The man lunged at Frank awkwardly, throwing a wild punch that Frank easily ducked. He was so off balanced that Frank was able to catch his arm and twist it behind his back. The man screamed in pain. Before he could mount any other form of attack, Frank yanked out a pair of handcuffs and placed them on the man's wrists. Frank looked around and saw that he and the man had attracted an audience. It always amazed him how the slightest sign of trouble could bring nosy people out of the woodwork. Most of them had their cell phones out, recording the event. He glanced around and saw that some people had even come out onto their porches to watch.

"Hey, what the hell are you doing?" the man asked.

"Isn't it obvious? I'm placing you under arrest."

"Placing me under arrest? For what?"

"Well, for starters, assault on a police officer."

"What? Man, I didn't know you were a police officer."

"I told you that I was a police officer when I was trying to restrain you. If you would've listened instead of acting like a damn fool, you would have heard me. You can come out now, ma'am," Frank said when he noticed the woman peeking from behind a parked car.

"Take him to jail! Take his abusive ass to jail!" she yelled.

"Jail? Oh, come on baby, you know I wasn't going to hurt you. I just wanted to talk to you."

Frank looked down at the man and shook his head.

"To hell with that," she said. "That's the last time you're going to put you hands on me!"

As the woman got closer, Frank noticed that she had a black eye. That revelation quickly caused his temper to flare. In his opinion, any man who beat up on a woman wasn't any kind of man at all. Frank grabbed the man by the collar and snatched him to his feet.

"What happened to her eye?"

"Huh? Man, I don't know," the man lied.

"Oh, you don't huh? Miss, what happened to your eye?"

"That bastard slapped me!"

"She's lying!"

"I am not!"

"Okay, that's enough! Both of you be quiet."

Frank sympathized with the woman's plight, but the entire situation was getting on his nerves. He had planned on relaxing for the rest of the day with a cold beer in one hand and his TV remote in the other when this nonsense occurred.

"What's your name miss.?"

"Felicia."

"Felicia what?"

"Felicia Gray."

"Okay Ms. Gray. Tell me what happened."

Black Viper

"Man, I knew it! Every time a man and a woman get into it, y'all always take the woman's side!" the man yelled.

"You damn right I'm taking her side! She was running for her life trying to get away from you, and she has a black eye, so if I were you, I would shut my damn mouth and pray that I don't get into any more trouble than I'm already in!"

Frank then turned his attention back to Felicia. "Go ahead Ms. Gray."

"Well, this asshole's birthday is next weekend, so me and his brother, Vince, was planning to throw him a surprise party. We met up yesterday at Tizzano's Party Center in Euclid to drop off the down payment. He paid half, and I paid half! That's why we were together, dumb ass! Wasn't nobody cheating on you!"

The woman's eyes bore a hole straight through her attacker. The man felt so stupid that all he could do was drop his head.

"I'm sorry. I really thought you two were having an affair."

"You oughta be sorry. I tried to tell you I wasn't cheating on you, but you wouldn't listen!"

"What's your name, sir?"

"Rodney. Rodney Sims."

"Well, Mr. Sims, your woman-beating ass is gong to jail," Frank said, patting him on the shoulder.

"Come on man. It's just a little misunderstanding."

"I'm afraid it's much more than that. Domestic Violence is a felony."

Frank was getting angrier by the minute. He hated men who tried to act so tough when it came to assaulting females but were total cowards when it came time to face the consequences for their actions. A wide smile broke onto his face when he saw a police cruiser approaching.

"Looks like your ride is here, tough guy." Frank roughly yanked Rodney toward the curb. The police cruiser stopped in front of them. Frank waited patiently as the officer cut the engine and got out of the car.

"Detective Stone. I hope you have a good reason for interrupting my dinner," Officer Duncan said, with a smile. Officer

Anthony Duncan was an imposing man to say the least. He stood at an even six foot seven inches tall and weighed a very solid three hundred pounds. His bald head was as shiny as a glass marble. His arms were so muscular, that he often had to wear short sleeve shirts to be comfortable.

"Oh, you're going to love this. This piece of crap right here, Mr. Rodney Sims, likes to hit women."

The smile slowly eroded from Officer Duncan's face. When he was eight years old, his mother was killed by her live-in boyfriend of two years. The youngster had to sit helpless on many occasions while his mother was pummeled into submission, so any man who put his hands on a woman in a harmful kind of way was the lowest kind of scum to him.

"Is that right?" he said, scowling. "Well, in that case, you have the right to remain silent. If you give up that right, anything you say can and will be held against you in a court of law. You have the right to an attorney. If you can't afford an attorney, one will be appointed to you."

Officer Duncan then clutched his massive hand around the fabric of Rodney's front collar, yanked him forward, and looked him straight in the eyes. His next set of words were barely above a whisper, but the menacing tone in which he said them nearly caused Rodney to urinate on himself.

"And if you give me any trouble or lip on the way to the station, I reserve the right to beat you to a bloody pulp."

Officer Duncan then gently pushed Rodney back and gave him a sinister grin. "Now, do you understand these rights as I have explained them to you?"

Before Rodney could answer the question, Officer Duncan was opening the back of the cruiser and roughly shoving him inside.

"Man, y'all can't do this to me," Rodney yelled, just before the door closed.

"You wanna bet?" Officer Duncan said.

Frank nodded in satisfaction as he watched the cruiser disappear down the street. He turned back around to see the victim,

Felicia Gray, sitting on her steps rubbing the side of her face. He walked up to her and knelt in front of her.

"Ms. Gray, I'm going to ask you something and I need you to be completely honest with me, okay?"

Felicia didn't answer verbally. Instead, she just nodded.

"Has Mr. Sims ever put his hands on you before?"

Felicia took a deep breath before answering. She'd known in her heart that this day was coming. On at least three other occasions, Rodney had gotten jealous for little to no reason and assaulted her. She swore on her mother's grave that the next time he did it would be his last. Well, the next time was finally here. She had to decide. Thankfully, they didn't have kids together so that wasn't an issue. She also earned a decent salary, so she didn't have to depend on him to take care of her. Right then and there, Felicia Gray decided that she'd had enough. Rodney Sims would never again use her as his punching bag.

"Yes Detective, he has."

Frank nodded knowingly. He was also cautiously optimistic. He'd seen how this movie played out a thousand times before. More times than not, the woman would recant her story, and the man would get off scot-free. Sadly, when the curtain was pulled on love stories of this ilk, quite often either the woman or the man was residing in a casket. He hoped this would end differently.

"Then you know what you have to do, right?"

"Press charges?"

"Exactly. So, do you need a ride down to the police station?"

"No, I'll just get Vincent to take me."

"Vincent. His brother?"

Felicia nodded and ran her hand across her face. When she looked back at Frank, he was staring at her quizzically.

"I know what you're thinking, but you're wrong. I have no romantic interest in Vincent at all, and he doesn't have any in me. As a matter of fact, he's been talking about proposing to his girlfriend."

"Actually, that's not all I was thinking," Frank said. "You mean to tell me that Rodney Sim's own brother would take you to the police station so you can press charges against him?"

"Yes, he would. Truth be told, Detective, Vincent has been trying to get me to leave Rodney for the last year. They've gotten into quite a few arguments about his treatment of me. They may be brothers, but they are total opposites."

"That's good to hear. I can't tell you how many women I've seen end up in a coffin because they refused to let go of a man who didn't have her best interest at heart. I pray to God that you stand by your decision to leave him. Do you have somewhere to go while he's locked up?"

Felicia looked at Frank and smirked. After glancing back at the front door and then back at Frank she said, "Detective, I don't need to go anywhere. This is my place. My name is one the deed, so I don't need to move. Rodney is the one who's going to be moving. How long is he going to be locked up?"

"That all depends. He's going to be in jail at least seventy-two hours, but if he can't make bail when you press charges, he'll probably be locked up longer than that."

"Good. That will give me more than enough time to get his crap out of here and get the locks changed."

Frank looked deep into Felicia's eyes in search of sincerity, and although he couldn't be one hundred percent sure, he believed that this was a woman who'd reached the end of her rope. Even so, he had to make the next statement to make sure that she got the message.

"You know, Ms. Sims, it makes absolutely no sense for you to press charges against this man, then turn around and take him back."

With steely eyes and a confidence that he didn't see in her a few minutes ago, Felicia Gray said, "I'm not going to take him back, Detective. I'm done."

"Good. Now, do you need medical attention?"

"No, I'm fine."

"Okay. What I need you to do now is call Mr. Sim's brother, tell him what happened, and ask him to take you to the police station to fill out a report and file charges."

"Now?"

"Yes, now. The sooner you do that, the sooner we can get this situation resolved."

"Okay. Thank you, Detective. If you weren't here I don't what he would have done to me."

"No problem ma'am. Just doing my job." Frank then helped her up and into her house. After she closed the door, Frank made his way back across the street. He looked around saw that there were still people mulling about, whispering to each other and it annoyed him.

"Okay, people, let's go. Nothing to see here. go on about your business."

"Is there a law against us standing here?" a young man with a white Du-Rag wrapped around his head asked. He had a look on his face that said he wanted to argue, and Frank was more than willing to give him his money's worth.

"As a matter of fact, there is. It's called loitering, smart ass."

"Wow, for real? With all the crime in this city, you're gonna bother us for loitering?"

Frank slowly walked up to the young man until he was right in front of him. "You know what, youngster? You're just like a lot of other citizens in this damn city. You'd rather stand around and watch a crime being committed than to get involved and try to prevent it."

"I didn't see any crime being committed."

"What if you had? Would you have gotten involved if I weren't here? Would you have stepped in and possibly saved that young woman's life when that asshole started beating on her? Because make no mistake, he was about to pummel that poor woman, and you and all the rest of these fine people out here weren't going to do a damn thing but pull out your cell phones and tape it. Now, like I said, move along before I run your ass in."

Frank turned on his heel and continued walking to his house. As he was walking away, he heard the young man mumble something inaudible under his breath. He started to turn around and say something but decided that it wasn't worth the trouble. As he reached the sidewalk, he turned to his right and saw Rhonda strolling down the sidewalk. She had a disturbed expression on her face, which caused Frank to stop dead in his tracks.

"You okay, honey?" he asked.

"Yeah, I'm okay. Just a little ticked off. Now I have to go inside and wash my hair before this milky smell settles in."

Frank threw his arm around his daughter and hugged her tightly. He knew that young ladies that age were terrified of being embarrassed and getting milk poured in her hair would certainly qualify as being embarrassed.

"Okay, honey," he said, sitting on the steps. "Why don't you tell your old man what happened."

Rhonda took a seat beside him. "But I thought you already knew. Wasn't you at the school today?"

"Yes, I was, but I want to hear I from you. That way I get the story from someone who was actually there."

"Well, I was still sitting down and eating with some of my friends, when that jerk Harold came over. He was with some of his stupid friends, so I guess he was trying to impress them. Anyway, he asked me if I wanted to go to the movies with him this weekend. When I told him no, his friends started laughing at him. I guess that embarrassed him, so he started talking about he was doing me a favor, and that I was lucky someone even asked me out. Then he had the nerve to call me ugly, so I told him that his mother was ugly."

Frank wanted to laugh so badly, that it was killing him, but knew he would be setting a bad example if he did, so he held it in.

"That's when he got mad and poured milk in my head. Dad, I was so embarrassed. I wanted to get up and smack the taste out of his mouth. Luckily, I didn't have to. Five minutes later Jr. showed up and beat the crap out of him."

A small smile slid across her lips as she said this. She was obviously proud of her brother for taking up for her.

"Yeah, I saw him when I came up to the school. Jr. really put a whipping on him."

"Dad, is Jr. in trouble? I mean, he was taking up for me, so any punishment you're going to give him, I'll take for him."

Frank's eyebrows shot up. He couldn't believe what he was hearing. He knew that his daughter was grateful to her brother, but he didn't think that she would be that grateful.

"Is that right?"

"Yeah," Rhonda said, shrugging her shoulders. "I mean, he did protect me."

Frank leaned over and kissed his daughter on the forehead.

"Tell you what. We'll talk about it when I get in the house, okay?"

"Okay daddy."

Rhonda got up and went inside the house, leaving her father sitting there. When he was sure that she was inside, Frank smiled. He loved the fact that his children were looking out for each other. The thought alone made him swell with pride.

"You have two very special kids there, Frank," Sadie said. She'd been so quiet; Frank had forgotten that she was still sitting on her porch. "Hopefully neither of them grows up to be like those two fools across the street."

"Well, hopefully she doesn't have to be bothered with that dude anymore."

"If you ask me, they had no business being together anyway. I've seen them argue on more than one occasion."

"Really? Have you ever saw him hit her?"

"Now you know better than that, Frank. Don't you think I would tell you if I'd seen something like that?"

"You're right, Sadie. Sorry. It just galls me to no end from a man to beat up on a woman. I hope she was serious when she said she was through with him."

"So do I. Those two are like chocolate and vanilla."

Frank laughed for five seconds before stopping abruptly. The realization hit him like a sledgehammer. That was it. The thing that had been nagging him about the case he and Amber had been working on. All along, he knew that he was missing something and now he knew what it was.

"Chocolate and Vanilla," he mumbled to himself.

Christopher Speight

24

Amber made a right into the cul-de-sac of a semi-affluent neighborhood. Since her son wasn't answering her calls, she decided to make a trip to her ex-husbands house and pay him a visit. It wasn't like him to ignore her and aimed to find out why he was being so evasive. She was worried sick about him and was beginning to wonder if she'd made an error in judgement by allowing him to go live with his father. Because of the nature of her job and hectic work schedule, Amber felt that it would be better if Ryan was with the parent that could spend the optimum amount of time with him.

A hint of envy bit into Amber as she took in the surroundings of the distinguished looking single-family homes. Every single lawn was immaculately manicured. Beautiful flowers protruded from fresh mulch, making each house look like the All-American home. Most of the houses were fenced in so that the couples who had children had no reason to worry about them stumbling into oncoming traffic. The entire community was friendly and peaceful. Amber shook her head as she pulled into Roger's driveway. It had only been a year since she and Roger's divorce had become final. Amber would never admit this to Roger, but she missed living in the large house. It was a far cry from the two-bedroom apartment she now resided in.

After cutting the engine, Amber took a deep breath and tried to calm her nerves. She was pissed that her son hadn't returned her phone calls and aimed to tell so but didn't want to go overboard.

She got out of her car and walked up the stoned walkway to the front door. She was just getting ready to ring the doorbell, when she heard laughter coming from the back of the house. She listened closely to see if she could pick up anything. When she couldn't, Amber proceeded to slowly make her way around the side of the house.

She stopped just before she got to the edge of the grass and peeked around the domicile. Her face twisted as she saw her ex-husband lying on a lounge chair. Lying next to him was a young lady with curly black hair and a curvaceous body. Her back was facing Amber, so she couldn't get a good look at the woman's face. What really got her blood boiling, however, was the activity she saw going on in the swimming pool.

Standing in the shallow end of the pool was her son Ryan. The smile on his face was so wide, it looked like it would crack at any moment. The reason for his jubilation, a young lady with fire-engine red hair had her legs wrapped around his waist. She was smiling just as hard as he was. The two of them were just about to share a kiss when Amber's piercing voice sliced through the air.

"Ryan Davis, what in the hell do you think you're doing?"

Ryan jumped at the sound of his mother's voice. Slowly, the young lady peeled herself off Ryan and pushed away from him. Not knowing what to do, she sank into the pool until only her head was above the water.

"Ma! Uh, what are you doing here?"

"I should be asking you the same damn question. Your father said that you were having migraines again, but from the looks of it, you're doing just fine!"

Ryan glanced toward his father, who had a smirk plastered on his face.

"Don't look at your father! Get out of that pool, right now! I want to talk to you!"

Without waiting for a response, Amber stormed toward the entrance to the back of the house. Embarrassment overtook Ryan. It doubled when he heard the girl in the pool snickering. He climbed out of the pool and grabbed his towel that was lying on a nearby chair. After drying off, he slowly made his way into the house. Ryan looked back toward his father. It puzzled him why he hadn't said anything.

"Uh, Dad? Are you coming inside to help me deal with Mom?"

"I'll be in there in a minute son," Roger said, his eyes glued to his companion's chest.

With a deep sigh, Ryan trudged forward. He knew what was about to transpire but was powerless to stop it. He'd been ducking his mother's calls. He'd begged his father not to tell her about the headaches, but Roger told him that he had little choice. When Amber agreed to let Ryan move in with his father, one of the few conditions she gave him was that he was to notify her about any and all health-related problems Ryan may have. Both of them knew that he was prone to having migraines, but the medication that the doctor had given him had been working so well, Ryan hadn't had an episode in quite some time. Because of this, Ryan had mistakenly thought that he was cured of the migraines and had ceased taking his medication. As soon as Ryan entered the house, he felt his mother's hot gaze on him. Amber stood there with her arms folded, leaning back on her right leg.

"Look Ma, I know what you're about to say, but—"

"Why in the hell have you been avoiding my calls?" she cut him off.

"I haven't, Ma. I mean, I just been busy, that's all."

"Busy with what?"

"School," he lied. Amber looked at him for two seconds and shook her head. It was all the time she needed to pick up on the fact that he was lying.

"So that's what we're doing now? We're lying to each other?"

Ryan opened his mouth to say something, but quickly closed it. His mother had always been able to read him like a book, and just because they didn't live together anymore, that hadn't changed.

"I'm waiting Ryan. Why have you been avoiding me?"

Ryan didn't want to tell his mother that he had been becoming increasingly interested in girls and that he didn't have time for her because he was busy chasing them. It would hurt her feelings and he didn't want to do that. Ryan was stuck. He didn't know what to say. Fortunately, he didn't have to say anything.

"Amber, you really need to call before just showing up like this," Roger said, coming into the house.

It was easy to see why Amber fell for Roger. He was a handsome man, standing six foot two, with a shaved head and smooth cocoa-colored skin. He wasn't overly buffed up, but he did have a physique that made most men envious. An electrical contractor by trade, Roger had owned his own business for the last fifteen years. Had he been able to keep his penis in his pants, he and Amber would probably still be married.

"Call? My son lives here! I don't *have* to call you every time I want to see him!"

"Oh, is that right? Why, because you're the police?"

"Me being a cop has nothing to do with it!" Amber yelled. She was getting louder by the second.

"First of all, Amber, you need to calm the hell down. Now, if you want the truth, Ryan is starting to get interested in girls. That's why he hasn't been as available as he normally is."

Hurt flashed in Amber's eyes. Roger saw it immediately. He knew the look well, mainly because he'd inflicted his share of pain on her.

"And don't look like that. The way he's feeling has nothing to do with you. The boy is growing up Amber. It's only natural that he's interested in girls." Amber took a deep breath. She hated to admit it, but her ex had a point. Ryan *was* growing up. She still didn't like the fact that some girl had her legs wrapped around him in a swimming pool, and she aimed to tell both of them about it. For now, however, she wanted to let her son know that she understood. Amber walked over to Ryan and threw her arms around him. She closed her eyes and hugged him tightly.

"I'm sorry baby. I know you're growing up and I guess I'm just going to have to get used to that. Look, your father told me that you were having migraines again. That's why I'm here. Are you still taking your medication?"

"Yeah, I mean, I was."

"Wait a minute. What the hell do you mean, you 'was'?" Roger asked. He had no idea that Ryan had stopped taking his mediation.

"I mean, I wasn't getting any headaches, so I stopped taking the pills."

"What the hell do you mean you stopped taking them? Have you lost your damn mind?" Roger screamed.

"Hey, stop yelling at him like that! Maybe if you paid more attention to what was going on in his life and less attention to entertaining your little slutty girlfriends, this would have never happened!"

"Amber, it's none of your business who I keep time with! We're not married anymore!" Amber's nostril's flared. She gritted her teeth and balled her fists up so tight, that her nails dug into her palms. She raised her finger to say something to Roger but balked when she saw the look on her son's face.

"Ryan, go outside so me and your father can talk. No— scratch that," she said when she remembered that there were two scantily clad dressed females outside. "Go upstairs."

"How come he can't go back outside?" Roger asked. He knew exactly what Amber was doing and he didn't like it. In his opinion, boys would be boys and he didn't see anything wrong with Ryan entertaining the young girl.

"Because I told him to go upstairs!" Knowing that he wasn't about to win this battle, Roger threw up his hands. He watched as Ryan trotted up the stairs and into his room. Before Amber could begin reading Roger the riot act, the sliding glass door opened and the woman who'd been lying next to Roger stuck her head inside.

"Roger, baby, how much longer are you going to be in here? I'm getting lonely here?"

"Just give me a few minutes, Janice. I'll be back out in a bit."

The woman shrugged and headed back to the pool area. She purposely left the sliding glass door cracked, attempting to hear what was being said. Not missing a beat, Amber quickly went over and slammed it shut.

"Nosy heifer," she said loud enough for Janice to hear it. After closing the door, Amber walked over to Roger and raised her finger. She was so close to him, that she could look up and see his nose hairs.

"Let me tell you something, Roger. I don't give a damn what sluts you have patrolling in and out of here, as long as my son isn't affected by it," she hissed.

Roger folded his arms and cocked his head to the side. "You know, if I didn't know any better, I'd think you were jealous."

A low snicker emitted from Amber's mouth. It soon turned into full-blown laughter. It continued for another ten seconds before she spoke again.

"Roger, let me tell you something. You can bring Ms. America in here and there would be no way I would be jealous, and do you know why? Because I don't give a damn about anything you do. You know, I'm starting to regret letting him live here."

"Regret letting him live here? Okay, Amber, now you sound crazy."

"Why? Because I don't want my son to pick up on your womanizing ways?" Before Roger could answer the question, the sliding doors opened again.

"Rooggerrr," Janice said sexily.

"What the hell do you want?" Amber snapped. She didn't have anything against the woman personally, but she was starting to get on her nerves.

"Excuse you?"

"I *said,* what the hell do you want? Don't you see we're discussing our son?"

"First of all, I wasn't talking to you. I was talking to Roger!"

"Well, bitch, I was talking to *you.* Take your ass back outside and wait!"

Before Roger could stop her, Janice had stomped over to Amber and got in her face. "What the hell did you just call me?" she asked.

"I think you heard me, and you need to get out of my face!"

"And what if I don't?"

Roger extended his arms between the two women and tried to push them apart. It was a little more difficult than he anticipated, as each woman stood her ground.

"Roger, you better get your little girlfriend before I—" Amber didn't have time to finish her sentence as Janice roared and swung a wild right hand in her direction. Being the skilled cop that she was, Amber easily ducked the oncoming blow. As fast as lightning, she grabbed Janice's arm and twisted it behind her back. Janice howled in pain.

Black Viper

"Wow! Really Roger? You're dating a chick who assaults a police officer?"

"Police officer? Roger, you didn't tell me she was a police officer."

"Yes, she is, and guess what? You're going to jail for assault, Ms. Thing."

"Oh, come on, Amber, do we really have to do this?" Roger whined.

He'd been seeing Janice for a couple of weeks and was hoping that tonight was the night she would let him score. Now, because of her temper, that didn't seem to be in the cards. Amber smiled as she reached behind her back and pulled out a set of handcuffs. After clamping them on her wrists, Amber shoved her down into a chair.

"You have the right to remain silent," Amber began.

"Roger, please. Don't let her do this to me," Janice cried.

"Okay hold up. Amber can I talk to you in the other room, please?"

Amber glared at Janice as Roger led her through a foyer and into another room. After coming to a stop, he wheeled to face her and held up his hands.

"Amber, I'm sorry. She does have a slight temper."

"What the hell are *you* sorry for? *She's* the one who attacked a police detective."

"Amber, she didn't know you were a cop."

"And that makes it okay?"

"No, it doesn't, and I apologize for it. Please don't arrest her."

Amber stared at Roger, deciding whether she would do him a favor or run the woman in. It was her sworn duty to put criminals in jail, but because she wanted to prove a point, she was going to let Janice slide. . .this time.

"I'll tell you what, Roger. Even though I know you're going to be banging that tramp later tonight, I'm going to cut her some slack. The last thing I want is for you to think I'm jealous of any broad you bring over here. Our marriage is done, so I don't give a damn what you do. But just know this. If I get just one inkling that my son is being affected by you rolling your little playmates through here, I'm coming after you for custody of him. Oh, and one more thing. That young redhead has to go, or your little playmate goes to jail."

Without saying another word, Amber turned and walked back into the room where Janice was handcuffed. She looked down at the woman's tear-streaked face and grunted a laugh.

"Guess what? Today's your lucky day. Because I don't feel like filling out paperwork for the next two hours, I'm going to cut you some slack."

Amber leaned down and got nose to nose with Janice before issuing her next statement.

"But if you ever try to attack me again, not only will I take your ass to jail. I'll beat the brakes off you before I do. Are we clear?"

Janice's head slowly nodded up and down.

"Good." Amber yanked Janice up rougher than she had to. She then spun her around and took off the handcuffs.

"Now go back outside while I finish talking to my son's father."

Janice rubbed her wrists as she made her back outside. Every second or two, she would send a wicked glare Amber's way. When she was completely out of the house, Amber turned to Roger and told him in no uncertain terms that she would be keeping an eye on how he behaved around her son. She then walked up the steps and knocked on Ryan's door, and she didn't give a care in the world whether Roger liked it or not. Five minutes into her conversation with him, her cell phone went off.

25

Dusk had nearly descended upon the Ohio streets when Amber pulled into the crowded parking lot of *Johnny Blue's*. *Johnny Blue's* was a sport's bar located in the city of Beachwood, roughly ten and a half miles, or twenty-seven minutes from the city of Cleveland, provided you were driving instead off taking the bus. Beachwood was an upscale neighborhood where many white-collar workers resided. Because it was such a low crime area, the running joke for years was that the Euclid Police Department was pretty much paid just to sit around and eat doughnuts. However, neither the mayor nor anyone on the Police Force took it personally. All parties involved knew that it was in good fun, and it actually added a sense of levity to an already dangerous and stressful occupation. Although the two Police Forces had sporadically butted heads in the past, the two divisions respected each other immensely. Franklin Stone had quite a few friends that worked in the Police Department, and the majority of them frequently visited *Johnny Blues*. In his opinion, it was a good a place as any to inform Amber of his newest thoughts concerning the murder investigations.

After cutting the engine, Amber took a deep breath, leaned back, and closed her eyes. It had been a long day, and instead of soaking in her tube listening to some H.E.R with a glass of wine in her hand, she was sitting in the parking lot of *Johnny Blue's*, nursing a slight headache. She didn't understand why Frank couldn't simply give her the information over the phone but arguing with the senior detective wasn't a wise move.

"I could use a drink," she mumbled as she thought back to her spat with Roger. She couldn't believe that he'd had the nerve to allow their teenage son to be hugged up with some floozy in his swimming pool. The young woman had her arms wrapped around Ryan's neck looking like she was two seconds from sticking her tongue down his throat. Amber had seen that movie before, and it almost always ended with the girl getting pregnant.

"I am entirely too young to be a grandmother," she'd told Ryan just before leaving her ex's house. Five minutes had passed before Amber got out of her vehicle and made her way toward the entrance. The closer she got to the door, the more relaxed she began to feel, as the smooth sounds of jazz leaked into her ears and massaged her eardrums. A light smile creased the corners of her mouth as she entered. It had been a while since Amber had been to *Johnny Blue's*, so she'd forgotten about the strict music code the owner enforced. Tow days out of the week, Johnny employed a DJ from the hours of seven to eleven. Tonight happened to be jazz night. The next night would be R&B night. However, the one hard rule Johnny had, was that under no circumstance was rap music allowed to be played. Speculation and rumors swirled about why Johnny had instituted this rule, but the simple fact of the matter was, he just didn't like rap. To be perfectly blunt, he hated it. At a time like this, that was more than okay with Amber. Although she did have a generous amount of rap songs downloaded onto the iTunes account of her cell phone, she had no desire to listen to Drake, Trilly Hydro, or any other of the new wave artists at this moment.

The second she entered the bar, the entire ambiance of Johnny Blue's calmed her spirit. She inhaled sharply and caught an intoxicating whiff of the barbecue wings that were being prepared for some lucky customer. It was only then that her stomach reminded her that she'd been neglecting it. She thought back to the last time she'd eaten something and realized that her last meal had been a Three Musketeer's bar four hours earlier.

Amber's eyes darted around the facility until she spotted Frank. He was sitting at the end of the bar, sipping a tall mug of beer. She smiled as she took in his masculine physique and confident posture. She wanted so badly to tell him how she felt about him but knew that she couldn't. . .at least not yet. She had to wait and see if things would fall into place, but for now she would continue to be his partner in the fight against crime.

Black Viper

"Hey," she said as she slid onto the stool next to him.

"Hey. You okay?" Frank asked.

"Of course. Why wouldn't I be?" Amber asked.

"I don't know. You just sounded a little upset when I called you. That's why I insisted that you meet me here instead of telling you on the phone. You sounded like you needed a drink."

"Do I ever."

Frank motioned for the bartender to come over. He chugged down the rest of his beer down and set the empty mug on the bar.

"Another one, Frank?"

"Yep. Get the lady one too."

"No problem. Oh, hey, Amber. Long time, no see," the bartender said when he noticed her.

"What's going on Charlie?"

"Nothing but the rent, pretty lady."

"Hell, Charlie, that's going on for all of us," Frank said, laughing.

"I guess you got a point there."

"You know what Charlie? I don't want a beer. Bring me a Chocolate Martini, and could you please put in an order of barbecue wings for me? I'm starving!"

"You got it, Amber." Charlie then picked up Frank's empty mug and scurried away to get their drinks. He'd been tending bar at Johnny Blue's long enough to know when two officers wanted to have a private conversation.

"So, what's this earth-shattering theory you've come up with?" Amber asked.

Frank smiled as he stood up from the bar stool. "I'll tell you when I get back," he said.

"When you get back? Where the hell are you going?"

"To the bathroom, but while I'm gone, I want you to think about the case. What's the one thing that both of the murders have in common? If you figure it out before I get back, your drink and your wings are on me."

Frank smiled even harder as he walked away. He loved challenging his partner in that manner. One thing he could be assured of though, was that she was up for the test. He could tell from the second he talked to her on the phone that she was under some stress, so he decided that he would get her mind off whatever was ailing her and force her to concentrate on something productive.

Frank hadn't been gone ten seconds before a short, bald man came and plopped down next to Amber. Amber rolled her eyes and turned to look at the television hanging on the wall behind the bar. She could feel his eyes roaming over her body but continued to ignore him. She was hoping that he would get the hint and leave her alone, but unfortunately, she was his choice for the night.

"Good evening, gorgeous. What's shaking?" he said.

"Thanks Charlie," Amber said, shortly after the bartender set her drink down. Charlie shot a look toward the man. He tried to get his attention so that he could give him a friendly warning, but the man's eyes continued to be glued to Amber. When the guy wouldn't look at him, Charlie gave up, shrugged his shoulders, and walked away. Since he didn't recognize the man, Charlie knew that he was probably either new to the area or had never visited *Johnny Blues* before. If he had, he would have known that it wasn't the typical bar where you pick up women.

"Chocolate Martini, huh? Looks like someone has had a hell of a day." The man pressed on.

Tiring of the stranger's flirting, Amber turned to him and gave him a chilly look cold enough to freeze fire.

"Someone's sitting there," she said coldly.

"I know. Me," the man said smugly. "Look baby, why don't we get out of here and go back to my place?"

"I'd like to, but I have something more important to do tonight."

"Now, what could you have to do that's more important than spending time with a great guy like me?"

"Anything. Now beat it."

The man's smile, which was charming at first, slowly faded and was replaced by an evil grin. A vein creased the middle of his forehead, and his light skin turned red with embarrassment.

"Oh, I see you're one of those type of broads, huh?"

"What type of broad?"

"The ones that think they're better than everyone else."

"Look, mister. I don't know what the hell your problem is, but I suggest you—"

Before Amber could finish her sentence, the man grabbed her wrist. Had he taken a quick look around the place, he would have seen that every set of eyes in the bar was now staring at him. Amber stared at his hand for a few seconds and then raised her eyes to meet his.

"Mister," she began, "you have exactly three seconds to take your hands off me."

"Oh yeah? And what if I don't?"

"If you don't, by the time the ambulance gets you to the hospital, they'll have to piece your body back together," Frank said, approaching the bar.

"What the hell do you have to do with it?"

The man flinched when Frank reached into his coat. His eyes got wide when he saw the gold shield clutched in Frank's palm.

"Damn," the man said, knowing that he'd messed up. His luck quickly went from bad to worse. Upon hearing Amber whistle, he looked back to her and saw the same kind of shield swinging from a chain clutched in her hand. The look in her eyes told him that he might have made a bad decision. Slowly, he released her wrist.

"You know, you're the second person today to try to assault a police officer. I let the last one slide. Tell me why I should let you get away with it."

"Officer, I—"

"Detective!" she corrected him.

"Okay, look, Detective. I'm sorry. I didn't know you were—"

The man never got a chance to finish his sentence before Amber backhanded him to the floor. It was unacceptable behavior for an officer of the law, and she knew it. Luckily, she had an out. The fact that the man had grabbed her wrist made her striking him a matter of self-defense. With a snarl on his face, the man got up and stared daggers at her.

"Buddy, I think it's time for you to leave," Frank said, sliding between Amber and the man. The man gave Amber one last look before exiting the bar. Frank looked back at Amber and shook his head.

"I can't leave you alone for five minutes," he said, sitting back down on the stool next to her.

"Hey, I was just sitting here minding my own damn business. Charlie here can vouch for me, right Charlie?"

"Absolutely, Detective."

Amber held her hands open as if to say, "I told you." She then reached down, picked up her drink, and took a healthy sip.

"I hope those wings are coming soon, Charlie. I'm about to starve to death." Right on cue, a cute waitress with straight blond hair sauntered over carrying a tray filled with Amber's food. As soon as she set it down, Amber dug in.

"Charlie, have you ever seen that guy in here before?"

"Nope."

"Well, that explains it. Anybody who lives around here or has been in here before knows that Johnny Blues is a place where cops hang out. No one in their right mind would come in here causing trouble."

"I know. Apparently, he didn't know where he was."

Frank nodded his head in agreement before turning his attention back to Amber.

"So, Detective Davis, have you figured out the connection between the two murders yet?" Amber stopped in mid-chew, snapping her head around and looking at Frank like he'd lost his mind. After swallowing her food, she began to speak.

"Did you not see me being harassed by that clown when you came out of the bathroom? As a matter of fact, what took you so damn long? I thought it only took a man a few seconds to relieve himself."

The look on Amber's face revealed annoyance and irritableness. Her voice indicated that she was being standoffish. Frank stared at her for a few seconds before closing the distance between the two of them.

"Detective, I don't know what your problem is, but I suggest that you adjust your tone when your talking to the senior detective. Do I make myself clear, Detective Davis?"

"Yes sir," Amber said humbly.

Frank placed his hands on her shoulders. "Hey, whatever it is, if you ever want to talk about it, I'm here okay?"

"Okay."

Frank stepped back and took a deep breath. His partner wasn't easily shaken, so whatever it was that had her on edge, he hoped she could get it under control. Since he wasn't sure where her head was, Frank decided to just tell her what theory he'd come up with.

"Well, I've been thinking about the two cases, and the one thing that makes them similar is that both couples were mixed couples." Amber cocked her head and looked up toward the ceiling. She thought back to the two crime scenes and instantly felt like an untrained rookie. Slapping herself in the head Amber uttered, "Well, I'll be damned."

"Don't be too hard on yourself, Amber. Hell, it took a comment from my neighbor Sadie for me to figure it out."

Amber smiled. She suddenly didn't feel like an incompetent detective. It wasn't that she had low self-esteem, but the obvious clue that she had missed made her feel that she was slipping.

Another thought occurred to her while she was thinking about what Frank had told her. Her mouth fell open as she looked at Frank.

"I've already thought of it," Frank said, reading her mind.

"Captain Snyder is not going to like this," Amber said, shaking her head.

Not at all," Frank cosigned.

Christopher Speight

26

Although the occasion was far more tenuous than it was when they'd first dined there, Reds was still the same romantic restaurant it was when they went there on their first date. Reds was famous for its seafood. Nearly every resident within a twenty-five miles radius had heard about the succulent crab legs and perfectly seasoned shrimp. Even the appetizer menu caused customer's mouths to water. The lobster bisque soup was to die for, as was the moist and tender crab cakes. Red's only drawback was that it was a bit pricey, but anyone who'd had the pleasure of dining there before knew that their exorbitant prices were well worth it.

The crab cakes had always been a favorite of Marie Snyder's. She'd never had them before going to Reds and decided to throw caution to the wind by ordering them. One bite. That's all it took for her to get hooked. From then on out, Marie made sure to order them whenever she visited the place. That's why she was especially disappointed that they wouldn't be available for the next couple of weeks. She stared at the waitress just long enough to make the young lady uncomfortable before responding.

"Out of crab cakes? Are you freaking kidding me? I've been coming here for years and this has never happened. Could you please explain to me what's going on?"

"I understand, ma'am, and I'm very sorry, but the problem isn't on our end. Our suppliers have done a recall on crab meat. From what I understand, there's been speculation of possible contamination, so the manager doesn't want to take any chances."

Marie shook her head and rolled her eyes. Her mouth had been watering for crab cakes from Red's for nearly two weeks.

"Can't they just make them without the crab meat?"

As soon as the words left Marie's mouth, she wanted snatch them back. The urge to slap herself across the face set in, knowing that she's just made an absurd statement.

"Crab cakes without crab meat ma'am? So basically, you want an egg and mayonnaise patty?" the waitress asked, citing the second and third main ingredients in crab cakes.

Her husband, Donald, who was sitting across the table from her, did his best to hide his annoyance at his wife's ignorant statement. Marie thought about how silly her statement had been and chuckled.

"You know what? Delete that question. I don't know what the hell I was thinking. Let me just have the lobster dinner with asparagus and a baked potato."

The waitress remained stone faced as she wrote down Marie's order.

"And for you, sir?" she asked.

Donald took his time gazing over the menu as the waitress patiently waited.

"Oh my God," Marie mumbled, which only served to make Donald take longer.

Another twenty seconds passed before he said, "You know? I think I'm gonna switch it up today. I think I'll take the prime rib, with mashed potatoes and green beans."

"Excellent choice, sir. Would either of you like anything to drink?"

"Just bottled water for me, please," Marie said.

"And for you sir?"

Donald stared at Marie for a few seconds before shaking his head. "You now what? Forget the bottled water. Bring us a bottle of red wine."

The waitress's eyes traveled from Marie to Donald. She opened her mouth to verify the change with Marie, but Donald cut her off.

"That will be all. Thank you," he said, dismissing the waitress as if he were a teacher dismissing his students at the end of class. Marie glared at Donald. He glared right back. Not wanting to reveal the true potency of her anger, Marie took a deep breath and tried to calm down.

"You see, Donald, that's what I'm talking about. You're always trying to control me."

"Oh please, Marie. No one's trying to control you. I just think you're a little tense and need to relax."

"I don't need you telling me what I need and what I don't need."

Donald sighed and rubbed his forehead. "Jesus, Marie, why are you always so damned defensive?"

"I'm not being defensive."

"The hell if you're not! Every time I say anything to you, you act like I'm offending you," Donald said, a little louder than he intended to.

Marie smirked and folded her arms. "Now I know you don't want me to get loud in here," she warned.

Donald held up his hands. He knew firsthand how capable his wife was of being extremely loud when she felt it necessary.

"Sorry. I didn't mean to raise my voice. It's just that—"

"Is everything okay over here?" a young man asked, approaching their table.

"Who the hell are you?" Donald asked, angrily. The young man had some nerve to butt into his and his wife's business.

"I asked if everything was okay over here," the stranger said, ignoring Donald's question.

"None of your damn business! Whatever is going on over here is between my wife me. Beat it!"

"Wait. Did you say that Captain Snyder is your wife?" the young man asked.

"Yes. Wife. And who in the hell are you, anyway?"

"This is Officer Timothy Jordan," Marie told her husband.

"Well, his ass needs to be out somewhere fighting crime instead of dipping into our business!"

Timothy's countenance turned hard. He wanted to punch Donald in the face.

"Sorry boss. I didn't know he was your husband. I thought you were in some kind of trouble or something," he said. He continued to stare daggers at Donald as he spoke.

"What are you doing here, Tim?"

"Me and a few of the other officers thought we'd spoil ourselves tonight and check this place out. We've heard good things about it."

Marie looked in the direction where Tim had come from and saw two other officers staring at them.

"Tim, go back to your table. Everything is fine here."

"Yes ma'am, and like I said, I'm sorry. I didn't know that he was your husband. Frankly, I think you can do better," Timothy said, just above a whisper.

"What the hell did you just say?" Donald demanded.

"Hey, you're out of line Jordan! Now apologize to my husband," Marie told him.

Upon hearing his wife come to his defense, Donald folded his arms and shot Timothy a condescending look. The fire in Timothy Jordan's eyes could've burned a hole directly through Donald. He softened his facial expression after taking a quick look at his boss.

"Sorry, sir," he said, just before turning and heading back toward his table. The other two officers, who had stood up and were ready in case they were needed, were also staring in Marie's direction. After locking eyes with their captain, they nodded their heads as a show of respect. She nodded and turned back around to continue her evening with her husband.

27

"You must really be a great boss. That guy was ready to fight me over you," Donald said, shaking his head.

"He wasn't going to fight you Donald. He just wanted to make sure I was okay."

"Is that right?" Donald leaned to the side and glanced toward the table where Officer Jordan and his co-workers were seated.

"I beg to differ. He still looks like he wants to take a swing at me."

"Oh, please. Like I told you, he just wanted to make sure that I was okay."

"Why are you defending that clown?"

"I'm not defending him. I'm just telling you."

Donald cocked his head. He looked at his wife and then back toward Timothy's table and frowned.

"What the hell are you frowning about?" Marie asked.

"You know, if I didn't know any better, I would think you and that youngster had something going on."

Marie's facial expression twisted. Anger bubbled up in her gut. She couldn't tell if her husband was serious or just joking around, but either way he had a lot of nerve.

"Something going on? Have you lost your damn mind?"

"Not at all. As a matter of fact, it looks like he's got a crush on you."

"Whatever Donald."

"Jesus Christ, I was just joking around, Marie."

"That's your problem Donald. You're always joking around."

"Look, I'm sorry, okay? Now, can we discuss why our marriage is going down the toilet?"

"Our marriage is going down the toilet because you want me to give up my career for you. You want me to walk around the house bare foot and pregnant." *That, and your cheating ass ways, she thought, silently.*

"Come on Marie. I never said that."

"No, you didn't say it, but you damn sure implied it."

"How Marie? How in the hell did I ever imply that?"

Marie looked at her husband like he had two heads. "What do you mean how? How many times over the last six months have I heard you tell the kids that I love my job more than I love my family?"

"First of all, Donald, our kids are grown. Gary is twenty-two and Kylie is twenty, so you can stop trying to blow smoke up their behinds about me loving my job more than I love them. They know better than that, and quite frankly, I resent you for putting that in their heads."

"Oh, I didn't have to put anything in their heads, Marie. They're not blind. They can see the lack of time you spend with us."

"Gary is busy chasing girls and Kylie is busy with college. They have their own lives and are not concerned with how much time I spend at the precinct."

"Uh, should I come back later?" the waitress asked.

"No, everything's fine."

"Okay. Your food will arrive shortly," the waitress told them as she poured an equal amount of wine into both glasses. Donald smiled as he picked up his glass and encouraged Marie to do the same. Following his lead, Marie gave him a light smile and lifted her glass in the air.

"Let's toast," Donald said.

"To what?"

"To getting back on track."

Marie forced a smile. She appreciated what her husband was doing but it was too little, too late. Especially since she'd found out that he was having an affair. She took a few sips of wine and Donald immediately refilled her glass. Marie gave Donald a strange look before smirking.

"If I didn't know any better, I'd think you were trying to get me drunk."

"And why would I have to do that? Were married. I shouldn't have to get you drunk anymore."

"Is that right?"

Donald felt his nature rise. He wanted his wife so badly, that he seriously thought about telling the waitress to box up their food. Slowly the smile on Donald's face began to disappear as Marie reached into her pocket and pulled out her cell phone. She looked at the ID and saw that it was Frank. The minute her phone rang, Donald knew that there was a good chance that their dinner was about to come to an abrupt end. He prayed that wasn't the case, but he wasn't holding out hope.

"Yeah Frank. What's going on?"

"Hi Captain Snyder. I'm sorry to call you on your day off, but Amber and I think we may have discovered a connection between the two cases."

"Well, don't keep me in suspense Detective. What is it?"

Just before Frank could reveal to her what he and his partner had discovered, a loud crashing sound reverberated from outside the restaurant. It was so loud, Frank could hear it on the other end of the phone.

"Captain! Captain! Are you okay, ma'am?" he yelled.

"Yes, I'm fine. Something's going on outside. I'll have to call you back."

Marie hung up before Frank had a chance to respond. Leaping to her feet, she quickly made her way to the exit to see what had transpired. Donald was right on her heels. Not because he was worried that something would happen to her, but because he was nosy.

"Get back, everyone," she said, holding her up badge. Marie forcefully pushed her way through the crowd. Once she got to the door and pushed it open, she quickly noticed what had caused the loud bang. Smashed headfirst into a telephone pole was a shiny black 2018 Cadillac Escalade.

"Hey! Everyone sit back down," Marie yelled, when she turned around and saw the crowd standing near her. She looked toward the table where Timothy Jordan and the other officers had been sitting and was surprised to see that they had left.

"Damn! You," she said, pointing at the waitress. "Call 911! Donald, stay inside. I'm gong to go out there and see if anyone is hurt!"

Donald opened his mouth to object, but Marie had already turned and headed outside before he could. Onlookers were already taking out their cell phones, getting ready to snap pictures. Marie didn't have time to admonish them. She had to make sure that whoever was in the vehicle was okay. Before getting to the car, she surveyed the scene. The hood was bent so badly, that it looked like a tent. One of the tires was flat. The headlights were both shattered on impact. The grill was broken into small pieces scattered across the ground.

The Cadillac symbol that normally rested on the front of the vehicle had disengaged from the truck and was now a good thirty feet away from it. Marie ran to the driver's side of the car and glanced inside. The air bag had deployed, and the head of a middle-aged African American woman lay motionless on it. A slow stream of blood ran from her nose. Her eyes were half shut. Marie slowly and carefully began opening the door. It was barely halfway open when the strong smell of liquor slapped her in the face.

"I should have known," she mumbled.

Once she got the door completely open and was sure that the woman wouldn't fall out, Marie zeroed in on the woman's chest. A sigh of relief filled her body when she saw that the woman was breathing.

"Ma'am, can you hear me?" she asked, hoping that she could jar the woman awake.

"Is she okay?" a voice behind her asked.

Marie turned to see who it was and instantly got pissed.

"Donald, I told you to wait inside!"

"Hey, don't yell at me, and the only reason I came out here was because I was worried about . . . Jesus Christ, what the hell has she been drinking?"

Marie was just about to read him the riot act when the ambulance came streaking down the street.

"Donald, please go back inside and let me do my job. I'll be back in as soon as the EMT's take her away."

"But—"

"But nothing, Donald. Please go."

"This has nothing to do with your job, does it? You're making me go back inside because I'm white."

A twisted frown formed on Marie's face for a few seconds before she burst into laughter. She wanted to get mad, but her husband's ability to make her laugh had surfaced once again. His sense of humor was one of the things that attracted her to Donald in the first place.

"Donald, please," she said, still chuckling.

"Okay, okay, I'm going," he said, scampering away.

The ambulance pulled to a stop on the opposite side of the street. Marie watched as two paramedics got out and quickly made their way to where the accident had occurred. When they were close enough, Marie showed her badge and identified herself.

"How bad is it, Detective?" one of them asked. He was a freckled-faced Caucasian man with a slicked-back hair and a tattoo on his hand that read simply 'I save lives.' Marie thought that it was narcissistic, but at the moment, she had neither the time nor the energy to debate him on it.

"I'm not sure. She was unconscious when I got out here. Judging from the odor permeating from the vehicle, I suspect that alcohol was involved."

"Has she moved at all since you arrived?"

"No, she hasn't, and I was careful not to move her," Marie said.

"Good." Speaking to the other paramedic, an overweight black man, he said, "Go get the gurney and bring a pair of shears as we may have to cut this seat belt off of her." The other paramedic, a slightly overweight black man nodded and scampered off.

"Miss! Are you awake? Can you hear me?" the sound of the paramedics voice caused the woman to stir slightly. A low moan emitted from her throat as she tried to sit up.

"Don't move yet ma'am," Freckle-Face cautioned. Just then, Joe returned, pushing the gurney.

"Ready Mark?" he asked.

Mark nodded as he tried unsuccessfully to release the latch on the seat belt.

"Dammit! Hand me the shears, Joe."

Mark took the shears from his partner and cut the straps holding the seat belt in place. After doing that, the two paramedics carefully removed the woman from the SUV and placed her on the gurney. Just as they were putting her in the ambulance, a Cleveland patrol car pulled up. Two policemen jumped out of the car and headed straight to the back of the ambulance. Marie decided to stay close to the woman's vehicle, just in case anyone had thoughts of burglarizing it. She watched as the paramedic named Mark pointed in her direction. The two uniformed officers nodded and headed her way.

"Good morning Detective. I'm Officer Patrick Graham. This here is my partner, Officer Marvin Black. The EMT worker informed us that you were the first to arrive on the scene. Would you like to tell us what happened?" Officer Graham asked as his partner pulled out a pen and pad and prepared to take notes.

"Well, from what I gather, the woman being taken away in the ambulance crashed into this light pole."

"Was she being chased? Speeding? Texting?"

"I honestly have no idea. I didn't see the accident when it occurred. I was inside the restaurant having dinner with my husband at the time. We heard a loud bang and I came out to investigate."

Officer Black lifted his head to see around the damaged vehicle and directly into Red's.

"Would that happen to be your husband with his head sticking out of the restaurant door?" Officer Black asked, grinning. Marie took a couple of steps and glanced toward the restaurant.

"Yes, that would be his nosey ass," she said frowning. With a jerk of her thumb, Marie indicated to her husband that she wanted him to go back inside the restaurant. Other people in the restaurant were staring through the window, but she was powerless to stop them.

"Anyway," Marie said, directing her attention back to Officers Graham and Black, "when I came outside and made my way over here, I looked inside and saw an African American female slumped over the steering wheel.

Black Viper

"Damn," Officer Black said, staring at the front of the vehicle. "She must've been traveling at a pretty decent rate of speed in order to do this kind of damage."

"That would be my guess," Marie agreed.

"Pat, I'm going to go back to the car and radio this in and have a tow truck sent over." Officer Black scurried away to make the necessary arrangements. While he was gone, Officer Graham put on a pair of rubber gloves and got ready to inspect the vehicle. Since Marie had already informed him that she'd smelled alcohol when she opened the door, probable cause had been initiated. That allowed the officer to search the vehicle without the driver's consent. Still, he wanted to be sure that he'd heard her right.

"Now, you did say she reeked of alcohol, right Detective?"

"That's right," Marie answered. She had no illusions of why he was asking that particular question. The officer nodded triumphantly as he proceeded to rifle through the SUV. Although he was only doing his job by conducting the search, it was clear that Officer Graham was intent on finding something illegal.

"Aha," he said, as he reached under the driver's seat and pulled out a half-empty bottle of vodka. "Wow, she drank half the vodka." Officer Graham then opened the glove compartment and rambled inside of it. He almost looked disappointed when he couldn't find anything else. However, his mood perked up when he reached into the console and found a small bag filled with a white powdery substance. He lifted the bag to eye level, shook it couple of times, and smirked.

"Well well well, what have we here?" he asked, condescendingly.

"Looks like cocaine to me," Marie said.

"Yeah, me too. I'll bet she was zooted out of her mind when she crashed the truck."

"Yeah, looks like it," Marie said sadly. It was bad enough that the woman was on her way to the hospital because she'd wrecked her car as a result of drunk driving. Now, it appeared that she might have been under the influence of drugs as well. When she noticed the satisfaction in the officer's eyes at discovering the illegal substance, she knew that it was time for her to go.

Christopher Speight

28

When Marie finally re-entered the restaurant, many of the occupants, including her husband, had retaken their seats. However, there were still a handful that continued to have their faces pressed against the glass windows attempting to see the commotion through to its conclusion. Marie thought about telling them to sit their nosey asses down, but since they weren't breaking any laws, what would be the point? When she got back to her table, she immediately noticed the frown on her husband's face. He was leaning back in his chair, sipping his glass of wine. His piercing, blue eyes had followed her from the moment she'd re-entered Red's until the second she'd sat back across from him.

"Why are you looking at me like that?" she asked.

Donald shook his head. "No reason at all, Marie."

"Donald, what should I have done? I'm an officer of the law. I couldn't just ignore the situation."

"Marie, I know that you're an officer of the law, but I'm a husband who hasn't been laid in months."

Marie's eyes narrowed into slits. The upper right corner of her mouth twisted into a half smirk.

"Are you *sure* about that?"

"What? Of course, I'm sure. What kind of question is that?"

"I'm just asking."

"Marie, I know that you're not about to tell me that you think I'm cheating on you. I never have, and I never will," Donald said.

"Look, Donald, I'm not about to discuss this here. We can talk about this at home."

Donald leaned across the table. He gazed into Marie's eyes and stared at her. "Look. No one's cheating on you. You are my wife, and I want some sex from you tonight. Are we clear?"

Marie smirked.

"Yes Donald, we're clear. Now if you will excuse me, I'm going to leave so that I can stop at Veronica's Secret and get something nice so that I can look sexy for our night of passion," she said sarcastically. Marie then got up and strolled toward the exit. Suddenly, she wasn't very hungry.

29

Donald watched with lust as his wife sauntered out of the restaurant. His loins jumped as he watched her stroll away. He didn't give a damn about her having an attitude. He wanted to screw his wife tonight and he wasn't going to take no for an answer. He felt terrible for sleeping around on his wife, but Marie hadn't shown any sexual interest in him in quite some time and he had needs . . . needs that could only be fulfilled through physical contact. Only the waitress's voice was able to break his trance.

"I take it you want me to box the rest of your food up for you?" she asked when she saw that his wife had left.

"How'd you guess?" Donald asked.

Growing up in Solon, Ohio, a suburb of Cleveland, Donald's interaction with minorities were minimal at best. Although he did associate with African Americans daily in high school, the student population still consisted of fifteen Caucasians to one African American. Donald went through high school hearing the jokes and off-color remarks about Black people. To his credit, he never participated in the derogatory statements. He could never wrap his mind around why some individuals were so hateful. The way he saw it, all people were created equal. All blood was red, and all shit stank. His sister Irene, on the other hand, felt slightly different. Although she wasn't an all encompassed racist, she did let it be known that she didn't want to get too friendly with people of the opposite color. She didn't have a problem conversing with them from time to time, but she wasn't about to stop and have a drink with them after work. That was where she drew the line. Hence, her icy relationship with her sister-in-law. Despite her brother pleading with her to be a part of the happiest day of her life, Irene decided that it would be best if she skipped the event. Donald loved his sister dearly, but he never forgave her for her absence. Nowadays, the two barely spoke.

As soon as the waitress returned with Donald's boxed up food, he made a beeline to the door.

"Damn," he heard a female voice stutter. He didn't have to wonder what she was marveling at. Donald had had a raging hard on ever since his wife had left. Slightly embarrassed, he quickened his pace. He had to make a quick stop and hoped like hell that his boner would subside before he got there. He checked his watch and saw that he had just enough time to pick up his Viagra prescription. After pulling into the flow of traffic, Donald reached into his pocket and took out his cell phone. He hastily punched in the number to CVS pharmacy and waited for someone to answer the call. It rang just long enough to make him frustrated before someone picked up.

"CVS pharmacy, how may I help you?" a gruff voice sounded from the other end.

"Todd?"

"Yes, this is Todd, how may I help you?"

"Todd, this is Donald Snyder."

"Oh, hey Donald. What's going on buddy?"

Donald had been a CVS customer for years and Todd had worked there for nearly the same amount of time, so it was natural that the two of them would become friends. On some weekends, they even went golfing together.

"I need my prescription refilled."

"No problem, buddy. Let me just run it through the computer right quick." A few seconds went by before Todd spoke again.

"Uh, it looks like you don't have any more refills, my friend."

"What? No refills?"

"Nope. Sorry about that. I'm going to have to call your doctor tomorrow and—"

"Tomorrow? Todd, I need those pills tonight, man."

"Sorry, buddy, I don't know what to tell you. It's much too late to call it in tonight. As a matter of fact, it would be a minor miracle if the physician even responded to the phone this time of day."

"Todd please man. Look, I've got this romantic night all planned out with my wife. The last thing I need is for my equipment to malfunction. There's got to be something you can do for me."

Todd remained silent. He'd been a pharmacist for the last seven years. He loved his job and didn't appreciate someone asking him to put it on the line because they were desperate to screw their wife— a friend.

"What the hell are you asking me to do, Donald?"

"Come on man. No one is going to miss one pill," Donald said, practically begging.

"Donald, you must be out of your damn mind if you think. . . hold on a second." Todd pressed the hold button, took a deep breath, and collected himself.

"Are you okay, Mr. Mason?" one of the pharmacy technicians asked.

"Yes, I'm fine."

The young lady gave Todd a skeptical look. It was clear that she didn't believe him but chose to let the matter drop. An idea suddenly formed in Todd's head. He wasn't about to put his job in jeopardy, but since Donald had been such a loyal customer and a good friend, he decided to help him out . . . at a cost.

"Donald? You still there?" he asked, placing the phone back to his ear.

"Yes, I'm still here."

Todd covered his mouth and whispered so that his co-workers couldn't hear him. "Look, meet me in the parking lot in ten minutes," he said.

"Okay, thanks." Donald disconnected the call and waited for Todd to come out of the pharmacy. He'd pulled into the parking lot five minutes ago. Every minute seemed like five as he waited for Todd to emerge. Eight minutes later, Todd came out of the store. He looked around slowly in search of Donald's car. Once he spotted it, he quickly jogged over to it. Donald hit the unlock button just as Todd reached for the doorknob. He slid into the passenger's seat, slammed the door shut, and shot a disbelieving glance toward Donald.

"Man, you have a lot of nerve, asking me to steal some damn Viagra pills."

"First of all, it wasn't some pills: it was just *one* pill."

"Regardless of whether it was one pill or a thousand, you still have a hell of a nerve to ask me to do that."

"Oh my God, dude, are you going to help me out or give me a damn lecture?" Todd raised an eyebrow.

"You're talking a lot of shit for someone who needs a favor, my friend."

Donald opened his mouth to protest but quickly closed it. His friend had a point and he knew it. A great night of passion awaited him, and all he had to do was not mess it up.

"You're right. I apologize. Did you get it?" Donald asked. Todd stared at him for a few seconds before reaching into his pocket and pulling out a blue pill wrapped in tissue paper. Donald scrunched up his nose up.

"Man, what the hell? You wrapped it in toilet tissue?"

"Look, I wasn't about to get reported and fired because you want to bump uglies with your wife tonight. Now, do you want it or not?"

Donald sighed and nodded his head. He wasn't about to let what the pill was packaged in deter him from performing for his wife. He reached for the tissue, but Todd quickly pulled it away.

"That'll be twenty dollars, please."

"Twenty dollars?"

"Twenty dollars."

"Wait a minute. You stole the damn thing, and now you want to charge me twenty dollars for it?"

"First of all, I didn't steal anything. This belongs to me. My doctor wrote me a prescription for them two weeks ago. I know damn well you didn't think I was going to risk my license stealing you a Viagra pill, and since I had to pay for them so do you."

Todd smiled as he held out his hand. Donald frowned as he pulled his wallet out of his back pocket. He opened it and snatched the money out of it with such disdain that he nearly tore it.

"Here!" he said, shoving the money into Todd's hand.

"Nice doing business with you," Todd responded as he exchanged the pill for the money and exited the vehicle. He looked back through the window and gave Donald the thumbs-up.

Black Viper

Donald responded by giving him the finger. He was pissed that Todd had requested that he pay for the pill. Donald looked down at the tissue paper for a few seconds before slowly opening it. A large smile fell across his face when he saw the small blue pill. He peeled out of the parking lot and headed home.

As soon as he got there, he jumped in the shower. When he was done, he lotioned himself up and splashed on some Polo cologne. Marie often complimented how good he smelled when he put it on. Donald then lit some candles in the bedroom and put on romantic music. After that he threw his robe on and went into the kitchen, where he proceeded to pour himself a glass of wine.

When he walked into the living room, the hairs on the back of his neck stood up. For some reason, he felt like he was being watched. His eyes slowly scanned the room, searching for anything out of the ordinary. When he didn't see anything, he shrugged his shoulders and made his way to the couch.

Donald smiled from ear to ear as he thought about the night ahead. He couldn't wait to get his beautiful wife in the bed, and ravage her body. His manhood grew, and as much as he tried to resist, he couldn't help but run his hand down his leg and grope himself. Donald closed his eyes and began to fantasize about how it was going to be making love to his lovely wife. It had been so long, he was beginning to wonder if she found him attractive anymore. The way she'd behaved at the restaurant however, erased that thought from his mind.

He took a sip from his glass, set it down on the table, and threw both of his arms back, resting them on the couch. Thoughts of the hot time they had on their honeymoon flashed through his mind. The reflections caused him to become fully erect, and he hadn't even taken the Viagra yet. He started to wonder if he was going to need it at all. The thought of what he was looking forward to had him feeling like he hadn't felt in months.

"Baby, I can't wait," he said to himself.

"The wait is gonna be longer than you think," a hard voice whispered into his ear.

Donald's eyes suddenly popped open. He was about to sit up but before he could, he felt a thin wire loop around his neck. His eyes began to protrude from his skull as the wire tightened. He desperately tried to use his hands to push himself off the couch. He soon discovered using that tactic was a mistake. Trying to rise from the sofa caused the wire to tighten even more. Gasping for air, Donald fell back on the couch and tried to push his fingers between the wire and his neck, but the fact that it had begun to bite into his flesh made it nearly impossible to do so.

Blood began to seep from under the wire and ran down Donald's neck. His eyes began to bulge out of their sockets. He tried to speak but the pressure from the wire smothered his voice box. For added support, Donald's assailant put both feet on the back of the sofa. With the added pressure, it didn't take Donald long to pass out.

"You know, this wouldn't be happening to you if you weren't such a slime bucket."

Those were the last words Donald heard before he slipped into the afterlife.

30

"Captain! Captain, what's going on?" Frank yelled into his cell phone.

After having his return calls to her go directly to voicemail, Detective Stone shoved his cell phone back into his pocket. He hoped to high hell that his boss wasn't in any danger. He thought about calling 911 but quickly realized that he had little to no information to give them.

It scared the daylights out of him to think that Marie could be in some sort of danger, but the only thing he could do at this point was wait for his cell phone to ring. It wasn't in his pocket three seconds before it began to buzz. Thinking that it may be his captain, Frank hurriedly snatched it out.

"Hey, did you get in touch with Captain Snyder?" Amber asked.

"Yeah, but I wasn't able to tell her about our theory."

"Why not?"

"Well, it seems that when I called her, she was in the process of investigating an accident."

"What? Where?"

"I have no idea. She hung up on me before I had a chance to ascertain any more information."

"Oh wow. I hope everything is alright."

"So do I."

"Are you going to try to call her back?"

"I tried to, a couple of times before you called, but I wasn't able to reach her."

"Hmmm . . . I don't like the sound of this Frank. She could be in real trouble."

"I don't think there's any need to worry Amber. If she needed assistance, I'm sure she would have called it in. Besides, the way she sounded on the phone gave me the impression that it was just a routine accident."

Frank said this more to reassure himself than Amber. His gut told him that everything was okay, but his numerous years of experience told him that anything was possible. He decided to trust his gut and wait a while before trying to contact her again.

"Okay partner. If you say so."

"Don't worry. I'll call her later, on and find out what's going on."

"Okay, thanks."

After disconnecting the call, Frank headed home. It was disappointing to him that he couldn't tell his boss about Amber's and his theory. He thought about the case and immediately became disgusted. He never could understand what the color of a person's skin had to do with who they fell in love with. He thought about his boss and her husband, whom he'd met on several occasions, and remembered how happy they had seemed to be together. Frank wasn't naïve, so he knew that Marie and her husband sometimes went through a rough patch in their marriage. He also knew that was normal, not only for them, but for virtually every married couple in America.

It took Frank less than ten minutes to get home. Once inside of his house, he dropped down on his couch and undid his tie. For some reason, he felt tired. He'd been experiencing that a lot lately. His stomach growled, alerting him that he hadn't eaten since early afternoon. Although he didn't feel like it, Frank got up and made his way to the kitchen. He stopped in the entryway and smiled when he saw his daughter sitting at the table eating a slice of leftover pizza.

"Hey sweetheart. Is there any left for me or did your brother demolish the rest of it?"

"Hey Daddy," Rhonda squealed. With joy in her eyes, she jumped up and flew into her father's arms. She wrapped her arms around him and hugged him tightly.

"Wow. It looks like someone is glad to see me."

"I'm always glad to see you Daddy."

"I'm always glad to see you too honey."

Black Viper

Frank kissed his daughter on the forehead and headed for the refrigerator. He frowned when he saw that there was only one slice of pizza left. With a twisted expression on his face, he turned to look at Rhonda.

"Hey, don't look at me. This is only my second slice. Captain Caveman up there ate four," she said, pointing toward Frank Jr.'s room.

Frank took a deep breath and shook his head. He should have known that his greedy son wouldn't leave much of anything.

"Oh well. It looks like it's cold cuts for me tonight."

Frank opened one of the drawers in the refrigerator and took out a package of turkey meat. After grabbing the jar of mayonnaise, he opened a separate drawer and took out a pack of cheese slices, a head of lettuce, and a tomato that had already been cut in half.

"Looks like I need to go grocery shopping," he said when he opened the bread box and discovered that there was only a half loaf of bread left.

"You sure do Dad. We're all out of cookies."

Frank looked up to see Frank Jr. stroll into the kitchen. Frank Sr gave his son a disbelieving look.

"I just bought two packs of cookies the other day. You mean to tell me that you two have eaten them up already?"

"Don't blame me, dad. The cookie monster is responsible for that," Rhonda said. "I only had a few."

"Snitch," Frank Jr. said to his sister.

"Whatever. I'm not taking the fall for you," she said, laughing.

Frank Sr. walked up to his son and folded his arms. An incredulous look passed over his face as he shook his head.

"First of all, why did you eat four slices of pizza, knowing that it was supposed to be our dinner for tonight? And second, why in the world did you eat damn near two packs of cookies in a matter of three days? What's the matter with you, boy? You got a tapeworm or something?" Frank Sr. asked.

"A what?"

"A tapeworm."

"What the heck is a tapeworm?"

"Never mind. From now on, don't touch any sweets in this house without checking with me first."

Frank Jr. frowned and cut his eyes at his sister. In his eyes, it was all her fault.

"And don't even think about blaming your sister. You're the one who scoffed down those cookies, so if you want to get mad at someone, get mad at yourself. Now answer my first question. Why did you eat so many slices of pizza?"

"Sorry Dad. I was just real hungry after practice."

Frank was just about to admonish his son for his lack of courtesy when he was interrupted by the doorbell. Seeing this as an opportunity to escape his father's wrath, Frank Jr. bolted from the kitchen.

"I'll get it," he said, quickly exiting the room.

Although Frank Sr. knew the true motive behind his son's hasty departure, he allowed him to leave anyway. Besides, someone had to answer the door. About a minute later, Frank Jr. returned to the kitchen. A strange look resided on his face.

"What is it, son? Who was at the door?"

Frank Jr. looked at his sister, then back toward the front door.

"Uh . . . dad, someone is here to see you," he said, sheepishly.

The strange look on his face caused Frank Sr. to become concerned. When he walked into the living room, however, he was met with a pleasant surprise. At least he hoped it was a pleasant surprise. Standing in his hallway, looking as radiant as she did when he'd first met her, was Principal Grace Ponder.

She'd ditched the conservative work attire she wore while at her place of employment and now had on a pair of tight-fitting jeans and a white blouse. A pair of brown sandals showed off her freshly painted toenails. The white polish matched her blouse perfectly. Her hair, which had been pulled back into a ponytail while she was at work, now hung freely around her shoulders.

"Uh . . . hello, Ms. Ponder," Frank Sr. stammered. He was as shocked as his children that she'd visited him.

"Good evening Mr. Stone. First off, I would like to apologize to you for coming to your home unannounced."

"It's quite all right, Ms. Ponder. Please come in and take a seat." Frank ushered her away from the front door and into the living room. Frank Jr. and Rhonda peeked their heads into the living room, attempting to hear what was going on.

"Frank, what did you do?" Rhonda whispered to her brother.

"Me? I didn't do anything. What did *you* do?" he shot back.

"Oh, please. I ain't did jack. If anybody did something, it was you."

"Stop talking so loud. Daddy's gonna hear you."

Neither of them wanted that. They wanted to remain right where they were so that they could eavesdrop on the conversation. Unfortunately, their father had other plans.

"Frank! Rhonda! Stop eavesdropping and go to your rooms so I can talk to Ms. Ponder."

Disappointment was etched onto their faces as they headed for their rooms. Principal Ponder noticed their worried expressions and decided to put their minds at ease.

"No need to worry, kids. Neither of you is in any trouble."

"Thank God," Frank Jr. said. He was so glad that Grace Ponder's visit didn't have anything to do with him, he practically ran to his room. Ronda, on the other hand, had a different thought process altogether.

If neither one of us is in trouble, then what the heck is she doing here? she wondered.

Just before disappearing through the doorway, she glanced over her shoulder just in time to see Grace smile at her father. It was a scene that didn't sit well with her at all. A frown remained on her face until she reached her room. When Frank was sure that his children couldn't hear them, he turned his attention back to Principal Ponder. Since she had just stated that neither of them was in trouble, his curiosity piqued about why she was there. Seeing the perplexed look on his face, Grace figured she needed to get to the point of her visit.

"I know you're wondering why I'm here, Mr. Stone, so I'll just say. I received a call today from Yolonda Green. She was still highly ticked off about what Frank Jr. did to her son, so much so that she threatened to take legal action against the school and Frank Jr."

Frank cocked his head and smirked. "So, let me get this straight. This little punk starts a fight with my son, comes out on the losing end, and now his mother wants to sue everybody?"

"Yes, that's about the size of it. Since you're a police officer, I wanted to get your professional opinion on whether she has a case."

Frank took a deep breath and leaned back on the sofa. He rubbed his chin and thought back to the day of the altercation. He'd made it a point to visually examine the other young man when he entered the principal's office. From what he remembered; the boy didn't look like he'd suffered any significant injuries. Only a few bumps and bruises, but he decided to ask Ms. Ponder to make sure.

"Did you see the kid today?" he asked.

"Yes. Anytime I give students alternative learning as a punishment, I go by and check to make sure they are there."

"How did he look?"

"What do you mean?"

"I mean, how did he look? Did it look like he had any broken bones on anything like that?"

"Not hardly. As a matter of fact, when I stopped by the room, he looked like he was busy annoying someone else."

"That figures. I guess he hasn't learned his lesson yet."

"Apparently not. Somehow, though, I don't think he will be bothering your son or daughter again," Grace said, trying unsuccessfully to suppress a slight chuckle.

"Not if he knows what's good for him." As soon as he said it, Frank wanted to take it back. It made him sound like he was advocating violence, which wasn't true. He immediately held his hands in the air.

"I'm sorry. I shouldn't have said that."

"It's quite all right," Grace said, smiling. "Like I told you in my office, I'm glad your son beat the brakes off that little punk."

Frank's loins began to stir as Grace's lips curled into a radiant smile. He pinched his wedding ring and turned it a couple of times.

"Now I'm the one who needs to apologize. As a principal, I shouldn't be sounding like I'm promoting violence between my students, but . . . I'm sorry. That kid is just a pain in the ass. Back to my original question though. Do you think Yolonda Green has a case against us?"

Frank slowly shook his head.

"Nah, I doubt it. The kid didn't seem to suffer any significant injuries. Kids get into fights at school all the time, so I don't see how this is any different. From the looks of it, this Yolonda Green is just upset because her son came out on the short end of the stick. I'd be willing to bet anything that if the situation were reversed and her son was victorious, she wouldn't be bitching about it at all."

Grace nodded her head in agreement. Frank's words had re-affirmed what she'd thought all along, but because he was a cop, she wanted his opinion. However, if she was being totally honest with herself, it wasn't the only reason she stopped over. Ever since she'd seen him at the school, she'd been having erotic thoughts about him. Frank was just her cup of tea. Tall, dark, and extremely handsome. She loved the protector type of man, and who better to protect you than a police officer? But as much as she yearned to get to know him better, the wedding ring on his finger said that he was off-limits. So even though she was attracted to him, Grace wasn't a homewrecker.

"So, is your wife in? I'd love to meet her."

"Huh?"

"Your wife," she said, pointing to his wedding band.

"Oh, she's not here."

"Really? I'd better hurry and leave then. I don't want to catch a beatdown."

"You don't have to worry about that."

"Really? And just why not?"

"It's complicated."

"Oh? How so?"

Grace knew that she was pushing the envelope, but she couldn't help herself. Frank was fascinating to her and even if she couldn't have him for herself, she wanted to know more about him. Frank stared at her for a few seconds. He was surprised at her audacity and although he liked her, he wasn't about to disclose anything in his personal life to her. He was just about to tell her so when his doorbell rang again. When he got up to answer it, Grace stood up with him.

"Oh my God, I didn't realize it was this late," she said, looking at her watch. "I really must go. Thank you for your time and your advice. I have to admit that I was a little worried about that woman's threat," she half-lied.

"No problem, Ms. Ponder."

"Please, call me Grace."

"Okay, Grace. Thanks for coming by." As Frank ushered her toward the door, he couldn't help but look down at her apple-shaped behind. Once again, he rubbed his wedding band to ward off the impending heat that threatened to surge through his body. When he opened the door to let her out, Amber stepped inside.

"Frank! We have an emer—oh, I didn't realize that you had company," she said, looking Grace up and down.

"Amber, this is Grace Ponder. She's the principal at St. Joseph's High School."

"Nice to meet you," Amber said dryly. Frank and Grace shot each other a quick glance. Amber's tone wasn't lost on either of them.

"Likewise. Thanks again, Frank."

Amber gave Grace the once-over as she walked past her.

"Your new girlfriend?" she asked when Grace was out of earshot.

"Not at all, and you know that I'm married so stop talking crazy. Like I said, she's my kids' principal."

"Really? What's she doing over here? Helping them with their homework?"

"Don't be a smart-ass. Just tell me what you were about to say when you first got here."

Amber took a deep breath and got ready to deliver the shocking news.

31

After giving a brief synopsis of what had transpired at Marie Snyder's house, the sound of Amber's voice wasn't heard again until she and Frank had reached Marie's house. Frank found that very peculiar. Amber was the chatty type, so the fact that she remained silent seemed strange to him. He wanted to inquire about the murder of their captain's husband but given her surly attitude, he decided to wait until they got there and investigate it for himself.

Twice he'd asked her if anything was bothering her and both times, she told him that she was fine. Frank wasn't a stupid man. He knew that something was bothering his partner, but he was smart enough to keep quiet and not aggravate the situation. For one brief moment, he wondered if she had gotten jealous when she'd seen Grace, but that would be absurd . . . wouldn't it? Even though Frank's wife was still in a comatose state, he was still a happily married man and Amber knew that.

When they finally arrived at the captain's residence, Amber quickly cut the engine and got out of the car. She moved toward the house so swiftly that Frank had to jog lightly just to catch up to her before she reached the front door.

"Hey, hold up a second," he said, grabbing her hand as she reached for the doorknob.

"Look, Detective, I don't know what the hell your problem is, but you need to leave it outside of these doors. Our captain and friend is in there, devastated by the loss of her husband, so I'm going to need you to focus on the job at hand. Got it?"

Amber drew in a long breath and blew it into the air. Her partner was one hundred percent right, and she knew it.

"Okay, Frank. I hear you. I'm sorry. I just had a few things on my mind, but I'm good now," she lied. She was still feeling some kind of way about Grace being there, but she knew she had to push her feelings to the side.

"Good. Now let's go in here and see about Marie."

The two detectives entered the house and were immediately overcome with sadness and grief. Grisly murder scenes weren't new to them. This situation, however, was completely different. One of their own had suffered a profound personal loss. Marie's place was packed with law enforcement officers and family members. Normally, civilians wouldn't be allowed within fifty feet of a murder scene, but special privileges were granted sine Marie was a captain. The looks on her coworkers' faces ranged from sadness to rage. Frank understood exactly how they felt. Whoever had murdered Donald Snyder had unknowingly declared war on the entire department.

When Frank and Amber entered the living room, Amber nearly threw up at the sight of Donald Snyder's neck hanging open.

"Oh my God," she mumbled, covering her mouth. "Who is God's name could have done this to Donald?"

"I don't know, but this seems personal," Frank said, looking around.

"What makes you say that?"

"Look around, Detective. It doesn't appear that there was any struggle here."

"So, you think that he knew his killer?"

"It's quite possible."

Just then Timothy Jordan walked into the living room and greeted them.

"Hello Detectives," he said, somberly.

"Hey,. Tim. Where's Marie?"

"She's in the kitchen with her daughter."

"How's she holding up?" Amber asked.

"Not good, but she's doing her best to stay strong for her kid," Tim said, leading them into the kitchen.

When they got there, the sight before them nearly broke their hearts. Marie's daughter Kylie sat at the kitchen table with her face in her hands. She was crying uncontrollably. Tears ran down both of her arms. Marie had her arms wrapped tightly around her daughter. Her chin rested on Kylie's shoulder and she too had a river of tears flowing down her cheeks. Frank walked up behind her and placed a soft hand on her shoulder.

"Captain, I would like to extend my sincere condolences to you and your children. If there is anything I can do, please let me know."

Marie was numb. All she could do was nod her head. Frank grabbed Amber gently by the arm and whispered instructions into her ear. Amber nodded and, in turn, whispered into Timothy's ear.

"Okay," he whispered. Timothy and Amber left the kitchen and made their way outside. Amber wanted to question him independently from the other officers.

"Wow, I just can't believe this," Amber said once they got outside.

"I know right? This is crazy! Who in their right mind would kill a cop's spouse?"

"Someone who's apparently not afraid of the police."

"What's your gut feeling?" Tim asked.

"Well, without thoroughly examining the crime scene, I would say that this is a crime of passion."

Timothy continued to stare at Amber as if he were waiting for her to expound further. When she didn't, he pressed forward.

"So what would make you say that?"

"Well, first of all, there was no sign of a struggle anywhere and nothing is missing, so it wasn't a robbery. Seems like it was personal."

"You think so?"

"That would be my guess."

"So why do you—"

"Look, Timothy. I have a few questions to ask you," Amber said, cutting him off. He was on a fishing expedition, and she wasn't about to let him bait her.

"Uh, okay, Detective. What is it?"

"Well, for starters, and don't get offended by this, but what are you doing here?"

Timothy was taken aback by her question, but Amber refused to retract it. She knew her captain well enough to know that she would not have called Timothy, so it was gnawing at her about how he ended up there.

"What's that supposed to mean? You know, I did give you the courtesy of calling you and giving you a heads-up when I got here and found out what was going on."

"That's what I mean. What were you doing here in the first place?"

Timothy thought about lying, but quickly decided against it. The truth was going to come out about him and Donald having words at the restaurant, so he figured he might as well get ahead of it.

"Actually, I came by to apologize to Captain Snyder. I was just about to ring the doorbell when I heard her scream. I didn't know what was going on, but my instincts told me to get in there in a hurry. That's when I went in and saw her staring at her husband in shock."

"Apologize? Apologize for what, Tim?"

"Well, me and a couple of other officers were having dinner at this place called Red's and we heard a commotion coming from another table. When I looked up, I saw that it was Captain Snyder, so I decided to go over and check it out."

"So, basically, what you're telling me is that you interrupted her dinner with her husband because they were having an argument."

"Look, Detective, I had no idea that the man she was arguing with was her husband. Hell, I didn't even know that she was married. I just saw some white man raising his voice to my Captain and decided to see what the problem was." There was something about the way Timothy said white man that made Amber look at him differently.

You mean you decided to take advantage of the opportunity to kiss her ass, Amber wanted to say.

"Tim, did it ever occur to you that the man Captain Snyder was with might have been a business associate? Or even another law enforcement officer that she was having a disagreement with?"

"I guess not," Timothy said, shrugging his shoulders.

"Well, did you see anything or anyone that looked suspicious when you arrived?"

Tim thought for a second before slowly shaking his head from side to side. "No, not anything that I can think of."

Amber cocked her head slightly. She found it hard to believe that a trained officer of the law could get to a crime scene and not notice anything.

"Interesting," she said. "So, who were the other officers you had dinner with?"

"Carla and Ryan."

"Carla Johnson and Ryan Turner?"

"Yes. Why? What does that have to do with anything?" he asked, slightly annoyed at her line of questioning.

"Nothing at all. I just felt like being nosy," Amber replied with a smile.

"Oh, okay," Timothy said, relaxing a bit. "For a minute there, I was starting to feel like a suspect."

"Why would you think that?"

"Because it sounded like you were interrogating me."

"Nah, like I said, I was just being nosy."

Just then the door opened, and Frank came out of the house. Worry lines were etched into his forehead.

"Excuse me Detectives, but I'm going to go back inside and see if I can be of any assistance," Timothy said. He nodded his head at Frank as he walked past him and back into Captain Snyder's house. Frank nodded back but decided to wait until the young officer was gone to begin speaking.

"So what did he have to say?"

"Well, apparently, he and two other officers were at the same restaurant that Captain Snyder and her husband were."

"Really? That's interesting. Anything else?"

"From what he told me, he saw her arguing with her husband and went over to see what was going on."

Frank raised an eyebrow.

"He said he didn't know that was her husband."

"It doesn't matter. Captain Snyder is more than capable of taking care of herself."

"Yeah, I know that and you know that. But Tim is a relative rookie to the job, so he doesn't have a clue. To be honest, I think he just took advantage of the situation and decided to suck up."

Frank shook his head and laughed. "Amber, you think everyone is trying to suck up."

"That's because in most cases, they are. But there was one thing that bothered me about our conversation, though."

"And . . . that would be . . .", Frank asked when Amber hesitated.

"I got the impression that he was disgusted by the fact that Captain Snyder was married to a white man."

Frank gave her a peculiar look. He hadn't gotten that vibe from Timothy when he'd first met him.

"What gave you that impression?" he asked.

"Just the way he looked when he said, 'white man.' It almost appeared that he wanted to throw up when he said it."

"Hmmm. Maybe we should have a talk with him about that at some point. For right now though, we need to go back inside and support our captain."

32

Marie Snyder sat inside Grace Baptist Church in silence. Her head hung low. Her grief-stricken soul ached. Tears dripped from her eyes and splashed onto the dark blue carpet. As a skillful soloist belted out a soulful rendition of "Amazing Grace", Marie thought about the good times she'd shared with her husband. She thought about the time they took the kids to the park and played Twister in the grass. She thought about the time they spent three passion filled-nights in a bed-and-breakfast in Norwalk, Ohio. Those memories caused a slight smile to grace her lips.

As much as she remembered the good times however, she was also filled with loathing. The last six months of their marriage had been anything but fulfilling. Her bastard of a husband had been sleeping around on her with some floozy he routinely met at a bar. When Marie noticed changes in his behavior, she decided to hire a private investigator and have him followed. The PI not only provided her with pictures but also audio. It turned Marie's stomach to hear him talk about how he was sick and tired of his sexless marriage. If only he would have come to her, maybe they could have worked it out.

From her right, she heard the soft whimpers of Kylie. Marie leaned back and wrapped a reassuring arm around her daughter. Kylie leaned sideways and rested her head on her mother's shoulder. Out of the corner of her eye, she saw Gary, who was sitting on her left, lean forward and place his head in his hands. She placed her left hand on the back of his neck and stroked it gently. Marie was worried about her son. He hadn't spoken a word since finding out about his father's death. His face had remained stoic, although his mother could see the pain in his eyes. She now worried that he was on the verge of a breakdown.

"Everything's going to be okay, guys. Everything's going to be okay."

Much to her surprise, Gary stood up and stormed out of the sanctuary. She wanted to go after him to make sure that he was all right, but Kylie had begun to sob harder, so there was no way she could leave her. She just had to hope and pray that he could pull himself together.

Marie closed her eyes and hugged her daughter tightly. She kissed her on the forehead and silently asked the Almighty to take the pain away for her children as well as herself. When she opened her eyes, she was shocked to see Irene standing over her, staring down at her. Her blond hair was spiraled on top of her head. Her blue eyes were ice cold as she stood there glowering.

Sensing that something was amiss, Kylie shifted her body to the right and moved away from her mother. Her young eyes traveled from one woman to the other. She knew that they didn't care for each other but hoped that they were respectful enough of her father's homegoing that they wouldn't make a scene. Not wanting to look like a subordinate, Marie stood up to face her. The two women were similar in stature, so they were pretty much eye to eye. The look in Irene's eyes told Marie to brace for a showdown. She gritted her teeth and stiffened her spine in anticipation of her sister-in-law making a scene. Much to Marie's surprise, however, Irene did something totally unexpected and out of character. She lunged forward . . . and enclosed Marie in a loving bearhug.

"I'm so sorry, Marie. I know you loved my brother."

"Yes, Irene, I did."

Irene squeezed Marie tighter and, for a split second, Marie actually thought that her sister-in-law gave a damn about her. That thought quickly vanished when Irene whispered something into her ear that caused a cold chill to run down her spine.

"But I loved him more, and since I blame you for this, I'm going to spend the rest of my natural life making you pay for it."

Marie pulled back and looked deep into Irene's eyes. "Did you just threaten an officer of the law?"

A sinister smile appeared on Irene's face as she prepared to answer the question. She'd never been arrested before, but for one brief second, she thought about chancing it by slapping Marie across the face.

"Of course not. I would never threaten an officer of the law, Captain Snyder. But like I said, this is all your fault."

"Irene, someone broke into our home and murdered my husband. Please tell me how this is *my* fault."

"You married him," Irene spat. "Had you not dug your venomous, nigger claws into him he would still be alive."

Marie's mouth fell open. She was genuinely shocked. It took every ounce of her willpower not to choke the life out of her.

"Irene . . . I advise you to get the hell out of here before I do something that I'm going to regret."

"Just remember my words," Irene said, before turning and walking back toward the casket. She took one last look at it before making her way up the aisle and through the exit.

From the other side of the room, Frank and Amber witnessed the entire exchange. They'd heard rumblings that Marie didn't get along with her in-laws, but no one had ever been bold enough, or stupid enough, to ask Marie about it.

"Wow. What do you think they were saying to each other?" Amber asked.

"Your guess is as good as mine, but from the look on Captain Snyder's face, they won't be having lunch with each other anytime soon."

Christopher Speight

33

Marie sat on the toilet with her elbows on her thighs and her head in her palms. She was exhausted. Although she knew they meant well, having Donald's friends and family as well as hers constantly in her space during the repast had been more tiring than working a sixteen-hour shift. All she wanted to do was go home, relax, and comfort her children.

After she was done, she opened the stall and walked toward the sink. While she was washing her hands, the bathroom door opened and in walked Officer Carla Johnson. She was an athletically built woman who stood a shade under six feet tall. Her skin was the color of bronze. Her black, shoulder length hair was curled inward at the shoulders with the front cut in a bang. Casually, Carla strolled over next to Marie and stood in front of the sink beside her. Just as she opened her mouth to speak, two other officers came into the bathroom. One of them walked into the stall vacated by Marie and closed the door. The other one walked to a mirror and started fondling with her hair. Carla gave her a quick glance before turning her attention back to Marie and continuing with her statement.

"Once again, Captain, I'm sorry about your husband," she said.

"Thank you, Carla. I appreciate that."

"You must be exhausted."

"I am. This all feels like a bad dream."

"I'm sure it does ma'am. Please let me know if there is anything I can do."

"Thank you, Carla. I'll do that."

Marie then gave Carla a weak smile and headed for the exit.

Christopher Speight

34

It was seven o'clock Saturday morning when a few rays from the sun decided to slide through the blinds and break through Frank's eyelids. Instead of turning his body so that they weren't such an annoyance, Frank decided that he would get up, make himself a cup of coffee, and sit on his porch. Sitting up in his bed, he stretched his arms high above his head and yawned before using the forefingers on each hand to push the sleep from the corners of his eyes.

When he felt that he was awake enough, Frank got out of his bed and threw on his robe. Afterwards, he made his way downstairs and into his kitchen. He didn't know why, but something told him to make an entire pot of coffee instead of the one or two cups he usually made. Franklin Stone was a man who followed his instincts, so without a second thought he filled the coffee pot to the line marked full and pressed the on button.

While the coffee was brewing, he walked to his front door, opened it, and peered out. He was surprised to see that it was foggy outside. He looked at the clock on the wall and saw that it was going on seven fifteen. The kids would be up in another couple of hours, and it would be time for them to visit wife.

A few minutes later, Frank walked back into the kitchen and poured himself a cup of steaming hot java, complete with one cream and five sugars. As the saying goes, Frank liked coffee in his sugar. After taking a sip, he slowly strolled toward the front door. Thoughts of his wife dominated his mind as he pushed it open and walked outside. Frank closed his eyes and took in a deep breath of fresh air.

"Good morning early riser," he heard someone address him. Frank opened his eyes to see Sadie sitting in her chair, smiling at him.

"Good morning. What the devil are you doing up this time of the morning, old lady?"

"Old lady? Who you calling old lady? I got your old lady," she said, crossing her arms over her chest.

"Hey, I don't want no problems," Frank said with a smile.

"Oh, I know that. You don't want this smoke youngster."

Sadie held up both fists as if she were getting ready to go twelve rounds. Frank twisted his lips at hearing her use such a hip analogy.

"What? You didn't know I was cool and hip?"

"I guess not."

"Well, you know now. You got any more coffee brewing in there or is that the last cup?"

"One cup of java, coming right up old . . . I mean *young* lady." Frank laughed out loud as he made his way back into the house. When he came back outside, he was met with a stern frown.

"You know, you're not to old for me to put you over my knee and give you a good spanking."

"I'm just teasing you Sadie. You know I love you."

"Um hmm," Sadie mumbled as she reached out and took the cup with both hands. A light breeze passed through and caused her to shiver slightly.

"You okay?" Frank asked her.

"Always," she responded with a smile. "I'm surprised that you're not in there cooking breakfast for you and the kiddies."

"Not today. I'm going to surprise them by taking them to McDonald's."

Sadie opened her mouth and stuck out her tongue, pretending like she was gaging.

"What?"

"McDonald's? That processed crap will kill you."

Frank looked at Sadie likes she'd lost her mind. "Wait a minute. As I recalled, I bought you McDonald's last week, and you sat up here and scoffed it down like it was the last meal you were ever going to eat on earth. Now you want to sit here and act like it ain't good enough for my kids?"

"There is a major difference between me and your kids. I'm sixty-three years old. I've pretty much lived my life. I'm headed toward the finish line, but those babies have a lot of living to do and

I'd hate to see their lives cut short because you were too lazy to cook them a decent breakfast."

"Well, one fast-food breakfast ain't going to kill them. Besides, I don't feel like cooking this morning. I mean, come on Sadie. You know good and damn well both of them will be excited as hell to get some McDonald's. As a matter of fact, I don't know of any kid who doesn't like Micky Dee's."

"Well, I guess you have a point there. It's still not good for them long term though."

All Frank could do was shrug. He knew better than to argue with Sadie. He couldn't remember the last time he'd won an argument with her and he was sure that today wasn't going to be the day he went on a winning streak.

"What's that on your robe, Frank?" she asked.

Frank looked down at the front of his robe but didn't see anything. "Where?"

"Right there, on your sleeve."

Frank looked at both of his sleeves but still didn't see anything. "What are you talking about? I don't see anything."

"I swear, you men are so blind," Sadie said, reaching for him. "Come here."

With a confused look on his face, Frank took a few steps forward. It wasn't until Sadie reached for his arm that Frank realized what was going on. He tried to move back, but with speed belying her sixty-three years, Sadie grabbed his arm and pinched him twice.

"Ouch!"

"What did I tell you about using those bad words?"

"Doggonnit, Sadie! The kids ain't out here."

"No, but *I'm* out here, and I demand my respect, even from you Detective Stone."

Frank rubbed his stinging arm. He wanted to get mad at Sadie, but he just couldn't bring himself to do so. She was so sweet and friendly that she could commit cold-blooded murder, and he couldn't get angry with her.

"Sorry Sadie."

"That's more like it. Now, I didn't want to ask, but since it doesn't seem like you're going to tell me, I'm just going to ask. Who was that model-looking broad I saw leaving here the other day?"

"Huh?"

"Huh, my behind. You know just what the heck I'm talking about."

"Oh, you're talking about Ms. Ponder. She's the principal at Frank Jr. and Rhonda's school," he said with a dismissive gesture.

"Is that right? Well, in all of my years of living, I've never heard of a principal making a house call."

"No, you don't understand, Sadie. The only reason she came by was because of the fight Frank Jr. got into at school. She wanted to let me know that the boy's mother is talking about pressing charges against Jr."

"Pressing charges? My goodness, how bad did Jr. beat this boy?" Sadie asked with concern. She loved Frank's kids as if they were her own grandchildren, and it would break her heart to see either one of their lives ruined over some nonsense.

"Not bad at all. Just a few bumps and bruises. I think the boy's pride and ego were hurt more than anything else."

"Oh, okay," Sadie said with a sigh of relief.

"From what I hear, the kid is a troublemaker and so is his mother."

"Yeah, sounds like it. But back to you and this Ms. Ponder, mister. You mean to tell me that she couldn't *call* you with that information?"

"I supposed she could've."

"Well, why do you think she didn't?"

"Sadie, I don't know."

"Yes, you do."

Frank blushed. "Look, Sadie, I'm a married man."

"Does *she* know that?"

"Uh, I'm sure she does," he said, looking down at his wedding ring.

"What makes you so sure she saw your ring? What makes you so sure that she even *cares*?"

Black Viper

"Sadie, you're making way too much out of this."

"We'll see," Sadie said, as she took another sip of her coffee.

Christopher Speight

35

"And now, by the power invested in me, by the State of Ohio, I now pronounce you man and wife. Tyrone, you may now salute your bride!"

Tyrone Powers looked down at his bride, Monica Andrews Powers, with an adoration that he'd never looked at any other woman before with. From the moment he laid eyes on her, he knew that she was his soulmate.

Monica, on the other hand, thought he was an arrogant jerk and wanted to wring her friend's neck for even introducing her to Tyrone. Truth be told, Monica didn't even want to go to the all-star gala. She'd worked sixty hours that week and all she wanted to do was sit at home, watch DVR reruns of Jeopardy, and eat ice cream. Betty thought that she was doing Monica a favor by getting her out of the house and introducing her to a different class of people. Because she was a press secretary for the Cleveland Indians, Betty had access to every player on the team. Tyrone Powers just happened to be an all-star pitcher for the Cleveland Indians. It was Betty who had guided him through a steroid scandal and helped him not only prove his innocence but repair his reputation. Tyrone was so grateful, that he promised Betty that no matter what event was being held, she and a plus–one would always be allowed in. He proved that he was a man of his word by flexing his considerable muscle and making sure that she was welcome to attend the party.

Betty was ecstatic. She immediately got on the phone and called Monica. It took a bit of coaxing, but Monica finally agreed to go.

That was a little over a year ago, and now the two of them were about to embark on a lifelong journey of love and happiness. Monica beamed as she closed her eyes and waited for her husband's lips to connect with hers. The two of them melted into each other. The wedding attendees cheered loudly. Some even whistled cat calls. The kiss seemed to last longer than the actual ceremony. The two of them smiled and waved at the crowd as they paraded up the aisle, out of the sanctuary, and into the waiting limousine. Following closely behind them was the twenty-person wedding party. Tyrone spared no expense for the wedding. Monica's wedding dress cost nearly $40,000. Her wedding ring, all ten carats of it, was rumored to cost around $75,000.

Because of Tyrone's celebrity status and financial resources, it was easy for him to hire security and off–duty police officers to ensure that the reception was void of party crashers and people who got too drunk to control themselves. Tyrone wasn't too worried about it, but was prepared just in case someone wanted to act up.

The reception was like a who's who in the sports world. Nearly all of Tyrone's teammates were there, not to mention players from the NFL and the NBA. Despite the many famous faces, however, the only thing on Tyrone and Monica's minds was getting to their hotel room and tearing each other's clothes off. Anyone with eyes could see that they were lusting for each other all night. Whether they were dancing, posing for photographs, or interacting with the wedding guests, the two of them just couldn't seem to keep their hands off each other. All night long, they were watching the clock, anticipating a night of sizzling love making.

As the reception neared its end, the more and more excited they became. Twice that evening they'd considered sneaking off to fulfill their sexual desires but decided that it would be better to wait until they got to the hotel. The next morning, they would board a plane and head off to the Bahamas for a week. When the last guest had left, and the final light switch had been flipped, Tyrone and Monica all but ran to their hotel room. Since the wedding reception was held in the downstairs ballroom of the hotel, all they had to do was hop on an elevator and ride it up to their penthouse suite.

From the moment the elevator closed, they were all over each other. Tyrone grabbed Monica's hand and pulled her toward him. His hand went to the back of her head and gripped it softly. Just like he had at the wedding ceremony, Tyrone leaned down and gently pressed his lips against his new bride's. His manhood stiffened and pressed firmly against her lower abdomen. Heat rushed through Monica's body as she wrapped her arms around his waist and hugged him tightly. The heat index rose inside the elevator and caused a bead of sweat to appear on Tyrone's forehead.

When the elevator reached the penthouse and the door opened, Tyrone and Monica were still in the throes of passion. It took them a full fifteen seconds to realize that doors were open, and the elevator had come to a stop. As they were stepping off the elevator, someone was getting on.

"Newlyweds huh?" the person said and smiled.

"How'd you guess?" Monica said as she stared deeply into her husband's eyes.

Just before the elevator closed, Tyrone shot a glance inside the elevator. He did a double take when he caught a glimpse of the person's face. He thought he recognized it, but the elevator closed before he could be sure.

"Oh my God, baby, I can't wait to get you inside the hotel room," Monica said as she reached down and fondled his manhood. She couldn't wait to feel her new husband inside of her. The two of them continued to paw at each other as they made their way down the hall.

By the time they reached the door to their room, they were like two dogs in heat. As soon as they got inside their room, Tyrone bent his wife over the arm of a couch and took her from behind. Monica howled like a wolf as Tyrone roughly entered her. They went at it for the better part of ten minutes before they stripped and got into bed. Thirty minutes later, they were both breathing heavily and were wrapped in each other's arms.

"Oh God, baby, that was fantastic," Monica beamed. For her to marry a man who loved her unconditionally and who she loved unconditionally meant the world to her.

"You weren't so bad yourself, baby."

"Really, baby? You're not just saying that are you?"

Tyrone looked at Monica as if she were crazy.

"Are you serious? Hell, you know I'm not just saying that!"

"Calm down, baby. I was just checking. Anyway," Monica said as she rose from the bed, "I'm going to take a shower. I stink."

"Yeah, you do," Tyrone said, laughing.

"Whatever. It's your fault for getting me all sweaty and shit."

"Hey, you got me sweaty too now."

"But you're a man. Y'all are always sweaty."

Without warning, Tyrone jumped up and grabbed Monica in a bear hug.

"Oh really? Well maybe you should take some of this sweat off my hands," he said, rubbing his body up against hers.

"Ewww, that's nasty. Now I really need to take a shower," Monica said, laughing. "You could join me you know."

"That's not such a bad idea."

Monica smiled devilishly as she reached down and took hold of Tyrone's penis. Like a dog on a leash, she led him into the bathroom and into the shower.

"Damn, this thing is big. What the hell have you been feeding it all these years?"

Tyrone shrugged and smiled at the compliment. He loved it when Monica bragged on the size of his penis. The two of them proceeded to get into the shower. Had it been up to Tyrone, they would have gotten busy right in the shower, but Monica wanted to take advantage of the queen-sized waterbed in the suite. Although he was slightly disappointed, Tyrone respected Monica's wishes.

"Okay, I'm clean enough. I'll be in the bed waiting for you."

Tyrone then got out of the shower and dried off. He blew Monica a kiss and went off to wait for her. Monica felt blessed as she watched her husband walk away. She'd managed to snag a millionaire and find true love all at the same time. Betty had told her the horror stories about star athletes not really loving their wives and vice-versa. More often than not for the wife it was a matter of financial security. For the husband, it was a matter of having a smoking hot babe on his arm. For the most part, love never even entered the equation, although the word was thrown around quite often. For Tyrone and Monica however, it was different. The two of them genuinely loved and cared for each other.

Black Viper

Monica stayed in the shower for another ten minutes before she felt clean enough to crawl into her husband's arms. After drying off, Monica tip-toed into the bedroom. A broad smile was on her face as she heard the soulful sounds of Luther Vandross coming from the mobile speaker. She licked her lips seductively when she looked at the bed and saw Tyrone's naked body lying there. His smooth chocolate frame was so inviting, a small drip of moisture escaped from the corner of her lip. He was turned on his left side, his muscular back exposed and taut.

"I know you're not tired already, baby. This is our wedding night so you may as well get ready for me to put it on you all night long."

Monica slowly walked over to the bed and climbed in. With her right hand, she reached down and squeezed his butt. She placed her left hand on his shoulder as she planted soft kisses on the back of his shoulder. When Tyrone didn't move, she frowned.

"Oh, playing hard to get, huh?"

Monica continued her seduction of her new husband by letting her tongue travel from his shoulder down the middle of his back. When she got halfway down, she turned him over with the intent of performing fellatio on him.

Noticing that he didn't have an erection bruised her ego. She poked her lips out and lifted her head to look at him. As soon as she looked into his eyes, a piercing scream roared from Monica's throat. The hole in the middle of his forehead peered back at her. Blood leaked from the wound and ran down the bridge of his nose.

Monica quickly moved away from his body and onto the floor. She was still on her knees, screaming, when a strand of piano wire was wrapped around her throat. Monica had no idea where she found the strength, but less than a second later, she was on her feet fighting for her life. Reaching for the wire around her neck, Monica frantically tried to insert her fingers between it and her skin. When she failed to do so, she used her legs to push back against the person attacking her and drive their body into the wall. Tears flooded her eyes as her attacker held on tight.

Christopher Speight

A sharp pain shot through Monica's back as her attacker's knee pushed into the middle of it. Through her tears, Monica saw an ink pen lying on the dresser. Her sight was blurry because of the incessant crying she'd been doing, but she was sure that the object she was looking at was a ball point pen. In a last-ditch effort to save her life, she used her last bit of strength to drag her attacker toward the dresser. If she could just get to that ink pen lying there, she could use it as a weapon and save herself.

She was halfway there when the pressure in her back increased and forced her to her knees. Monica felt her strength abandoning her body. The reality of her impending demise was quickly starting to set in. Feeling that there was nothing she could do to save her life, Monica let her muscles relax and accepted the inevitable.

36

Frank awoke on a Sunday morning to the smell of burnt toast drifting through his nostrils. He looked at his clock sitting on his nightstand and realized that he had slept past his regular 'get up' time of nine o'clock. The previous day had pretty much drained every bit of energy he had. Although it had been Captain Snyder who'd lost a family member and not him, he could still feel her pain. Being at the funeral had caused him to think of his wife. Even though she was laid up in a hospital bed, she was still alive. His heart ached every time he saw her, but he would be devastated if that was no longer an option.

Captain Snyder was more than a boss to him. He considered her a friend. The sad look on her face had nearly broken his heart. He thought about Timothy Jordan and wondered if the young cop could possibly be the mastermind behind the brutal and senseless murders. From everything he gathered, the killings seemed to be racist in nature. Frank had seen his share of dirty cops in his day, and although Timothy Jordan didn't ring any alarms, Frank wasn't going to rule him out as one. Dealing with criminals for the last twenty years had taught him that no one was exempt when it came to committing a crime.

The prospect of Timothy Jordan being a dirty cop angered Frank. It also saddened him. There were enough crooked cops in existence without adding him to the ranks. As an African American man, he was well aware of the social injustices going on worldwide. The lives of innocent black men like Trayvon Martin and George Floyd have been snuffed out by racist officers. And although some racists, such as Donald Sterling, have been brought to light by their racist points of view, members of law enforcement seemed to be immune to the judicial system. It sickened him even more when he thought of the beautiful Black women who'd also become victims. Sandra Bland and Breonna Taylor were just two examples, although Frank was positive that there were many more that hadn't come to light or were just plain being covered up. Frank had no idea if Timothy Jordan was guilty of the infraction, but one thing was for certain. If he was, Frank was going to take him down. A knock on his bedroom door jarred him from his thoughts.

"Daddy? Are you still asleep?" A soft voice sounded through the door, causing a broad smile to spread across Frank's face. He didn't need x-ray vision to know that it was he precious baby girl on the other side of the door.

"No, baby, I'm awake."

"Can I come in?"

Frank raised an eyebrow. Very rarely did Rhonda ask to come into his bedroom. As a matter of fact, now that he thought about it, the times she knocked on his door were far and few between. He sat up in his bed, yawned, and stretched his limbs before answering her.

"Come on in, sweetheart."

Rhonda pushed open the door and entered with a large smile on her face. She was carrying a tray holding the burned toast, runny eggs, and grits that seemed to be drowning in water. A lump formed in Frank's throat. He was choked up at the fat that his daughter had made him breakfast, but he was also nauseated at the monstrosity that sat on a plate before him.

"Uh . . . Thanks, baby girl. You didn't have to do this though. You know I usually cook breakfast on Sundays."

"I know, Daddy. I just wanted to do something to show you that I love you."

Frank looked back down at the plate and forced a smile. He had no idea how he was going to be able to digest the plate of gob before him, but if meant keeping the smile attached to Rhonda's face, he would force himself to do just that. Just then, he heard a snicker coming from the doorway. Frank glanced up to see Frank Jr. leaning on the door frame. He could tell that his son was struggling to suppress his laughter. Rhonda frowned as she turned to face her brother. Her expression revealed that she was upset with her brother's amusement.

"What are you laughing at, big head?"

"Big head?"

"That's what I said," Rhonda replied, rolling her neck.

"Whatever. I'm just here to see Dad eat his scrumptious breakfast that you threw together. And I do mean *threw* together."

"Shut up!"

"Okay, you two, that's enough," Frank said, quickly defusing the argument.

"Daddy's gonna love this breakfast," Rhonda said, turning back to her father. "Here you go, Daddy," she said extending the tray toward him.

Frank Jr. covered his mouth with his hand to further conceal his smirk. Frank looked down at the badly cooked food and came up with a brilliant idea. He hated to do what he was about to do, but it was the only thing he could think of to get himself out of the jam he was in. he reached for the tray and 'accidentally' knocked the tray onto the floor.

"Daddy!" Rhonda shouted in horror.

"Oh my God, baby girl. I'm sorry! I'm so sorry!"

"Oh, daddy, I worked so hard on it too."

"I know you did, baby girl. I'm really sorry."

Rhonda looked down at the floor with sad eyes. She sniffled a couple of times, which made Frank feel like crap. Frank looked up at his son, who gave him a 'Now I know you did that on purpose look,' With sadness in her eyes, Rhonda turned to leave the room. Frank couldn't take it. He had to do something to make it up to his little girl.

"Rhonda, baby, hold up a second. Let me make it up to you."

"Make it up to me how?" she asked.

Frank had an answer already prepared.

"Well, I could take you and you brother to that restaurant y'all like so much."

"IHOP?" the two of them said in unison.

"Yep."

Frank Jr. and Rhonda both threw their hands in the air and celebrated.

"You two go get dressed and wait for me downstairs. I'll be down as soon as I clean up this mess and get dressed."

"Yes! Thank you, Daddy," Rhonda said, as she moved to leave the bedroom. As she walked past her brother, she looked at him and winked.

37

For the third time since they'd left, Frank glanced in his rearview mirror. He didn't know what was going on or why Frank Jr. choose to ride in the backseat with his sister, but he smelled a rat. Something was up. He could feel it in his gut.

"Okay. You two have been giggling ever since we left the house. Just what in the devil is so funny?" he asked.

"Nothing Dad. We're just back here chillin'," Frank Jr. said. Frank glanced at the rearview mirror again.

"Yeah, I can see that. But that's not what I asked you. I asked you what the two of you were laughing at."

"Oh, just something that happened at school the other day," Rhonda interjected. For the next ten seconds, silence engulfed the car.

"Well?" Frank Sr. said.

"Well what?" the kids said in unison.

"What happened in school that was so funny?"

Frank Jr. and Rhonda shot each other a glance. Neither of them had expected their father to ask that question. The look between them wasn't lost on him.

"Come on Dad? Really? You *really* want to know what went on in our school?" Rhonda asked.

"No, not everything. I just want to know what has my kids laughing like a couple of hyenas," Frank said, smiling.

"Just kid stuff, Dad, come on," Rhonda said, shrugging her shoulders.

"Yeah, okay," Frank said, willing to drop it for the moment.

He pulled into the restaurant's parking lot and found a spot near the entrance. He was surprised that the parking lot was so empty on a Sunday morning. He checked his watch and realized that it was almost eleven thirty.

"Guess it's not morning anymore," he mumbled to himself. Even though midday was approaching, Frank still had his taste buds set on breakfast food, pancakes in particular. The IHOP they were getting ready to enter did serve lunch, but Frank had his mind and heart set on pancakes. Apparently, so did his children.

"Man, I can't wait to get in there and put the smash on some chocolate chip pancakes," Frank Jr. said hungrily.

"As greedy as you are, I'll be surprised if you don't order everything on the menu," Rhonda cracked.

"Shut up Anna. You need to be eating everything on the menu, as skinny as you are."

"Whatever, bucket head."

Frank Sr. just shook his head and smiled. It amazed him at how the two of them went at it so much, but always had each other's back. he decided that he would call one of them on it once they began eating.

"Welcome to IHOP. Would you prefer a table or a booth?" a young waitress asked. As soon as Frank Jr. saw who it was asking the question, a vibrant smile spread across his face.

"Hey! I didn't know you worked here," he said.

Because of their father's imposing stature, the young lady couldn't see Frank Jr. or his sister walking in behind him. The smile the young lady returned to him was temporarily put on hold when she saw Rhonda. The two young ladies stared at each other for a few seconds before both of them rolled their eyes. Kisha's smile returned when she focused back on Frank Jr.

"Yeah, I started a few days ago," she said.

"Dad, you remember Kisha, right?"

"Yes, I do. It's nice to meet you again, young lady," Frank Sr. said, nodding his head in courtesy. Rhonda popped her lips, which earned her a nudge from her father. Something was going on between the two young ladies and if his son were going to continue seeing this girl, he would have to have to find out what it was and get to the bottom of it. It was one thing for someone to be rubbed the wrong way, but these two girls seemed to have a genuine dislike for each other.

"Nice to meet you again too, sir," she said. "Would you and your family like a table of a booth?"

"A table would be fine. Thanks."

Kisha turned and led Frank and his two children to a table in the rear corner of the restaurant.

"Someone will be with you to take your order in a moment."

Kisha continued to smile at Frank Jr. as she left. The gesture caused Frank Jr. to blush. Now he was really glad that his sister had tricked his father into bringing them here. Rhonda, on the other hand, shot daggers at Kisha as she walked away.

"Okay Rhonda, what's the story with you and that girl? You mean mugged her when I dropped Jr. off to meet her at the movies, and you're doing the same thing now. What's going on between you two?"

"I just don't like her," Rhonda stated flatly.

"Why not?"

"I don't know. I just don't," he lied.

"Rhonda, no one dislikes anyone for no reason. There has to be one."

Rhonda simply shrugged. There was indeed a reason that she didn't like Kisha, but she wasn't about to reveal it to her father and brother.

"I think she's just mad because Kisha is pretty and she's ugly," Frank Jr. said, laughing.

"Shut up, jerk!"

"Rhonda, lower your voice," Frank said, sternly.

"Sorry Daddy. He just gets on my nerves sometimes."

"And you," he said, glaring at his son. "I don't ever want to hear you call your sister ugly again, do you hear me?"

"Uh . . . okay. Sorry Dad."

Frank had a perplexed look on his face. He and his sister went at it all the time, so he couldn't understand why his father had seemed to get so upset with him this time. What he didn't know was that his father had seen many women's self-esteem destroyed by males drilling into their heads that their looks were inferior, even when they weren't. He'd seen quite a few women come into the precinct with their heads down and their spirits broken, all because some piece of shit man had ruined their self confidence with hateful words and candid putdowns. When Frank was sure that his son had gotten the message, he smiled slightly. After all, this was a family breakfast and he did want the mood to remain festive.

"Son, you baffle me at times," he said as he crossed his arms and cupped his chin with his thumb and forefinger.

"Huh? What are you talking about dad?"

"Like I said, you baffle me."

"What do you mean? How?"

"Well, you're always giving your sister a hard time and making fun of her."

"And . . . that's what big brothers do."

"Yet, you damn near beat that boy at your school to a bloody pulp."

"'Cause, that's what big brothers do," Frank Jr. said smiling at is little sister.

Frank Jr. couldn't dispute anything his father had just said. While it was true that he gave his sister a hard time, he wasn't going to let anyone else do it.

"Oooo, Daddy, you said a cuss word," Rhonda said, imitating a three year old.

"So what's you point?"

"Ms. Sadie's gonna get you for that."

Frank looked around the restaurant a few times, then looked back at his daughter. He held both of his hands in the air, palms up as a wry smile creased his lips.

"Well, Ms. Sadie ain't here, is she?"

"Well, I might just have to tell her what you said."

"Oh, is that right? You mean to tell me that you're going to snitch on your own father?"

"That's her—Queen Tattletale," Frank Jr. said.

"I'm not a tattletale, because if I was, I would tell Daddy about what you did in school last month."

Frank Jr. frowned. He had no idea what Rhonda was talking about. Immediately, he began to replay in his mind what he could have done that would land him in hot water with his father. Had he been paying attention to his sister, he would have seen her wink at her Dad.

"Girl, you're tripping. I ain't done crap," he said when he couldn't remember anything that he'd done. Frank Jr. then reached into his pocket and pulled out his cell phone.

"Whoa there, young man. Just what do you think you're doing?"

"Nothing. Just checking my email," he said, telling a half-truth. While it was true that he was going to check his email, he was also going to scroll Facebook.

"Liar. Your behind was about to get on Facebook," Rhonda said.

"And you know the rules. No social media when we're doing a family outing," Frank Sr. said, sternly.

"Yeah, jerk."

Frank Jr. looked at his father. "Dad, how come you never say anything to her when she calls me names?"

"'Cause when I call you names, I'm telling the truth," Rhonda said smartly.

"Rhonda," Frank Sr. said, looking at his daughter.

Ignoring his sister's verbal jab, Frank Jr. stared at his father as he waited for an answer. It had been bothering him for a while now that his father always seemed to let Rhonda slide on the snide remark she made toward him.

Frank Sr. weighed his options. He wanted to teach his son the proper way to conduct himself when dealing with a smart-mouthed female, but he didn't want his daughter to get the feeling that she could talk to a man however she saw fit. He decided to wait until he and Frank Jr. were alone to discuss the matter.

"We'll talk about it when we get home, all right?"

"Yeah, all right," Frank Jr. answered. He wasn't thrilled with his father brushing off his question, but he understood the look that Frank Sr. was giving him. *'Not in front of your sister'* it said.

"Is that Principal Ponder?" Rhonda asked, interrupting the conversation between father and son. Frank and Frank Jr. turned their heads toward the entrance just in time to see Grace Ponder point in their direction. Frank Jr. frowned as a greeter lead her to their table.

"Ah man, what the heck is she coming over here for?" he wondered.

"She's probably coming over here to tell Daddy what a disappointing student you are," Rhonda answered.

Frank Jr. cut his eyes at his sister. He was getting tired of her smart mouth. Seeing the tense look on his son's face, Frank Sr. figured that it was time to reign in his daughter.

"Rhonda, that's enough," he said, sternly.

"What I do?" Rhonda asked in her innocent tone.

Usually, the tone would soften her father's attitude toward her, but this time even he was getting tired of her shenanigans.

"You know what you've been doing. You've been picking at your brother ever since we go here, and I want you to stop. Understand me?"

A satisfied smirk slid across Frank Jr's face as Rhonda stuck out her lips and pouted. Frank Sr. didn't notice either of their facial expressions. He was too busy gawking at Grace Ponder. As soon as he'd gotten done chastising his daughter, he turned his attention back to the principal. It took every bit of self-control he had to keep the muscles in his face from forming a smile.

Grace Ponder, however, was smiling from ear to ear. Frank watched mesmerized as she glided across the floor and stopped at their table.

"Well hello, Detective Stone. I saw you guys as soon as I walked in. May I join you?" she asked.

"Sure," Frank said as he quickly stood up and pulled out a chair for her. Frank Jr. and Rhonda looked at each other. They were both speechless. Having their principal sit down and join them for breakfast was something that neither of them ever thought would happen. As the initial shock wore off, Frank Jr. and Rhonda had two very different thoughts going on in their heads. Frank Jr. started getting suspicious. It was the second time he'd seen Principal Ponder since he'd gotten into the fight at school. He was beginning to wonder if his father had secretly instructed her to keep an eye on him and report back to his father.

Rhonda, on the other hand, felt that Principal Ponder was trying to get close to her father and she didn't like it one bit. Even though her mother was laid up in a hospital bed comatose, that still didn't give her father any right to be seeing some other woman. It didn't matter that her father hadn't initiated either meeting between the two of them. That was beside the point. Rhonda didn't want anyone trying to replace her mother. Up until now, she'd always liked Principal Ponder, but that was slowly beginning to change.

"Good morning Frank Jr. and Rhonda. How are you two doing this morning?"

"Uh . . . I'm good," Frank Jr. said.

Rhonda remained silent. Her disdain for the entire situation wouldn't allow her to speak. Frank Sr. nudged his daughter. He didn't know why she suddenly had an attitude, but he wasn't about to be embarrassed by her behavior.

"Oh, sorry. Hi Ms. Ponder," she said unenthusiastically.

Grace Ponder barely noticed her dry tone. She was too busy focusing on Frank Sr. She'd been thinking about him a lot lately. Although she knew that he was off limits, it didn't stop her from being attracted to him. She wanted so badly to broach the subject of his wife to gauge where his head and his heart were but realized that now wasn't the time. Grace Ponder also knew that, technically, it wasn't illegal to date the parent of a student, but it was unethical to the highest order. She didn't care. Detective Frank Stone was her type of man. Tall, handsome, rugged, and employed.

Christopher Speight

38

The ride on the way home from the restaurant was quiet. Rhonda sat in the backseat seething from the fact that Grace Ponder had interrupted their family time. Sitting directly behind Frank Jr., she was able to see the right side of her father's face. She couldn't be sure, but she could have sworn that she'd seen remnants of a slight smile. This caused her to become even more irate. If Grace Ponder thought that she was going to wiggle her way into their lives and replace her mother, then she had another think coming. In Rhonda's eyes, Marilyn Stone was the greatest woman ever to walk the face of the earth, and no one would ever be able to take her place. Frank glanced in the rearview mirror and noted the sour expression on his daughter's face. Her arms were folded over her chest and her lips were poked out.

"What's your problem?" he asked.

"Nothing," she replied, flatly.

Frank cut his eyes to his son in the passenger's seat. Frank Jr. was busy reading Twitter feeds and wasn't paying attention to his father or his sister. Frank Sr. tapped his son on the shoulder to get his attention. When Jr. looked at him, Frank jerked his head In Rhonda's direction and shrugged his shoulders. His son responded by shrugging his own shoulders and giving his father a look that said, 'I don't know what the hell is wrong with her.' It still hadn't crossed Frank Jr.'s mind yet that his principal was hitting on his father. He still thought that it was some kind of conspiracy and that his father and Miss Ponder were in cahoots about something he may have done in school.

"Okay," Frank Sr. said, giving up his inquisition. "Well, since I'm off today, I was wondering if y'all wanted to go to the movies today. If not, then we can just find something on cable and order a couple of pizzas later."

Because he knew his children so well, Frank knew what the response would be before he even asked the question. Frank Jr. was seventeen years old and the last thing he wanted to do was be seen at the movies with is father, and he definitely didn't feel like sitting in front of a television watching some old, boring movie that his father was surely going to pick out. Besides, Frank Jr. had plans of his own.

"Uh, sorry Dad, but me and Wallace have plans."

"Oh yeah? What kinda plans?"

"We entered an X-box basketball tournament. The winner gets five hundred dollars."

Frank Sr. raised an eyebrow.

"Five hundred dollars? Are you sure this is a tournament?" he asked.

"Yes Dad, it's a tournament," he responded, knowing exactly what his father was getting at. Frank Jr. had already been hustled once trying to gamble, and Frank Sr. was determined not to let it happen again. It was roughly six months ago when he'd sent his son to the store to pick up a few items, but when Frank Jr. returned, not only did he not have the items, but he also didn't even have the money that his father gave him to get said items. A headache started to set in as he desperately tried to think of a good enough story to tell his father when he got home. The second he stepped inside the house though, his father knew that something was up

"What's wrong? And where's the stuff that I sent you to the store to buy?"

For one brief second, Frank Jr. thought about lying and saying that he'd gotten robbed, but just as quickly, common sense prevailed. His father would've seen right through that fib. For one, Frank Jr. didn't look like he'd been in any kind of altercation. His face bore no cuts, bruises, or scraps. Also, his knuckles were unmarked and if Frank Sr. knew anything about his son, he knew that he wouldn't go down without a fight. After bracing himself for an explosion, he went ahead and told his father the truth. He still hadn't understood how it had happened and now that he was explaining it to his father, he understood it even less. He was sure that he knew where the ace of spades was. He had already taken the man for twenty dollars and was positive that he could win even more.

Black Viper

As he finished telling his father the story, something dawned on him. The man had waited until Frank Jr. was confident enough to wager every dime he had before agreeing to up the ante. After telling his father the entire episode, Frank Jr. waited for his father to explode. Instead, Frank Sr. just shook his head and laughed.

"Son," he said to him, "you have just fallen for one of the oldest cons in the book." After taking Frank Jr. back to confront the con man, Frank Sr. sat his son down and had a long talk with him about gambling. Since Frank Jr. wasn't risking any of his own money, technically, he wasn't gambling.

"Yeah, okay. What about you, honey? You feel like watching a movie with the old man?"

"Whatever," Rhonda said, shrugging.

Now, Frank was beginning to get angry. He didn't know what Rhonda's problem was, but he wasn't going to tolerate any disrespect. As soon as he pulled into his driveway, he instructed Frank Jr. to go into the house wile he talked to his sister. Not wanting to get caught up in the storm brewing, Frank Jr. quickly exited the vehicle. Once he was inside the house, Frank Sr. turned and face his daughter.

"Look, Rhonda. I don't know what in the devil your problem is and quite frankly, I don't care. But whatever is on your mind either tell me about it or let it go, because I'm not going to tolerate you disrespecting me any longer. Do you understand me, young lady?"

"Yes sir."

"Good. Now, do we need to talk about something?"

"Not at all, Daddy."

Although Rhonda did want to confront her father and let him know how she felt about Grace Ponder injecting herself into their lives, she decided that now wasn't the time to do so. She didn't want to be rash and jump to conclusions. What if she was wrong? What if Grace Ponder was merely being friendly, and her showing up at IHOP was a coincidence? Then she would come off looking like a spoiled fool. That wouldn't have been a good look, and she would have embarrassed the hell out of her father, so she decided just to bide her time and keep a close eye on the situation.

"All right. Now, do you want to watch a movie later on?" he asked.

"That's fine, Daddy," she said, although she really didn't want to.

"Hey, don't let me twist your arm. If you don't want to . . ."

"No Daddy, it's fine. We can watch a movie." Rhonda knew that her father looked forward to spending time with his children. The last thing she wanted to do was blow him off and hurt his feelings. Frank Jr. blowing him off was different. Both she and her father expected him to chase girls and play videos games with his friends for hours. But she was his little girl. The light of his life. The apple of his eye. So even though she didn't feel like watching a movie, she sucked it up and made the sacrifice for him, because she would run out of numbers if she tried to count the sacrifices that he'd made over the years for her. Frank reached for the door handle, but Rhonda's voice stopped him in his tracks.

"Daddy, do you still love Mommy?"

Frank turned around with a surprised look on his face. It was the last question he ever expected either of his kids to ask him.

He was so surprised at the question that he thought he'd heard it wrong.

"Huh?? What did you just ask me??"

"I asked you if you still loved Mommy."

"Of course, I still love you mother . . . with all my heart," he said sincerely.

Rhonda looked into her father's eyes and instantly knew that he meant every word. That was just what she needed to hear. A large smile spread across her face. Without saying another word, she hopped out of the car and ran into the house. Just before she got into the house, Frank rolled down his window and called out to her.

"Hey! I'm going to run to the store and get us some snacks for us for tonight. Tell your brother that I'll be back in few minutes."

"Okay Daddy," she said just before disappearing into the house.

39

Rhonda waked into the house with a smile that could light up downtown Cleveland. A tremendous weight was lifted from her shoulders when her father told her that he still loved her mother. She figured as much, but it did her heart a world of good to hear him say it. She entered the kitchen to get a glass of water and was amazed to see Frank Jr. fixing a bowl of cereal.

"I know good and well you're not hungry. You just ate two stacks of pancakes, four sausage links, and two biscuits."

"And?"

"Dang, you're just greedy."

"Whatever. What did Dad want to talk to you about?"

"None of your business, nosey."

"Fine, you ain't got to tell me. I already know anyway."

"No, you don't," Rhonda said in an agitated manner. It irked her to no end the way her brother thought he knew everything.

"Yeah, I do. He was probably getting on you about your little snotty attitude."

"I didn't have no snotty attitude."

"Please! As soon as Ms. Ponder walked in the restaurant, you started acting like something crawled up your ass."

"Ooooh, I'm telling Dad!"

Frank Jr. looked at his sister and slowly shook his head.

"My God, you're such a snitch!"

"I ain't no snitch!"

"Then prove it. Keep your damn mouth shut!"

"I ain't gotta keep shit shut!" Rhonda's hand flew to her mouth. She would give anything to be able to push the word back down her throat, but it was too late. A shocked expression appeared on Frank Jr.'s face. He'd never heard his sister use foul language. A few seconds later, the stunned expression was replaced by a devious smirk.

"Now, you were going to tell dad what?" he asked.

"Oooooh, you make me sick!"

Rhonda stormed over to the sink and turned on the faucet. After filling her glass with water, she made her way back into the living room, where she grabbed the television remote and pressed the on button. After channel surfing for a few seconds, she heard her brother snickering from behind her.

"What the heck are you laughing at?" she asked.

"You. I just figured out what's wrong with you. You're mad because you think Ms. Ponder likes dad and you're afraid that he likes her back."

"Daddy doesn't like Ms. Ponder! He still loves Mama!"

Frank cocked his head and looked into his sister's eyes. He could see the sadness in them, and it made him feel bad. He took a deep breath, walked over to the couch, and dropped down next to her.

"Look, sis. I know you miss Mama. I miss her too. But sooner or later, we just have to face the facts that she may be in a coma for the rest of her life. Maybe it's time for Dad to move on."

"No! It's not time for him to move on! Mama will be okay! You'll see! God will see to it!"

Frank Jr. just stared at his sister sympathetically. Although he personally didn't believe that God would do a damn thing, he remembered what his father said about not crushing her faith. Frank Jr. put his arm around his sister and gave her a tight hug. His gut feeling told him that he would have to comfort her quite a bit in the coming days.

40

It didn't take Detective Stone long to figure out why his daughter had such an attitude. From the second Grace Ponder arrived at their table, Rhonda's entire demeanor changed. She became argumentative and very combative. A small sliver of guilt ran through him as he began to realize what his daughter was doing. She was protecting her mother's turf. Frank smiled when he thought about how defensive his daughter was when it came to his wife. She missed her mother terribly and prayed every night that she would come out of her comatose state and re-join their family. Although Frank was reluctant to admit it to himself, he found it harder and harder to have faith with each passing day. It seemed as if the prayers of his, his daughter's, his son's, and anyone else praying for his wife were going unanswered.

If that wasn't bad enough, he was now presented with a new challenge. Better yet . . . a temptation. Grace Ponder was one of the most beautiful women he'd seen in a long time. In his opinion, she was the only woman he'd seen that had even come close to Marilyn's beauty. He felt guilty for being attracted to her and, for some strange reason, he felt even guiltier that she was attracted to him. He was sure that he hadn't done anything to provoke that.

Frank spun his wedding ring back and forth around his finger as he sat at a red light, He smiled as he thought of the day he and his wife exchanged nuptials so many years ago. He was so deep in his thoughts that he remained sitting there after the light had turned green. A loud-sounding horn from a beat-up Ford Taurus jarred him back to the present. As he pressed down on the pedal and continued on his way, Frank realized that he was coming up on his destination. He parkee his vehicle, cut the engine, and looked around. At this moment, that he fully understood how powerful a hold his love for his wife had on him.

Frank took a deep breath and exited the vehicle. Slowly, he made his way toward the hospital entrance. What started as a simple trip to the store turned into Frank's desire and need to see his wife. He couldn't explain it, but the closer he got to her room, the guiltier he felt. Even though he hadn't done anything wrong, just being in Grace's presence had him feeling like he was unfaithful to Marilyn. He knew it wasn't true, but that's how he felt.

When Frank reached his wife's room, he stopped. He took a deep breath and tried to collect himself. When he felt that he'd pulled himself together enough, he entered the room. His stomach was in knots as he moved toward her bed. He frowned when he felt his cell phone vibrate in his pocket. After taking it out, Frank turned it off without looking at the screen. He didn't know who it was, and he didn't care. Whoever it was, they were just going to have to wait. He needed to do this. While he enjoyed bringing his kids to see their mother, right now Frank needed time with his wife. Alone.

He looked at her and smiled as he reached down and grabbed her hand. A single tear leaked from his right eye and ran down his cheek as he gently stroked her hand. The monotone sound that went off every two seconds was harmless. But to Frank, the beeping sounds were more painful than any gunshot could ever be. Each one felt like a dagger of death, plunging in and out of his heart. Frank remained silent for a few seconds before doing something that he'd become all too familiar with doing. He closed his eyes and got down on his knees. He then clasped his hands together and began reciting the Lord's Prayer. When he finished, he began speaking to his wife.

"Marilyn, baby. I'm sorry. My God, I'm sorry. Had it not been for me asking you to pick up Frank Jr., this would've never happened. I love you, baby. And just know, I will never betray our love or our vows. I will honor them forever, until death do us part."

When Frank opened his eyes, the nurse was standing next to him. Her eyes were watery as she held a box of Kleenex in her hand. She plucked two from the box and handed them to Frank. Until that moment, Frank hadn't realized that he'd been crying.

"Thank you," he said, taking the Kleenex from her and wiping his eyes.

"Are you okay, Detective Stone?"

Frank cleared his throat.

"Yes, I will be," he said.

"Okay. I'll be out of your hair in a few seconds. I just need to check a few things, and then I'll leave you alone with your wife."

The nurse moved as fast as she could. She didn't want to infringe upon Frank any more than she had to. It had touched her deeply to see a man showing genuine care and love for his wife. But there was something else. She knew the question that Frank was going to ask her, and seeing him in the state he was in, she would rather not answer it. She was almost out of the room when he called out to her.

"Uh, excuse me Nadine, but has there been any change?"

It broke Nadine's heart to have to tell him the sad truth

"I'm sorry, Mr. Stone, but no. there hadn't been."

Frank expected as much, but he still had to ask. A little bit of hope was better than none at all. Frank stayed there with his wife for another fifteen minutes before getting ready to leave. However, just before he did, he lifted Marilyn's hand up his face and used it to massage his cheek. Her touch alone seemed to cause a calm to fall over him. It also seemed to strengthen him. But being here with her all by himself seemed to connect the two of them in a way that only they could understand. After leaning down and kissing Marilyn on her cheek, Frank whispered into her ear.

"I love you, baby. Please, come back to me."

Christopher Speight

41

When Frank got home, he walked into the house and was pleasantly surprised by what he saw. Sitting on the couch, wrapped in each other's arms were Frank Jr. and Rhonda. They were both sound asleep. Frank didn't have to think long to know what was going on. It was obvious to him that Rhonda was still upset about Grace showing up at the restaurant and her brother provided her a shoulder to cry on. The sight warmed his heart. Instead of disturbing them, Frank went outside on the porch.

"Good afternoon, Mr. Detective."

Frank turned to see Sadie sitting in her chair, thumbing through a newspaper.

"Hey, Sadie. What's going on?"

"Not much. Just sitting here, enjoying some of this good weather. I see you were out and about this morning."

"And just how do you know that?"

"I heard your garage door open up."

"Let me guess. You were up exercising again, right?"

"You know it," Sadie responded, as she flexed her bicep muscle.

"You know, Sadie, you really should slow down on your physical fitness activities. You don't want to overdo it," Frank warned.

As usual, Sadie paid him no mind. After staring at him for a few seconds, she simply rolled her eyes and waved him off.

"I'm serious, Sadie. A woman your age shouldn't be—"

"A woman my age shouldn't be what?" she said, cutting him off.

Frank knew that he was borderline pissing Sadie off, but he cared too much about her to bite his tongue on what he felt was important.

"Exerting herself with strenuous activity," he said, completing his sentence.

"You've got a lot of nerve. You fight crime and dodge bullets from bad guys for a living and you're worried about me doing a few exercises?"

"Sadie, that's different. I do that stuff because it's my job."

"Oh, okay. So, I guess I'm just supposed to knit blankets and do crossword puzzles all day, is that it?"

"No, of course not. I mean, I understand that you want to get some exercise in. That's a good thing. All I'm saying is that you shouldn't overexert yourself."

"And just what in the devil makes you think I do that?"

Frank opened his mouth to answer but was at a loss for words . . . because he had no concrete proof that Sadie was overexerting herself. All he had to go on was a fruitless hypothesis.

"Yeah, that's what I thought. Your behind is just guessing," she said.

"I'm sorry, Sadie, I didn't mean to offend you. I just don't know what I would do without you."

"Ah, that's so sweet. But hear this, Franklin Stone. There is nothing that is going to happen to me until the good Lord sees fit. Now, park your behind in one of these chairs while I go pour us a cup o' joe."

Sadie then ended the conversation by getting up and going into her house. As Frank trudged down his steps and made his way across his lawn and up Sadie's steps all he could do was smile. He dropped into the chair next to the one Sadie had sat in and waited for her to return. A few minutes later, Sadie walked back onto the porch with two cups of steaming, hot coffee. The two of them had drank coffee on the porch for years, so she knew exactly how he liked it.

"I suppose you still like coffee with your sugar?" she cracked.

"Very funny, old woman, and yes. With two creams." Frank couldn't drink a cup of coffee unless it had at least five tablespoons full of sugar in it. He received the cup from Sadie and took a sip. The liquid slightly burned his tongue, causing him to wince.

"Wow, that's hot," he acknowledged.

Black Viper

"Yeah, I've heard that it's supposed to be," Sadie said with a smirk.

"Smart-ass." As soon as the words left his mouth, Frank knew what was about to happen. He braced himself for the sting of one of Sadie's pinches. However, what he hadn't planned on, was that she was going to give him a double dose.

"Hey! I only cussed once, and it wasn't a real cuss word at that," he said, rubbing the spot where she pinched him a second time.

"It was the way you used it mister."

"But why did you pinch me twice?"

"Well, the first one was because of what you said. The second one was for something you said that I wasn't around to hear."

Frank burst out laughing. This old woman was something else. He loved her as if she were a blood member of his own family and would kill to protect her.

"So, where did you go off to this morning?"

"I took the kids to IHOP."

"Oh. I know they loved that."

"Well, it was the least I could do, after accidentally dropping the food Rhonda cooked for me this morning," Frank said with a wry smile.

"Hmmm, from the sound of your voice, dropping it on the floor was no accident."

Frank turned his head toward his porch and glanced at his front door. He then turned back to Sadie, leaned over, and whispered into her ear.

"It wasn't an accident, Sadie. You should've seen that monstrosity she brought into my bedroom for me to eat."

"Really?" Sadie said, surprised. "I thought you told me that your wife taught her how to cook."

"She did, so I don't know what the hell happened this morning," Frank said, sticking out his arm ready to accept his punishment.

Sadie held up her hands.

"I'll just put that on in the bank. Let's get back to this terrible breakfast, though. What was wrong with it?"

"Well, the toast was burnt crispy black, the grits were watery, and eggs were running like Usain Bolt. I mean, I really hated to trick her like that, but there was no way I was going to be able to eat that stuff," Frank said, looking back again at his door to make sure that his daughter wasn't eavesdropping.

Sadie looked at Frank and shook her head.

"What?"

"And you call yourself a detective."

"What the heck are you talking about?"

"I'm disappointed in you Frank. Don't you know when you're being played? Think about it. You told me that Marilyn taught Rhonda how to cook, right?"

"Yeah, so."

"So, do you honestly think that she could mess up three different foods in one cooking session?"

After thinking about it for a few seconds, Frank closed his eyes, smiled, and shook his head.

"Yep. In the immortal words of Malcolm X, My brother, you've been bamboozled, hoodwinked, led astray, run amuck—"

"Okay, okay, I get the picture. That sneaky little rug rat. No wonder she and Jr. were sitting in the back seat together laughing on our way there."

"Yeah, she set you up good."

"I forgive her though. That's my baby, even though she acted like a total brat at the restaurant."

"Oh yeah? What did she do?"

"Well, I think she got mad because Grace showed up there while we were there."

"Grace? The woman who came to your house the other day?" Your kids' principal?"

"Yes."

Sadie gave Frank a disbelieving look.

"Sadie, I didn't invite her. I didn't even know she was coming. Had I known that, I probably wouldn't've gone there."

"Probably?"

"You know what I mean," Frank said, exasperated.

"Oh, I know what you mean, all right," Sadie said with a sly smirk.

"Sadie, nothing is going on between me and Grace."

"I believe you Frank. I really do. Let me ask you something though. Why are you calling this woman by her first name? It's not like you two are old friends."

Frank was at a loss for words. Now that he thought about it, it did look suspect. He pressed the sides of his temples and rubbed. Suddenly, he was getting a headache. Sadie placed a hand on his shoulder.

"You're attracted to her, aren't you?"

"I don't know, Sadie," he said, shaking his head.

"Well, my friend, I've been around a long time, so I know. But believe it or not, that's not the worst part of it."

Frank looked at her with a confused look.

"What do you mean?"

"The worse part of all of this is that she's attracted to you. Let me ask you something. When you saw her in the restaurant, did you invite her to join y'all, or did she invite herself?"

"Actually, she invited herself."

"That's what I thought," Sadie said, nodding her head. "Does this woman know that your married?"

"I assume so. I mean, we never talked about it, but I'm pretty sure she sees the wedding ring on my finger."

"Well, don't be surprised if she gets aggressive coming after you."

Frank looked at his ring and then at Sadie.

"What? You think just because you have a ring on, that she won't come after you? Frank, you've seen this woman three times in the last week, and not one time has she asked about your wife, has she? I'll answer that for you. No. That means one of two things. She either thinks that you're separated or that your wife is dead because, trust me, she's wondering why she's never seen her. Come on, Frank. Everything I'm telling you; you already know."

Frank wasn't dense. He knew in his heart that everything Sadie had just told him was the truth. It was apparent that his attraction to Grace Ponder wasn't letting him see it.

"What you should've done when she invited herself to sit with y'all is politely tell her that you wanted to spend some time with your kids alone."

"You're right, Sadie. That was a mistake."

"Yes, that was *definitely* a mistake."

"The thing I hate most of all is that it upset Rhonda."

"Well, I don't mean to sound like I don't care, but Rhonda will be okay. She's not going to like anyone other than her mother. I'm more worried about how *you're* going to handle this. It's not like you're an old man, and I know you get lonely at times. Please, let me finish," she said when Frank opened his mouth to speak.

"You're a man, and you have needs. But please don't mistake that need for anything other than that. Even though Marilyn is in the hospital, she's still breathing, and she's still your wife.

Remember that when your loneliness overcomes you, and you give in to it."

"Sadie, if you mean by that what I think you mean, you don't even have to worry about it. Just because I'm attracted to a woman doesn't mean that I'm going to sleep with her."

Sadie smiled. Frank responded just the way she hoped he would. She knew that it had been tough on him ever since his wife's car accident, but so far, he'd stood strong. She just hoped that he would remain strong.

42

Marie Snyder sat on the edge of the bed and stared at the floor. Because her house was an active crime scene, the city had put her and her children up in a hotel suite in downtown Cleveland. She thought about her son, Gary, whose emotions continued to range from anger to sadness. He still hadn't spoken much since his father died, but when he did, he would either burst into tears or scream in anger. Marie was skeptical when he told her that he was going to hang out with a friend of his but decided that she would have to let him deal with the tragedy in his own way. She thought it would be her and her daughter spending time together in the hotel room until Kylie informed her that she was going to the library. Kylie had been mopping around the room all day and decided that the only way to get it off her mind was to study. So now, Marie was left alone, but she didn't mind. She needed a little time to herself anyway.

Since the police didn't have any suspects so far, police chief deemed it necessary to have guards posted in the hotel lobby. Every hour or so, one of them would come up to the room and make sure that Marie was okay. After their third visit to her room, annoyance began to set in. She told them that she and her kids were okay and to please not bother them for the rest of the day.

Marie rolled her eyes when she once again heard a knock on the door. She bit her bottom lips as she tried hard to control her temper. She thought about ignoring it, but the last thing she wanted was for officers guarding her to panic and break down the door.

With a heavy sigh, Marie got up and made her way toward the door. Thinking that she knew who was on the other side of it, she snatched the door open. She had fire in her eyes and was ready to unload on the officers for bothering her again. She was surprised, however, when she saw Frank and Amber standing there.

"Hi Cap. How are you doing?" Amber asked.

"I've been better guys. What are you doing here?"

"We came by to check on you and the kids," Frank said.

"You could have called."

"True, but we wanted to see for ourselves."

Marie stared at Frank and Amber for a few seconds before inviting them in. She led them into the entertainment area of the suite.

"I thought you were one of the officers that were assigned to protect me," Marie said, using air quotes.

"You sound like you think that's a bad idea," Amber replied.

"No, I know that they've been ordered to do it, but they're bugging the hell out of me. Every time I turn around, they're knocking on the door asking me if I'm all right. I'm just tired of seeing them. My kids aren't here, so I was just in here taking some time for myself. Who's working the crime scene?"

"Hughes and Phillips."

"Okay," she said, nodding her head in approval. Had it been up to her, Frank and Amber would be working the scene. But they were already investigating the two previous murders that happened in the last couple of weeks.

"Cap, why don't you let us take you out for a drink or two," Frank suggested.

"Yeah. It'll do you some good to get out," Amber chimed in.

Marie thought about what they were saying. Although she hadn't been out since she'd checked into the hotel, she didn't know if she was ready to bebothered with anyone outside of it yet. She was lonely though, and maybe it would do her some good to be around people who cared about her.

"Captain? What do you say?" Amber pressed.

Marie leaned her head from one side to the other, shrugged her shoulders, and smiled. It was the first time that she'd smiled since her husband had been murdered.

"Okay. I guess it would do me some good to get out a little bit. Let me throw on something presentable and get my purse."

Frank and Amber waited patiently for Marie to get ready. Frank rubbed his face and blew out a deep breath. He felt sorry for his boss.

He knew that she was going through a rough time in her life, but he'd never seen her as broken as she was right now.

"You okay Frank?" Amber asked.

"Yeah. I just feel bad for Marie."

"Yeah, me too. I hope getting her out of here for an hour or two lifts her spirits."

"Where did you want to take her?"

"Where else? We're taking her to Johnny Blue's."

Christopher Speight

43

As usual, Johnny Blue's was packed. Off duty cops once again flooded the place. The second Frank pulled into the parking lot, he wondered if they'd made a mistake by inviting Marie out for a drink. Although she was grateful that her fellow law enforcement officers were sympathetic to her plight and had her back, she didn't want to be bombarded by her contemporaries overwhelming her with condolences. After cutting the engine, he turned and looked at Amber.

"Hey, you two stay put for a second. I'll be right back."

Amber turned and looked into the back seat at Marie. Both of them were confused by Frank's actions.

Frank jogged across the parking lot and into the establishment. He went to the bar and got the bartender to get everyone's attention. Once the bartender had done so, Frank made a public service announcement.

"Listen, everybody. I know you've all have heard about what happened to Captain Snyder's husband, right?"

Many officers in the bar answered his question verbally, while others simply nodded.

"Well, Detective Davis and I went to visit her in her hotel room a short while ago. We convinced her to come out and have a drink with us, but I'm not sure that's she's ready to be bombarded by a bunch of condolences. I know you all mean well, but let's just let her come in here and have her space, okay?"

To a man, and woman, everyone in the bar agreed. The last thing they wanted to do was make things uncomfortable for their fellow law enforcement officer. Frank thanked everyone for their cooperation and headed back outside.

"Okay, let's go," he said when he got back to the car.

"What was that all about?" Amber asked.

"Just wanted to make sure that everything was good in there."

Amber and Marie followed Frank in. All eyes turned to them when they got inside. As several officers nodded to her in a show of respect, Frank quickly ushered Marie to a table in the back. As they made their way there, Frank realized that many people were present that weren't police officers, unlike the last time they were here.

"What'll you have Captain?" Frank asked.

"I'll just have a beer," Marie said. She actually wanted something much stronger, but she was afraid that if she got something of that caliber, she wouldn't be able to stop herself from breaking down. After Frank ordered the drinks, the three of them sat there in awkward silence for a few seconds. Marie was the first one to break the silence. Even though she was technically on leave, she was still a law enforcement officer and, therefore, thought like one.

"So how is the case on the two murders going? Have you found out anything new?"

Frank and Marie gave each other a surprised look. Talking about unsolved murders hadn't been on their agenda.

"Uh, you really want to talk about that now, Captain?" Amber asked.

"I don't see why not. The world hasn't stopped just because some scum bag decided to take my husband from me," she said, angrily. "Now, do you have anything new to report?"

"Well, actually, we do. Detective Davis and I have been brainstorming, and we think that both murders are related."

"Really? How so?"

"Well, the one thing that seems to be the constant in both cases is that the victims were interracial couples."

"Is that right? So now we're looking at a hate crime?" she said through gritted teeth.

"It would appear so, Captain. Of course, the district attorney would have to prove that for the charge to stick," Frank said.

Marie nodded her head in agreement. A few more seconds of silence went by before Marie addressed the elephant in the room.

"Detective Stone, do you think the murders in those two particular cases have anything to do with my husband being killed?"

Frank rubbed his chin as he pondered Marie's question.

"It's a possibility, but to be honest, Captain, it's too early to tell."

"Yeah, I think you're right," Marie agreed.

"It seems to fit, though," Amber said.

"I agree with that also. Nothing seemed to be missing, so I think we can pretty much rule out robbery as a motive. There was no sign of a struggle. The one thing I can't figure out is how the hell the killer got in, because I just can't see Frank leaving the front door unlocked."

"Here are your drinks, Officers," the waitress said, setting the beverages down on the table. "Let me know if you need anything else."

"Thanks Linda. You know, there seems to be quite a few civilians in here this evening," Frank said, glancing around.

"I know, right? We've actually been getting more and more civilians coming in here recently."

"Really? I wonder why," Amber asked.

"Well, just from talking to a couple of them, they feel safe here."

"Yeah, I guess that makes sense," Frank admitted. "I mean, who in their right mind is going to start trouble in a bar full of cops?"

Just then a loud grumbling sound was heard around the table.

"Excuse me," Marie said, embarrassed. It was then that she realized she hadn't eaten anything for the past ten hours. She'd skipped breakfast and lunch.

"On second thought, I think I will have a turkey burger, with mayo and cheese."

The waitress quickly took out her pad and jotted down Marie's order. Afterwards, she waited to see if either Frank or Amber was going to order something. Knowing that police officers often had police business on their minds, Linda decided to ask to make sure.

"Did either of you want anything?"

"Nothing for me, thanks," Frank said, holding up his hand.

"What about you, Detective Davis?"

"That turkey burger sounds pretty good. I think I'll have one too."

"Two turkey burgers coming right up," Linda said and scampered off.

Linda had been working at Johnny Blues for a little over five years. She had short black hair and was a bit on the plump side, but she was very friendly and cordial to everyone who came in.

"You okay Cap?" Frank asked when he noticed Marie staring into space.

"Huh? Oh yeah. Just trying to get myself together."

"Wow, that was fast," Amber said when Linda returned with their food.

"Eh, not too many people ordering food tonight. The cook isn't that busy."

"Well, I'm glad to get my food in a timely fashion, but this burger had better be done. Like Amber said, it got here rather quickly. The last thing I need is to walk out of here infected with salmonella poisoning."

Linda looked around slowly to make sure no other employee could hear her. When she felt she was in the clear, she looked back at Marie and smiled.

"I'll let you guys in on a little secret. The turkey burgers are already cooked when they get here. All we have to do is thaw them and warm them up. Shhh," Linda said as she put her finger to her lips.

To say that Marie was surprised was an understatement. She'd had one of Johnny Blues' turkey burgers before, and it tasted nothing like meat that had been cooked, frozen, thawed, and heated back up. This time was no different. Marie moaned in satisfaction as she bit into her sandwich. It was so juicy and seasoned to perfection, that she could have sworn that it had been specially made for her.

"Oh my God, is this good," she said, savoring every delicious bite. Marie didn't know if it was the fact that she hadn't eaten in so long or that the cook just happened to outdo himself, but this was the best turkey burger she'd ever tasted in her life. Seeing both Marie and Amber devour their meal, combined with the aroma coming from their burgers, caused Frank's stomach to rumble. He wasn't hungry, but he had to have one. He looked around for Linda to order himself one and did a double take when he saw Timothy Jordan, Carla Johnson, and Ryan Turner headed in their direction.

"Hey, guys. Hey, Cap. How are you doing?" Carla asked Maria.

Marie shrugged. "It comes and goes," she said softly. Carla slid into the booth next to Marie and put her arm around her. She was very fond of her boss.

"It's going to be okay, Cap. We're all here for you whenever you need us," she said, squeezing her boss tightly. Marie hugged her back. After they broke their embrace, Marie looked at Timothy.

"Hello Officer Jordan."

"Hi Captain Snyder. How are you holding up?"

"I'm surviving, but I can't say that it's been easy."

"I could only imagine," he said.

Marie starred at him for another few seconds before the sound of Ryan Turner stole her attention away.

"Captain Snyder, I am so sorry about your loss. My condolences to you and your family," he said sincerely.

"Thank you, Ryan. Your concern is much appreciated." Marie cut her eyes back to Timothy before closing them. She took a deep breath and blew it out slowly.

"You know, Donald had been on me for a few weeks to get cameras mounted around the house, but me, being the procrastinator that I am, kept putting it off. Had I not done that, we probably would have already caught the bastard that killed him."

"Don't do that, Cap. Don't blame yourself like that. This isn't your fault," Frank said to her.

"No? Then who's fault is it Detective? Because it sure as hell isn't my poor husband's."

Tears leaked from the corners of Marie's eyes. Amber reached down, grabbed a napkin out of the dispenser and handed it to her.

"I'm sorry, guys. I don't mean to be a wet blanket. I just can't believe that my husband is gone."

"You don't have anything to apologize to us for, Cap," Carla said. "I can't imagine that any one of us standing here would react differently if we were in your shoes."

"Thanks, Carla. I'm sorry, but maybe it was a mistake for me to come out so soon. I think it would be better if I went back to the hotel."

"No problem, Cap. We understand. We'll be glad to take you back to the hotel."

"You don't have to do that. You guys stay here and have fun. Carla, would you mind dropping me back off at the hotel? From what I'm being told, I won't be able to move back into my own home for a couple of days still."

"No problem at all, Cap. I'll be glad to," Carla said. After sliding out of the booth, Maria gave Frank, Amber, and Ryan hugs. When she got to Timothy Jordan, however, the hug became half-hearted. Noticing the difference between the way Marie hugged him and how she hugged the other officers, Timothy Jordan quickly separated his body from hers and took a step back. The strange look on her face caused him to glance toward the other officers. He opened his mouth to ask her why she gave him such a peculiar look but thought better of it.

"I'll talk to you two later," she told Frank and Amber. "If you hear anything from the investigating officers before I do, please let me know."

Since she was the captain of the police force, Marie doubted that they would get any information before she did, but she just wanted to be thorough. Frank continued to watch Marie closely as she and Carla headed toward the exit. Something about the entire scene seemed off to him. Marie was treating Timothy Jordan like he had the plague, and it had Frank wondering why.

"I'll be right back," he told the rest of them as he moved to follow Marie and Carla. When he got outside, Frank glanced around the parking lot, trying to locate the two ladies. It took him about five seconds to do so, but when he did, he yelled out to them. Hearing Frank's booming voice caused them to stop just before getting to Carla's car. Frank went into a light jog as he made his way toward the two women.

"Okay, Cap, what's going on?" he asked when he caught up to them.

The two women looked at each other and sighed. They hadn't planned on telling anyone this until they had proof, but since Frank sniffed out that something was up, they figured they might as well let him in on their thoughts.

"You guys may as well tell me what's going on. Or have you forgotten that I'm a super-human detective and will find out anyway," Frank said with a smile.

"Oh, brother," Carla said, rolling her eyes. "I guess we'd better tell him then. We wouldn't want him to figure it out by himself and make us look bad."

"I guess so," Marie said, smiling softly. "I asked Carla to keep an eye on Timothy Jordan. I thought it was very strange that he showed up at my house, claiming that he wanted to apologize. He could have done that the next day at the office."

Frank thought about what his captain was saying, and it made sense to him. He also thought about what Amber had told him regarding Timothy's apparent dislike for Caucasians and wondered how in the world the academy let a racist make it through their training program.

"That does sound suspicious. Well, please keep me in the loop. I'm going to go back inside and tell Amber that I'm ready to go."

"I'm sorry, Frank. I know you and Amber meant well, but I'm afraid that I'm not going to be good company tonight. I'm just going to have Carla take me back to the hotel."

Marie hugged Frank and walked around to the passenger's side door. She smiled faintly as she got inside.

"Don't worry, sir. I'll take good care of her," Carla said when she saw the worried look in Frank's eyes.

As Frank watched Carla pull out of the parking lot, he couldn't help but wonder if Marie and Carla were on to something. He would hate to think that Timothy Jordan was a racist, cold blooded killer, but Marie's instincts were usually spot on. He decided right then that he would have to keep a closer eye on the officer. Frank turned and started walking back toward the bar. Suddenly, he didn't feel like being there. He thought about calling the detectives assigned to the case and asking them if they had made any progress in the case but elected to wait until tomorrow. When he got back inside, he found Amber sitting by herself.

"Where the hell did Ryan and Timothy go?"

"The hell if I know. Timothy said he had something to do, and since Ryan rode with him, he had to leave too. You were out there kind of long. What's going on?" Amber asked.

"Well, come to find out, Marie has Carla keeping an eye on Timothy. Turns out, she's suspicious of him too."

"Really? Well, heaven help him if he turns out to be the one who killed Marie's husband."

"I hear you partner. Listen, I hate to leave you here alone, but I need to go home and spend time with my kids. I haven't really talked to them too much today."

"No problem, partner. After I finish this beer, I'm going to get out of here too."

"Okay. I'll see you tomorrow," Frank said as he reached into his back pocket and pulled out his wallet.

"What are you doing?"

"What does it look like? I'm paying for your beer."

"Thanks, Frank. I appreciate it."

"No problem, partner."

"You want to hear something funny, though? Jordan actually offered to pay for it, but when he reached for his wallet, it wasn't there."

Frank frowned. "You think he was pick-pocketed? In a police bar?"

"Nah. I think he just left it home or lost it somewhere."

"Yeah, that sounds about right. He does seem kind of . . . What's the word I'm looking for?"

"Goofy?" Amber answered with a light smile.

"Bingo! Well, let's just hope and pray that he's too goofy to commit murder. I'll see you tomorrow, partner."

"Wait, have you talked to either Hughes or Phillips?"

"Not yet. I'll probably give Hughes a call tomorrow and see if he found anything."

44

Frank Jr. lay back on his bed with his cell phone resting on his chest. He had just about dozed off when it vibrated. A smile spread across his face when he looked at the screen and saw who it was.

"What's happening, baby?" he asked, trying to sound cool.

"Not much. I told you I was going to call you back later. Why do you sound so surprised?"

"I'm not surprised. I was just messing with you," Frank Jr. lied. He knew he would have sounded stupid had he told her the real reason he answered the phone in that manner.

"Yeah, whatever. You know you've been sitting by the phone waiting for me to call."

"Oh, I see you think you all that, huh?"

"Nope. *You* think I'm all that," Kisha said, sassily.

Frank Jr. thought about what she'd just said before he responded. He wanted to craft a response that would complement her without causing her head to swell with arrogance.

"Well, let's just say that we *both* have it going on," he said, smoothly.

"Okay. I'll agree with that. We both have it going on. So, tell me," Kisha said, getting down to th4e real reason she called, "what happened between you and Harold? I heard you put the beat-down on him."

The admiration in her voice wasn't lost on Frank Jr. Apparently, Kisha thought highly of a man who could defend himself.

"That punk disrespected my sister and I had to put these hands on his ass."

"Oh, I see," Kisha said, slightly disappointed. She was hoping that their fight had something to do with her. It would have done her ego a world of good to know that he was defending her honor.

"What's wrong?" Frank Jr. asked, not catching on.

"Nothing. I was just wondering what went on between you two. Especially after what happened at the movie theatre."

It took a few seconds for the light bulb to go off in Frank Jr.'s head, but when it did, he realized what Kisha was thinking.

"Oh, don't get it twisted, though. I was ready, willing, and able to beat the brakes off that clown for bothering you too."

"For real?" Kisha asked, her smile lighting up her bedroom.

"You know it."

Before the conversation could go any further, Frank thought he heard sniffling coming from the hallway.

"Hey, Kisha, hold on for a second." Frank got up and strolled toward the hallway. He stood in front of his door for a few seconds, wondering if he was hearing things or if he actually did hear something. When he heard the sniffles a second time, however, he opened the door and peered out. He looked toward his sister's room and saw her just about to enter it.

"Rhonda? You okay, sis?"

"I'm okay," she said, nodding her head. Frank Jr. looked at her closely and could see tears dancing in her eyes. Something was definitely bothering her. Frank watched his sister as she went into her room and closed the door.

"Hey, Kisha. I'm going to have to call you back. Something is going on with my sister."

"Is she okay?"

"I'm not sure. I have to go check on her right quick." Without even saying goodbye, Frank Jr. hung up and headed toward Rhonda's room. He listened for a few seconds before knocking on the door.

"Rhonda? Can I come in?" he asked.

Rhonda remained silent. She honestly didn't feel like dealing with her brother's judgmental attitude.

"Rhonda?"

"Go away, Frank. I don't feel like talking right now."

Ignoring his sister's pleas. Frank Jr. turned the knob and cracked the door. He didn't want to barge in, but he was genuinely concerned about his sister.

"Well, that's just too bad, because I'm coming in anyway."

Black Viper

Frank Jr. slowly pushed the door open and walked into his sister's bedroom. He looked around and saw that her room was unusually unkempt. Rhonda was borderline OCD, so to see her room looking as shabby as it did let him know that something was weighing heavily on her mind. When he looked at his sister, she was staring daggers at him. Throwing caution to the wind, he walked over to her and sat down beside her on her bed. The two of them sat in silence for about ten seconds before Frank Jr. decided to speak first.

"Rhonda, are you going to tell me what's going on, or am I going to have to call Dad and tell him that you're in your room crying?"

"Ain't nobody crying, Frank."

"It doesn't matter," Frank said, shrugging his shoulders. "I'll tell him that you are anyway."

Rhonda rolled her eyes. There wasn't a doubt in her mind that her brother would make good on his threat and call their father.

"Look, Frank, this is something that we're just not going to see eye to eye on, so I really don't think we should talk about it."

Frank studied his sister closely. He could clearly see her struggling with her emotions. It was then that he decided to listen to what she had to say without judging her. Even though they had different views on certain things, he loved her dearly and would always be there for her.

"Just tell me what's bothering you, sis. I won't say a word. I'll just sit here and listen while you get it off your chest." Frank wrapped his arm around his sister and pulled her close. Rhonda responded by resting her head on his shoulder. After taking a deep breath, she commenced telling her big brother what waws on her mind.

"Frank, I just don't like Ms. Ponder intruding on our family time like that. She may be our principal, but she had no right to do that. And did you see the way Daddy looked at her? His eyes were about to pop out of his head! What about Mama? Did he forget that he has a wife? I don't like it Frank. I don't like it at all. I know Ms. Ponder is pretty, but she's nowhere near as pretty as Mama."

Rhonda pulled her head away from her brother's shoulder and looked him directly in the eyes. Frank Jr.'s heart nearly broke when he saw the tears that had welled up in them.

"Frank, do you think Daddy still loves Mama?"

"Of course, he still loves Mama. Didn't he tell you that already?"

"Then why is he messing around with Ms. Ponder?"

"What?? Rhonda, you're talking crazy. Just because she came to the same restaurant where we were doesn't mean that her and Dad are messing around."

"She came to our house too, Frank, and all I know is that when Mama gets out of the hospital, Ms. Ponder is going to have to find herself another target."

Frank Jr. wrapped his arms around his sister and again pulled her down on his shoulder. He didn't have the heart to tell her that their mother would probably never come home.

45

Mike Hughes sat behind the wheel of the police-issued Crown Victoria and stared intently at Marie Snyder's residence. He'd been doing so for the last fifteen minutes. It irked him to no end that neither he nor his partner, Detective Shelton Phillips had been able to find any clue as to who may have been responsible for the murder of Donald Snyder. Hughes took one last drag from his cigarette before flicking the butt out the window and onto the pavement. He then ran his meaty hand over his face, before shaking another one out of the pack and repeating the process. Phillips, who'd been occupying his time by looking at pictures of women on a dating site, cut his eyes toward his partner.

"Milton, how long are we going to sit here, man? I told you that I had plans later with this woman I met last week."

"Is that right?" Hughes said with a smirk. "Well, your plans are just going to have to wait, my friend. We have a murder to solve. And not just *any* murder, I remind you. We're talking about the murder of our captain's husband."

A frown formed on Phillips's face as he blew out a breath.

"No, Milton, you don't have to remind me."

"Then stop complaining and start using that lump sitting on your shoulders for more than housing a hat."

Phillips stared at his partner in disbelief. He and Hughes had traded wisecracks from time to time, but he had never insulted him up until now.

"What the hell is your problem, man?" he asked.

Hughes closed his eyes and leaned his head back against the headrest. He hadn't meant to be so short with Phillips, but he felt like they had missed something when they examined the crime scene.

"Sorry about that, partner," he apologized. "I didn't mean to snap at you, but something doesn't smell right. Normally, when this sort of senseless murder is committed, the perpetrator would almost always slip up somehow."

"True, but we went over that room with a fine-tooth comb and didn't find a thing—period. We even went over the adjoining rooms and still didn't find anything."

"Shelton, I'm telling you, as God is my witness, I'd be willing to bet every dime I have that we're overlooking something."

"Okay partner, I'll tell you what. Let's come back and give it one more shot tomorrow. But if we don't find anything, we close the crime scene and release the house back to Captain Snyder. Knowing her as I do, I'd bet she's tired of staying in that hotel."

Hughes chuckled. "Hell, I've known her longer than, you and I'd bet the same thing. Okay, partner, you've got yourself a deal."

Hughes started the engine and pulled off down the street. He was more than willing to come back the next day and let his partner prove to him that there was nothing to find. What his partner didn't know, however, was that Hughes had an ulterior motive for solving the case. Oh, he definitely wanted to find who'd killed Captain Snyder's husband. But if everything went according to plan, Marie Snyder would be taking an extended leave and he would be stepping right into her shoes. Although he kept it to himself, Detective Hughes was very disappointed when Marie was chosen as captain over him. It was a friendly competition. They were both vying for the job, but in the end, her length of service was the deciding factor. He wished her well, but the burn never completely went away.

As Hughes's taillights disappeared down the street, a sinister smile spread across the killer's lips. The opportunity that seemed non-existent a few seconds ago suddenly presented itself. The killer stealthy made a slow trek around Marie's house and up to her window. After completing the task in which they had come for, the killer disappeared into the night.

46

After dropping his partner off at home, Detective Hughes drove straight to the nearest Rite Aid and picked up a bottle of Tums. He had heartburn something terrible. Hughes actually suffered from acid reflux and was supposed to take Omeprazole once a day to relieve his discomfort. Unfortunately for his stomach, he hadn't taken his medication in a few days and it was starting to catch up with him. He could have easily waited until he got home to take his regular capsule, but then he would've had to argue with his wife Rose as to why he hadn't taken it. Hughes wasn't intentionally skipping his medication. The murder of Marie's husband had been weighing on his mind. He'd been on the force long enough to know that whoever killed Donald was an extreme threat to the rest of society. Anyone who had the gumption to kill a police officer's spouse was a definite threat to civilians.

By the time Hughes got home, it was nearly eight o' clock. His stomach rumbled so loudly, that he could clearly hear it over the garage door being opened. It reminded him that he hadn't eaten anything for the last ten hours. Hughes slid his thick frame out of the car and headed for the door. Upon entering his home, he heard the faint sounds of the television playing in the living room. Hughes smiled, already knowing what he would find once he got inside the room. He came to a stop in the doorway leading to the living room. Like she'd been so many times before, Rose was sitting on the love seat sound asleep. Her glasses were perched on the end of her nose. An open book rested on her chest. Rose was an avid reader. It was one of the things that had attracted Hughes to her. Ironically, though, he had never been much of a reader. Rose had been trying unsuccessfully to get him to do so for several years. Hughes reached down and carefully lifted the book off her chest. He looked at the titled and frowned.

"Street Banditz by C.J. Hudson," he mumbled. Hughes shook his head and laid the book back down on her chest. At first, Hughes couldn't understand what she saw in urban fiction. The more he got to know her, however, the more he realized that the genre and how she grew up had a lot in common. She was a young lady who'd been raised in the inner city of Cleveland, Ohio, but refused to let her surroundings define her. Not having the patience to attend a four-year university, Rose decided to try her hand at a two-year clerical trade school. She graduated at the top of her class, landed a job with a local consulting agency, and had been gainfully employed ever since. Although she was a working woman, Rose almost always made sure that there was something on the stove for her husband to eat when he got home, and tonight was no exception. Milton Hughes stared at his wife for a few more seconds before making his way into the kitchen.

Even though the kitchen lights were off, the small light above the stove illuminated the two pots sitting on the stove. In one pot was mixed vegetables, while the other one held perfectly whipped mashed potatoes. When Hughes opened the oven, his mouth began to water. Lying there perfectly seasoned and cooked to perfection was a pan filled with baked chicken breasts. After taking the chicken out of the oven, Hughes practically ran to the bathroom to wash his hands. When he returned to the kitchen, he was surprised to see that Rose had fixed his plate and set it on the table.

"Thanks, honey, but you didn't have to get up to do that. I could have fixed my own plate."

"No trouble at all, honey. I was getting up anyway," she said as she walked up to him and threw her arms around him. "Rough day?"

"Kind of," he answered.

Rose raised an eyebrow. Usually when she asked him that question, Hughes would simply say, "It is what it is," and leave it like that. To hear him admit that he had a rough day meant that something was weighing heavily on his mind.

"Really? What happened? Did Shelton bore you with stories of his women-conquering again?" she asked, trying to lighten the mood. "I swear, it seems like that man-whore is trying to sleep with every woman in the city."

"Nah, although it does seem like he sees a different woman every week."

"I guess he doesn't want to leave any female stone unturned. How's Marie doing?" Rose asked, getting to the crux of what she sensed was really bothering her husband.

"About as well as could be expected. It has to be rough on her. I can't imagine something happening to you," he said, hugging her tightly.

"I feel the same way about you. I must tell you though. It's not easy being the wife of a cop."

"I'm sure. Just know that I plan on coming home to you *every* night."

"You'd better," Rose said, looking him square in the eye. "Go ahead and eat your dinner. I'm going upstairs to shower. Hurry, and you just might get dessert to go with that meal," she said flirtatiously. Hughes didn't need an interpreter to know what his wife was getting at. He usually took his time eating a meal, but not tonight. So far, he hadn't gotten lucky investigating the case, but he was about to get lucky in other ways.

Christopher Speight

47

Detective Milton Hughes pulled in front of Marie Snyder's house and parked. The smile on his face was nearly bright enough to light up the entire street. It had been awhile since he and his wife had enjoyed such a passionate night. For one night, at least, Rose was able to get her husband to forget about the crime going on in the city of Cleveland and enjoy himself. Hughes continued to smile as he reached into a McDonald's bag and pulled out a breakfast sandwich. He unwrapped it and took a couple of bites before picking up the small cup of coffee. He had just scoffed down the last of his food when his partner, Shelton Phillips, pulled up behind him. Although Phillips had requested that his partner pick him up, Hughes declined. He had no desire to play chauffer to his partner today.

He glanced in the rearview mirror and watched as Phillips got out of his vehicle, stretched his limbs, and looked around. After doing so, he made his way to the driver's door and tapped lightly on the window. Hughes took his time acknowledging him as he pulled out a pack of cigarettes from his breast pocket. After shaking one out and sticking it between his lips, he opened the door and got out.

"Got a light?" he asked his partner.

"Hell no. You know I don't smoke," Phillips said with a frown. He noticed the look on his partner's face and inquired about it. "What the hell are you so happy about?"

"Let's just say that I had a good time with my wife last night."

"I guess so," Phillips said, an uncertain look on his face. "I still don't think we're going to find anything, though. Like I said yesterday, we've gone over that room with a fine-tooth comb and didn't find shit. I don't know why you think today is going to be any different."

"Maybe, maybe not. But we owe it to Captain Snyder to do everything we can to bring her husband's killer to justice. Now let's go." Hughes took one last drag off his cigarette and dropped the remainder of it to the pavement. Reaching into his coat pocket, he pulled out two pairs of latex gloves. He handed one pair to Phillips and pulled the other pair onto his hands. The two detectives then made their way to Marie Snyder's front door.

After letting themselves in, the detectives began looking over the same places they had examined the previous day. Thirty minutes later, they still hadn't found anything. Hughes ran his hand down the front of his face. He was becoming increasingly frustrated.

"I hate to say I told you so, but——"

"Shut up, Phillips! Just keep looking!" Hughes snapped.

"Yeah all right," Phillips said, rolling his eyes. The detectives searched for ten additional minutes before something occurred to Hughes. A loud roar emitted from his throat.

"The hell are you laughing at?" Phillips asked.

"My friend, we have been going about this all wrong. We've been looking inside this house or the better part of two days. Not one time have we searched around the perimeter of it."

"Damn . . . You're right. I'll get right on it," Phillips said and headed for the front door. He was gone for a little over five minutes before he came back with a large smile on his face. Hughes looked at him and cracked a smile of his own.

"From that shit-eating grin on your face, I take it you found something?"

"Absolutely," Phillips said, holding up a brown wallet.

"Where'd you find that?"

"On the right side of the house, lying on the ground, under the window."

A curious look fell across Hughes's face. He walked over to the window Phillips was referring to and lifted it up. Surprisingly, it opened without resistance. Hughes was slightly baffled. He was almost sure that he'd personally checked that window when he was here the previous day.

"You know, I could have sworn that this window was locked yesterday."

"Well, apparently, you were wrong. To me, it looks like the killer murdered Donald, made his escape by climbing through the window, and dropped his wallet on the ground."

Hughes stared at the window for a few seconds before shrugging his shoulders and turning his attention back to Phillips. Maybe he had made a mistake.

"Did you check inside?" he asked.

"Not yet. I figured you'd want to find out who the low-life scum was together."

Hughes smiled as he walked toward Phillips.

"You got that right. Open it up."

Phillips nodded as he flipped open the wallet. As soon as they laid eyes on the driver's license, their mouths dropped open. A lump formed in Hughes's throat. His eyes had to be playing tricks on him.

"This has to be a mistake," Hughes said, pulling out credit cards and reading the name on them.

"Not according to the name on these credit cards in here. As much as I hate to admit it. Donald Snyder's murderer is one of our own."

"Let's not jump to conclusions, Phillips. There are other reasons that Jordan's wallet would be lying where it was."

"Such as?"

"He could've walked around the perimeter like you just did."

"Well, it looks like we're just going to have to find out if that's true or not, aren't we?"

"I guess we do, partner. I guess we do."

48

When Detective Stone dropped his kids off at school, he was slightly surprised to see Principal Ponder walking out of the building and heading toward his car. He glanced in the rearview mirror just in time to see Rhonda rolling her eyes.

"Here comes your girlfriend," she mumbled.

Stone turned around and glared at his daughter.

"What did you just say?" he asked.

"Nothing, Dad."

"Little girl, you'd better mind your manners! I'm not going to tolerate any disrespect! Get out of this car and get your behind in that school!"

Armed with an attitude, Rhonda pulled the door latch and pushed the door open. Frank Jr. made to join her, but his father stopped him.

"Hold up a second, Jr. What the devil is your sister's problem?"

"Come on Dad. You know exactly what her problem is. She's afraid that you're going to forget about Mom and start dating Miss. Ponder."

Frank Sr. ran his hand down his face. He couldn't understand why his daughter was so worried about such a thing. He loved his wife, and no matter how attractive he thought Miss Ponder was, he was not about to break his marital vows with his wife.

"Lord have mercy. Son, nothing is going on between me and your principal. I've told your sister that before."

Frank Jr. eyed his father curiously. He wanted to believe him, but he couldn't help but notice the way his father looked at his principal.

"Are you sure Dad? I mean, nothing is going on between you and Miss Ponder?"

"Yes, son. I'm sure. I love your mother with all my heart, and no woman will ever come between that. Now, do I find her attractive? Yes, I do. But that has absolutely nothing to do with the love I have for your mother. No one will ever take her place."

"That's good to hear Dad. I'll talk to Rhonda and see if I can get through to her."

"Thanks, son. I appreciate that."

"No problem Dad. In the meantime, you need to make sure that Miss Ponder knows that you're a happily married man. See you at home."

As Frank Jr. got out of the car, Miss Ponder was just now making her way around to the driver's side.

"Good morning, young man."

"Good morning Miss Ponder." Frank Jr. gave his father a quick glance before heading into the building. Frank Sr. rolled down the window and greeted her.

"Good morning Miss Ponder. Is there something I can do for you?"

"Good morning. I just thought I'd let you know that Yolonda Green has decided that she's not going to sue anyone."

"Well, I'm glad that she's finally come to her senses. The only thing she would have accomplished is wasting the court's time."

An awkward silence hung in the air as the two of them stared at each other for a few seconds. Grace Ponder was just about to say something when a loud sounding bell interrupted her.

"Well, duty calls," she said, smiling.

"I hear you. I'm on the way to the office myself."

"Okay. It was nice to see you again, Detective Stone. Take care," Grace said as she walked away.

As he watched her walk back towards the building, Frank reached down and grabbed his wedding band. A wave of guilt surged through him as he thought about his wife. Although he hadn't done anything immoral, it weighed on him that he found another woman other than his wife attractive. Thoughts of his wedding day slid through his mind as he raised his wedding band to his mouth and kissed it. After taking one last glance at Grace Ponder, Frank pulled away from the curb and headed to the precinct.

49

When Detective Stone got to the precinct, he was surprised to see Captain Snyder's car sitting in the parking lot. From the information that he'd received, she was scheduled to be out on leave for at least the next two days. Just as he cut the engine, Amber pulled into the space next to him. She gave Frank a curious look when she too noticed their boss's car sitting there.

"What the hell is she doing here?" Amber asked after the two of them got out of their vehicles.

"Your guess is as good as mine," Frank answered. "Deputy Chief William Clark didn't exactly tell her how long she had to stay out."

"It still seems weird to me though . . . unless there's something we don't know about yet."

"Hmmm. I wonder if there's been a break in the case."

"That wouldn't have anything to do with the captain though. There's no way she would be allowed to work on her own case."

"I know that, Detective. But I'm sure that if something broke, they wouldn't keep it from her."

"Well, let's go inside and see, partner." Amber grabbed Frank by the arm and guided him toward the entrance. By the time they'd made it inside the building, he realized that she'd been massaging his bicep the entire way there. Frank cut his eyes at Amber, who in turn ignored him. As they approached Marie's office, Frank smoothly pulled his arm out of Amber's hold. The last thing he needed was for anyone to think that any improprieties going on.

"Come in, Detectives," Deputy Chief Clark said, waving them in.

Frank held the door open for Amber and then followed her in. By the looks on the faces of everyone sitting in the room, Frank knew that there had to have been a break in the case. He looked around and saw that Carla Johnson and Ryan Turner were also in attendance.

"Good morning, Captain, Deputy Chief. What's going on?"

Before either of them could answer, Hughes and Phillips made their way into the office. In Hughes's hand was a small bag carrying Timothy Jordan's wallet. He slowly made his way across the room and set the bag down on Marie's desk.

"What's that?" Amber asked.

"That, my dear partner, is a wallet we found outside of Captain Snyder's window this morning," Hughes said.

A bad feeling started to settle in the pit of Frank's stomach. Had this been an ordinary situation, the deputy chief would not be there. Something major was going on. Hughes opened the bag and took out the wallet. He glanced around at his fellow officers for a brief second before opening the wallet and taking out the driver's license. All eyes were glued to the identification as he laid if face up on the desk. Captain Snyder stared at it with fire in her eyes.

"So let me get this straight. Are you telling me that Officer Timothy Jordan killed my husband?" Marie said, seething.

"We really don't want to jump to that conclusion just yet ma'am."

"The hell do you mean, you don't want to jump to that conclusion? Can you think of any *other* reason that his wallet would beat my place?"

"Calm down Marie. I'm very sorry about what happened to your husband, but don't forget that you're here as a courtesy. You are in no way involved in this investigation whatsoever," the Deputy Chief reminded her.

"Sorry, sir," Marie said and sat back in her chair. Seeing the look on her face caused him to soften his stance.

"No, I'm sorry, Marie. I can't imagine what you're going through. Trust me though. If this Timothy Jordan is responsible for your husband's death, we'll nail his ass to the wall. By him being a cop, however, we're going to have to tread lightly on this. I'm sure once we bring him in, he's going to want to have his union rep present.

Captain, can you think of any reason this Timothy Jordan would want to see your husband dead?"

Marie thought about the scene at the restaurant. She thought about what she'd heard about Timothy Jordan seemingly not liking white men. She conveyed these thoughts to the deputy chief, who, in turn ordered Hughes and Phillips to go pick Timothy Jordan up.

"We're coming too," Frank said.

Christopher Speight

50

Timothy Jordan plopped down on his couch and took a deep breath. The blue flannel pajamas he wore clung to his skin as a light sweat covered his frame. He'd been searching for his wallet for the last hour and, so far, had come up empty. He rubbed his temples and tried to remember where he could have lost it. He wasn't so much worried about his credit cards. He only had two and he could easily cancel them and order replacements. But he didn't want to have to go through the trouble of waiting in the DMV line to get another license. However, from the looks of things, that's just what he was probably going to have to do.

Since it was his day off, Timothy figured that he'd sit around the house and relax all day. That plan changed when he decided to pay for Amber's sandwich the night before and discovered he was missing his wallet. Now he was tearing his apartment apart, searching for it. He was just about to go through his place a second time when someone rang his doorbell. Taking another deep breath, Timothy got up and headed toward the front door.

"I'm coming," he said, when someone pressed the doorbell a second time. When he got to the door, Timothy leaned in and peered through the peephole. He waws surprised to see Detectives Hughes, Phillips, Stone, and Davis standing there.

"Good afternoon, Detectives," he said after opening the door. "What's going on?"

"Good afternoon, Officer Jordan. We're here to tie up a few loose ends concerning the Donald Snyder murder."

"Uh, okay. Come on in." Timothy turned and lead his co-workers inside. "So, what's going on?"

"We just have a few questions," Hughes stated. "Now, when you went to Captain Snyder's house after her husband was murdered, what did you see?"

"What did I see? I'm sorry, sir, but I don't understand the question."

"It's a simple question, Officer Jordan. Did you see anyone leaving the premises? Did you notice anything suspicious while you were there? And since we're on the subject, why *were* you there?"

Timothy Jordan looked around at the hardened faces of the other detectives. It was then that he realized what was going on. He folded his arms defiantly.

"No, I didn't see anyone leaving the premises. No, I didn't notice anything suspicious, and as far as why I was there, I'm sure that you already know the answer to that question," Timothy said, cutting his eyes to Frank and Amber. He was positive that either one or both of them had already filled Hughes and Phillips in on the argument he'd had with Donald Snyder.

"Okay. Let's get to what you saw once you got inside."

"The only thing I saw when I got inside was my boss grieving over her husband. You know, if I didn't know any better, I would think that you guys view me as a suspect."

"*Should* we be looking at you as a suspect?" Phillips asked.

"Absolutely not."

"Okay, we have just one more question for you, Officer Jordan. Did you, at any time before any of the other officers got there, leave that house?"

"Leave that house? Of course not! I stayed there with my captain until other officers arrived on the scene."

"You didn't go outside at all?" Frank asked, hoping that Timothy Jordan would give himself an out.

"No, Detective Stone. Not at all."

The four detectives all looked one another. A foul expression was on Phillips's face as he shook his head in disgust.

"What?" Timothy Jordan asked.

"Well, the way we figure it, there was no damage done to the front door, so either Donald knew his killer and let him in, or the killer crawled in through a window, waited for Donald to come home, and murdered him when he got there."

With an exasperated look on his face, Timothy Jordan snorted out a laugh. His hands flew to his hips as he stood there in shock.

"You guys have *got* to be kidding me! What possible reason do I have to kill Donald Snyder?"

"Well, from what we understand, you did have a nasty exchange with him at Red's restaurant."

"Oh my God! I was coming to my captain's defense!"

"Coming to her defense? Against her husband?"

"Look, man. I didn't know that was her husband at the time. That's why I went by her house, to apologize to both of them."

"And you say you never left the house after the other officers came, correct?"

"No, no, no! how many times do I have to tell y'all that?"

Hughes looked at Phillips and smiled. He then looked at Frank, who had now closed his eyes and was rubbing his face. Amber took a deep breath as she crossed her arms and leaned back on one leg. Hughes then reached into his jacket pocket and pulled out the bag with Timothy's wallet inside.

"Well, if that's true, Officer Jordan, then why did we find your wallet outside next to the window?"

Timothy Jordan's face went slack. His mouth fell completely open.

"Where the hell did you find that?"

"We just told you where we found it, Officer Jordan. Now, do you have any idea how it got there?"

"How in the hell should I know?"

"Maybe we should talk about this down at the station," Hughes said.

Timothy opened his mouth, but nothing came out. Suddenly his throat felt very dry. He looked around at the accusatory faces, and a scowl appeared on his.

"Well, Officer Jordan? Are we going to do this the easy way or the hard way?"

"The easy way would be for my fellow law enforcement officers to take me at my word when I tell them that I had nothing to do with Donald Snyder's murder."

"Come on, son. You know we can't do that," Frank said.

A long pause went by before anyone spoke again.

"You know what? Fine! But when we get to the station, I want to call my union rep and my fuckin' lawyer!"

Timothy turned and headed to his bedroom.

"Where do you think you're going Officer?" Phillips asked him.

Timothy stopped in his tracks. He slowly turned back to face Phillips. With a scowl still plastered on his face, he slowly walked up to Phillips and stared him in the eye.

"I'm going to put on some damn clothes, *if* that's okay! Or would you rather have me sitting in the precinct with my dick hanging out?"

After getting dressed, Timothy Jordan was escorted out to the car and ushered into it. Twenty minutes later, he was sitting in an interrogation room waiting to speak to a lawyer.

51

Timothy Jordan sat stone-faced as Detectives Hughes and Phillips stared at him from across the table. His right fist was firmly placed inside his left palm, with his elbows resting on the table. His chin rested between the knuckles of his middle and forefinger. From the moment he sat down, his eyes had been closed. If the detectives didn't know any better, they would swear that he was asleep.

"Officer, why don't you just tell us what really happened?" Phillips said. In his mind, this was an open-and-shut case. Timothy Jordan slowly opened his eyes and looked up at Phillips.

"I've told you what really happened, so stop asking me stupid ass questions."

"Look, we understand. You got into it with Donald at a restaurant, went to his house to apologize, and things got out of hand. It happens."

"We can't help you if you don't tell us the truth, Jordan," Hughes chimed in.

Jordan's eyes narrowed into slits. He slowly raised his head up and suddenly slammed his fists down on the table hard enough to send an echo throughout the room.

"I'm telling you the damn truth!"

"Quite a temper you have there, Officer," Phillips said, smirking at Jordan.

Timothy Jordan stared at him for a few seconds before shaking his head and placing his chin back in its original position. Phillips opened his mouth to say something else, but never got the chance. Before the words could leave his mouth, the door swung open and in walked a pencil thin African American woman dressed in grey, pinstriped, business attire. The top of her hair was wrapped up in a bun and her face was caked with make-up. Her lips were laced with black lip stick. She was a very pretty lady. Her skin was the color of dark honey. Her heels click-clacked across the floor as she made her way over to the table. The sound of her briefcase slamming onto the top of the table seemed to startle everyone in the room. Her eyes darted from Hughes to Phillips then back to Hughes. She then looked down at Timothy Jordan, gave him a warm smile, and placed a reassuring hand on his shoulder.

"Detectives, now I *know* that you haven't been questioning this officer without his lawyer present," she said, the smile never leaving her face.

"And just who the hell are you supposed to be, Wonder Woman?" Phillips asked.

"Believe it or not Detective, I *have* been called that before. Now, if you want to know my real name, it's Beverly Hubbard. And since you like asking questions, maybe you can answer one for me. Why in God's name do you have my client in this sweat-box?"

"Your client is being accused of murdering his boss's husband. His wallet was found outside of a window of the house where said murder occurred."

Miss Hubbard stared at Phillips for a few seconds before turning her attention to Hughes. The two detectives looked at each other and then back at her.

"What?" Phillips asked.

"I'm still waiting on the punchline."

"What punchline?"

"The punchline to this joke. What you said, Detective, is in no way proof that my client committed any crime whatsoever."

"What about his wallet?" Hughes asked.

"What about it? That's not proof, and you know it."

"Your client was seen having a very loud argument with the victim an hour before the murder was committed."

"Argument? From the files I've read, my client was merely protecting his boss. He had no idea that the man was his boss's husband."

"Look, Counselor——"

Black Viper

"No, Detective, *you* look," Beverly said, cutting Hughes off, "unless you are prepared to arrest my client on a murder charge right now, he's about to get up, walk through that door, and go home."

Beverly crossed her arms and waited for Phillips's response. When it was clear that he wasn't going to offer one, she shrugged her shoulders, looked at Timothy Jordan, and said, "Let's go Mr. Jordan."

Timothy smirked as he arose from the chair and followed his lawyer from the room. As the two of them walked through the door, Timothy locked eyes with Marie Snyder. Although she wasn't allowed to be involved in the investigation, the deputy chief did extend her the courtesy of being present when Officer Jordan was questioned. Her stare burned a hole through her.

"Captain Snyder, I swear to God that I did not kill your husband," he said.

Marie Snyder didn't say a word. She just continued to stare at him. Timothy Jordan then looked at his partner, Carla Johnson. His eyes were pleading for her to believe him.

"Come on, Carla. You know me. You know I couldn't do anything like this."

"I don't know what to believe, Tim." Carla then turned and walked out of the precinct. It was her off day, and the only reason she was even there in the first place was that Timothy Jordan was her partner, and Clark wanted to see if she could add something to the investigation. Standing there taking it all in was Frank Stone. He had a perplexed look on his face. Something about this entire incident just didn't sit well with him. It all seemed a little too convenient to him. Frank decided right then and there that, before Marie was allowed to go back to her home, he would swing by there and check things out for himself.

Christopher Speight

52

From the time she'd left the airport until the Uber driver helped her retrieve her bags from the truck of his car, Catherine Samuels face was fixed in sadness. Although she'd had a fantastic time with her girlfriends on their two-week vacation to Hawaii, reality was beginning to set in that the trip was coming to an end. Catherine had saved up for an entire year to achieve her bucket list goal of going to Hawaii. Since she was single, unlike her two girlfriends, Catherine had no one to answer to. Because of this, she was more than willing to stay an extra week, but her friends had to get back to their husbands. Catherine thought long and hard about staying in Hawaii anyway but decided that she wouldn't have as much fun without her friends. She had one more week of vacation left, so she decided that she would just hit the gym every day and try to work off the ten pounds she gained lying around on the beach, eating sweets and drinking Mai Tais.

"Well, back to the real world," she said as the Uber driver carried her bags up the driveway. He stood there for a long moment waiting for Catherine to open the door. Instead of doing that, she reached into her purse, pulled out a ten-dollar bill, and handed it to him.

"You don't want me to take the bags in for you? I don't mind," he said.

"No thanks. I've got it from here."

The man shrugged, stuffed the money into his front pocket, and headed for his vehicle. Although he did think that Catherine was attractive, he was slightly offended that she seemed afraid to open her door while he was standing there. He gave her a mean look as he got into his car and drove away. Catherine couldn't care less. This was Cleveland, Ohio, and she wasn't about to take any chances. A victim she would not be on this day.

After entering her home and turning off the alarm, Catherine did a quick walk through to make sure that everything was just as she'd left it. When she discovered that it was, she went into the kitchen and poured herself a glass of wine. The turbulence she experienced on the flight home was so bad that she needed something to take the edge off and calm her nerves. When she finished, Catherine went into her living room and turned on the television. She then went to the camera app on her phone and connected it to her television via Bluetooth.

Even though it was evident that no one had been inside of her house, just before she'd left for vacation, Catherine had to chase a vagabond away from her home. The homeless man was sniffing around her garbage can for scraps of food, but Catherine felt that he was setting her up for a chance to break into her house. She wanted to make sure that he hadn't returned. Figuring that she wasn't going to see anything of substance, Catherine scrolled back just a few days. Although Catherine didn't see the bum, she did see something very interesting after watching the video for about half an hour.

The way her camera was set up, Catherine could clearly see a few of the homes that sat across the street. One of the houses she could see was that of a policewoman who lived directly across from her. Standing in front of the policewoman's house were two men holding a conversation. Catherine had seen enough episodes of Law & Order to know that the two men were detectives. She turned the volume up attempting to hear what they were saying, but they weren't talking loud enough. She watched them get back into their vehicle and drive away. Not ten seconds later, she witnessed someone dressed in a black hoodie sneak around the side of the policewoman's house. The figure looked around for a few seconds before placing what looked like a wallet on the ground.

"What the hell?" Catherine mumbled. After seeing this, she decided to scroll back further. Something was going on. She went back five more days and watched the same figure climb through her neighbor's side window. A few minutes later, she saw Donald Snyder enter his home. A bad feeling settled in the pit of her stomach. Something was wrong. Very, very wrong. Moments later, a lump formed in Catherine's throat as she saw the hooded figure climb out of the window and haul ass down the street. Her only regret was that she didn't get a clear look at the hooded figure's face.

Upon hearing a car door slam, Catherine jumped up and ran to the window. When she noticed the handsome man in a suit about to get in his vehicle, she quickly ran onto her porch and began yelling.

Christopher Speight

53

Frank Stone's mind continued to swirl as he walked out of the precinct and headed toward his car. He'd been a detective for a long time, and he couldn't ever remember a feeling in his gut like the one he was having now. When Phillips and Hughes first informed them that they'd found Timothy's wallet next to Maria Snyder's window, he had his doubts about the man's innocence. Now however, after taking one look deep into Timothy's eyes, he was beginning to have doubts about his guilt. As he got in his car, he heard Amber calling his name.

"You just gonna leave without saying anything to anybody?" she asked.

"I need to run home right quick. I forgot my badge," Frank told her. It was a weak lie and both of them knew it. Amber didn't know what bothered her more, the fact that her partner was lying to her or the fact that she didn't know why he was lying to her. She wanted to call him on it, but before she could, Frank started his car and pulled off.

"I'll be back in a few," he yelled out the window. Amber watched his taillights disappear down the street and wondered what secret Frank was keeping from her. Frank stared in his rearview mirror until Amber was a mere speck. He hated not letting her know what was going on, but this was something that he needed to do by himself. Had Amber been acting objectively, he wouldn't have minded taking her along. But from Frank's observations, she, like Detective Phillips, seemed to have already made up her mind about his guilt. Frank, however, wasn't so sure.

As he pulled up in front of Marie's house, his intensity and focus increased. Although he knew that Hughes and Phillips were capable detectives, he couldn't help but wonder if they had missed something. Frank got out of his car, walked up to the front of the house, and stopped. His eyes swept the home from side to side as he stood on the sidewalk. Finally, after staring at the house for a few minutes, he casually strolled toward the front steps. They creaked slightly as his thick frame pressed down against them.

"Dammit," Frank mumbled as he got close to the front door. It was then that he realized that he didn't have the key. His silent prayers were answered when he turned the knob, and the door slowly opened. Frank bent down and ducked under the yellow police tape that crossed the door.

As he entered the house, a feeling of sadness overcame him. He recalled the look on his captain's face when he entered her home after her husband had been murdered. It was a look that he would never forget. Frank had seen that look on the faces of the families of victims hundreds of times, but it affected him differently when it was someone he knew and cared about. Shaking off the emotional attachment, Frank went about the business of trying to find what the other two detectives missed.

He walked into the living where the murder had been committed and looked around. He then went to the couch and scanned the area where Donald's body was found. Dried blood rested on the fabric. The smell of death still lingered in the air. When Frank didn't see anything out of the ordinary, he decided to examine other areas of the room.

Ten minutes later, Frank still hadn't found anything. He began to get frustrated. He took a deep breath and messaged his temples. He glanced up at the mantel and got teary eyed when he saw all the pictures sitting there. Photos of Marie, her husband Donald, and their two kids filled every space on the mantel. The more Frank looked at the pictures, however, the more something seemed odd to him. It wasn't the photos that gave him pause. It was the frames. One frame in particular. It contained a picture of Donald and Marie sitting at a picnic table in the park. The frame stood out to Frank because of a tiny pin-sized hole near the bottom of it. Nine times out of ten, it would probably go unnoticed. But because Frank decided to think outside of the box, he quickly zeroed in on it.

He walked over to the mantel, picked up the frame, and turned it around. Frank quickly realized that this wasn't an ordinary frame.

Black Viper

This particular frame was fitted with a small camera. Frank examined the frame again and concluded that it was fairly new. He doubted if it was even a month old. Frank thought about calling Marie and asking her if she knew anything about the camera frame, but that would be breaking protocol. Any evidence or suspicious findings had to go through the chain of command or risk being ruled inadmissible. Frank reached into his pocket and pulled out a large baggie. Then he slipped the picture into it and headed for the door. He had just gotten to his car when he heard a high-pitched voice call out to him.

"Officer! Officer! I need to talk to you!"

When Frank turned around, he saw a pretty, brown-skinned woman running toward him from across the street. After placing the bag containing the picture inside of his vehicle, Frank closed the door and turned around to face the woman.

"What can I help you with ma'am?"

"Officer, I have—"

"Detective," Frank corrected her.

"Oh, sorry. Anyway, Detective, I have something I need you to look at."

Frank glanced at the photo lying on the passenger's seat and then back at the woman. "Ma'am I'm very busy right now."

"Detective, there is something you *need* to see, please."

After placing the picture in the glove compartment and locking the vehicle, Frank reluctantly followed the woman as she made her way back across the street. There was an urgency in her voice that caused him to grant her request. Frank had to half jog just to keep up with her. Just before she reached for the doorknob, Frank grabbed her arm.

"Miss, hold up a second," he said, pulling out a notepad. "Before I do anything else, I'm going to need to know your name."

"My name is Catherine. Catherine Samuels."

Frank quickly jotted her name down on the notepad. He was just about to ask her another question, but when he looked up, she had disappeared into her house. When Frank went inside, he could hear her moving around but had no idea where she was. "Miss Samuels?" He called out.

"In here. I'm in the living room," she answered.

Frank followed the voice to his left and found Catherine sitting on her couch, fumbling with the TV remote. After turning the television back on, she picked up her cell phone. Catherine then proceeded to show Frank videos of what had taken place at Marie Snyder's residence. From the moment the intruder climbed through Marie's window right up until the mysterious figure dropped what looked like a wallet next to the window, Catherine showed him everything. Her eyes dampened when she came to the part where the coroner's truck pulled up. Frank had her go back to the part where the intruder dropped the wallet. Five times he asked her to rewind it to see if he could get a good look at the culprit's face, but it was all for naught. The angle just wasn't good enough. One thing was for sure though. The figure in the picture was *not* Timothy Jordan.

"Dammit," Frank yelled, slamming his fist into his hand. "Excuse me for being blunt, but why in the hell didn't you come forward with this information earlier?" he snapped.

"Because I've been out of town for two weeks, that's why," Catherine said with an attitude. "I would think that the police would be grateful that I even came forward to share this information, but I guess I should've known better."

Catherine then folded her arms and gave Frank an incredulous glare. She was beyond pissed off. Here she was, trying to do her civic duty, and the detective was treating her like *she'd* done something wrong. Frank took a deep breath. The information that Catherine had just given him was extremely helpful. It cleared Timothy Jordan and left no doubt whatsoever that he'd been framed. But by whom? And why him?

"You're right Ms. Samuels. I do appreciate your help and I'm sorry that I snapped at you. Marie Snyder is more than my boss. She is also my friend, and I can't wait to catch the scumbag who did this to her husband."

The sad look in Detective Stone's eyes caused Catherine's stance to soften.

"I hope you catch him too, Detective. Marie is a nice lady. I hate to see her going through this."

"Thank you. Ms. Samuels. Is there any way you can email that video to me?"

"Probably, but I'll have to do it in increments. The file is pretty big."

"Okay. That's probably better anyway." Frank wrote down his personal email address and handed it to Catherine. "Please get it to me ASAP. A man nearly got arrested today for this crime, and the video can prove his innocence."

Christopher Speight

54

On his way back to the precinct, Frank called Amber and told her to meet him at Starbucks. He wanted to let her in on what he'd found out. Frank knew how much Amber liked Starbuck's White Chocolate Mochas and was hoping that he could soothe her hurt feelings by buying her one. There was no doubt in his mind that she would still be upset about him going to Marie's house without her.

Frank pulled into the Starbucks parking lot and was surprised to see that Amber was already there. He pulled beside her, looked at her, and smiled. Amber simply glared at him. After doing so for about ten seconds, she got out of her car and walked around to his driver's side. Frank sighed heavily as he reached for the door handle. He knew what was coming but was powerless to stop it. Amber's eyes were fixed on Frank the entire time as she waited patiently for him to get out of the car.

"Hey sunshine," he said, attempting to lighten the mood.

It didn't work.

"So, did you get your badge?" Amber asked, sarcastically. It was fairly evident that she hadn't believed that excuse when he'd told it to her earlier.

"Huh? Oh yeah, I got it."

Amber's mouth opened slightly, as she slowly shook her head.

"Franklin Stone, this is some bullshit, and you know it."

"Calm down, Amber. Come on, let me buy you a White Chocolate Mocha." Frank placed her hand on her shoulder, but she jerked away from him.

"I don't want any damn White Chocolate Mocha! I want you to stop lying to me!"

Frank held up his hands in surrender mode.

"Okay, Amber, okay. Look, let's just get in the car so we can talk about this."

With a scowl on her face, Amber stormed around to the passenger's side. When Frank went to open the door for her, she abruptly stopped him.

"I can do that myself," she snapped as she yanked the door open, got in, and slammed it shut.

Frank held up his hands and backed away. As slowly as he could, he walked back around to the driver's side and got in. In his eyes, any little time he gave her to calm down would be worth it.

After getting inside, Frank decided to get right into it. She was going to be pissed no matter how he approached it, so there was no need to waste any time.

"Okay, Amber, I'm going to tell you the truth."

Amber crossed her arms over her chest and waited.

"I didn't leave my badge at home."

"No shit, Sherlock. I figured that out already. Tell me something I don't know."

"Okay, I will. I went by Marie's house and checked out the crime scene for myself. I know that Hughes and Phillips are good detectives, but for some reason that I can't explain, I just got the feeling that they may have missed something."

"So, you don't think Timothy Jordan is guilty?"

"Do you?"

"Well, his wallet was found at the crime scene."

"That doesn't make him guilty, Amber. That's why I didn't take you with me. You seem to have already made your mind up about him."

Hurt flashed in Amber's eyes. Although his comments may not have been meant as a slight, she certainly took them that way.

"So, what are you saying Frank? That I'm incapable of being impartial?"

"What? Amber, I'm not saying that at all."

"Well, that's what it sounds like. And let's not forget that we're supposed to be partners. We're supposed to trust each other and have each other's backs!"

A single tear appeared in the corner of Amber's right eye, but she refused to let it fall. After listening to her side, Frank felt like a world-class jerk. He had hurt Amber. It was something that he hadn't intended to do, but he'd done it, nonetheless.

"You're right, Amber. I'm sorry. I should have trusted you to be the professional that I know you are. Please forgive me." Frank hung his head and waited for Amber to speak. The longer it took her, the worse he felt. Instead of making him feel like a bigger piece of shit, however, Amber took the high road.

"Don't worry about it, Frank. We all make mistakes. I forgive you. Let's just concentrated on the case. Did you find out anything new?"

Frank's spirits lifted. The last thing he wanted was to be at odds with his partner.

"As a matter of fact, I did," he said with enthusiasm.

"Well, don't keep me in suspense," she said.

"Well, the first thing I did was look around Marie's house to see if I could find anything that either Hughes or Phillips may have missed."

"Those guys are going to be just as pissed as I am when they find out you did that."

"They'll get over it."

"You think so, huh?"

"Yep."

"How can you be so sure?"

Frank didn't want to tell Amber what he really thought, which was that men didn't hold grudges like women did. She would swear he was being sexist, so he went with the next best option, which was also the truth.

"Because I'm going to let them take the credit for it."

"Yeah, that'll do it," Amber agreed. "So, what did you find?"

Frank smiled as he reached over, opened the glove compartment, and took out the picture he'd gotten from Marie's house.

"What is this?" Amber asked.

"Take a look at it. A *close* look, Frank added.

Amber looked at the photo of Marie and her husband and then at Frank. A confused expression landed on her face. She had no idea what she was supposed to be looking for. Shrugging her shoulders, she turned the picture over and looked at the back of it. To her, it seemed like a standard picture frame.

"Turn it back over and look at it closely," Frank said. Amber did what he suggested. That was when she noticed the small camera lens resting near the bottom. She squinted her eyes to get a closer look.

"Is this a camera lens?" she asked, although she already knew the answer.

"That's what it looks like to me. It was sitting on top of her mantel. Apparently, someone was filming the living room . . . and you know what that means," Frank said.

"Oh yes. Depending on how long the video goes back, we may have just cracked this case wide open."

"No. Hughes and Phillips may have just cracked this case wide opened."

Amber frowned.

"Yeah . . . about that. Why should they get all the credit?"

"Amber, they were assigned to the case."

"And? We're the ones who found the crucial evidence."

"Oh, *we* did huh?" Frank asked, emphasizing we.

"Yes, we! We are partners, aren't we?"

"Of course, we are."

"Then it's like I said. *We.*"

All Frank could do was laugh and shake his head. Truth be told, Amber had a point. Although Hughes and Phillips were assigned to the case, her partner was the one who'd discovered the camera picture frame. Still, Frank wasn't comfortable doing what she suggested.

"Amber, you have a point. But I just wouldn't feel right doing that. Not only would it show that we stepped on their toes, it would also make them look like idiots."

"They *are* idiots," Amber said, laughing.

"Be that as it may, we're not doing it."

"Okay," Amber said, jokingly crossing her arms and poking out her mouth like a small child.

"No need to pout, partner. I've also got something that should put a smile back on your face."

"Oh yeah? What?"

"It turns out that our fellow law enforcement officer is innocent."

Amber raised an eyebrow. Even though she would never admit it to Frank, she did think that Timothy was guilty.

"Really? And just how did you find that out?"

Right on cue, Frank's cell phone went off. It had taken a while for it to reach his cell phone, but Catherine's email had finally come through.

"Aha! Here it is," he said, excitedly.

"What?"

"Well, after I left Marie's house, a woman came running across the street telling me that she had something I needed to see."

"Which was?" Amber asked, when Frank hesitated.

Frank held up his finger, signaling for her to hold up a second. When he came to the part where the hooded figure was crawling through the window, he handed her the phone. Amber watched in silence as the sequence of events unfolded. Like Frank had earlier, Amber tried hard to make out the hooded figure, but the hood partially hid the face.

"Dammit! The video is grainy as hell. And the face is somewhat hidden. You're right about one thing, though. This is definitely *not* Timothy Jordan. Not tall enough or dark enough."

"My thoughts exactly."

"Well, hopefully, we won't even need the techies' help on this one," Amber said, holding up the picture frame.

"I hear you, partner. With any luck, our killer will be caught red-handed."

55

The tension surrounding the table was so thick, a chainsaw would have had trouble cutting through it. Four sets of eyes darted back and forth at one another. Four detectives, unflinching in their ways. Finally, a full twenty seconds later, after hearing what had gone down, Phillips decided to break the silence.

"Are you fucking kidding me, Frank? You mean to tell me that you went over to Captain Snyder's house after Hughes and I investigated the scene and went behind us like we were some rank amateurs?"

Frank looked around the crowded restaurant and sighed. One of the reasons he'd chosen this particular restaurant to tell Hughes and Phillips about going behind their back was that it was always busy. He didn't have to worry about either of them showing their asses. At least that's what he thought. Frank however, had severely underestimated how they would take the news. When he turned his attention back toward the table, Hughes was staring daggers at him. Unfazed, Frank stared them right back.

"Something on your mind, Hughes?" he asked.

"You damn right there's something on my mind. Who the hell do you think you are, Stone? You think you and your partner are better than me and mine?"

"Come on, Mike. You know damn well, that's not it."

"Well, it sure as hell looks that way!"

"Okay, you can just calm the hell down, both of you. What's done is done. Now, do you want to hear what we have to say or not?"

"I don't want to hear shit from you, Stone! You either Davis!"

"You know what? Fine! Let's go Frank!"

With fire in her eyes, Amber stood up from the table. She'd been biting her tongue ever since Hughes and Phillips had started ranting and raving. In her opinion, they weren't on the same level as she and Frank, but they were on the same side, so she had to subdue her attitude. Frank didn't budge. Neither did Hughes. Although he was supremely pissed that Frank had gone behind his back, he wanted to find out who had killed Marie's husband just as much as Frank did. Frank sensed it and motioned for Amber to sit back down. Hughes took a deep breath and leaned back.

"What do you have?" he asked.

"Hold up a second, Mike. I don't like this. This cocksucker went behind our backs to investigate the crime scene and now he wants to rub what he found in our faces? How do we know that he doesn't just want to take the credit himself?"

"Because if he did, he would have never told us about it," Hughes said, smirking.

Frank smirked back at him. They *were* on the same page. Frank looked at Amber and nodded. Amber reached down and picked up the bag containing the picture frame. She set it on the table and slid it across to Hughes.

"What the hell is that?" Phillips asked.

"It's a picture frame fitted with a video camera lens. It's probably connected to a cell phone," Hughes answered before either Frank or Amber could. "If I had to guess, I would say that it was connected to Donald's cell phone."

Frank smiled. He and Hughes were *definitely* on the same page.

"Wait. Do we even have access to Donald's cell phone?" Amber asked.

"Of course we do," Phillips said, now smiling as well. "We took it as evidence, but we haven't had a tech go through it yet."

"You guys *do* know what this means right?" Hughes said. "With this evidence, we can nail Timothy Jordan's ass to the wall."

Frank and Amber glanced at each other. They didn't know how Phillips would take the news that Timothy. Jordan was innocent. From the way he reacted at the police station, they both had to wonder if he would be disappointed if he was wrong.

"Why in the hell are you two looking at each other like that?" Hughes asked when he noticed the peculiar looks between the two detectives.

"Well, that brings me to the second piece of evidence that we've uncovered." Frank took his cell phone out of his pocket and pulled up the video. He then slid his phone to Hughes. He watched as Phillips leaned over and looked at the screen. Both of their faces went slack at what they saw. After viewing the video, they both looked up at Frank.

"Well, I'll be damned," Phillips said. "The asshole really is innocent, huh?"

"It would appear so," Hughes chimed in.

"Yep, looks like we owe that young man an apology," Frank said.

"Well, that can wait. Right now, we need to get this frame to Joe and see if he can pull whatever footage is on it from Donald's phone."

"I still don't know how I feel about you guys going behind our backs though, Frank. We're supposed to be a team," Phillips said.

"We *are* a team, Milton. That's why we're letting you guys take the credit for this."

Hughes and Phillips looked at each other curiously.

"Really?" Phillips asked, surprised. Had the situation been reversed, he would have never reciprocated the generosity that Frank and Amber were affording them.

"Yes, really," Frank said.

"Well, we definitely appreciate that. You know if the situation were reversed, we would do the same thing right?" Phillips said.

Frank and Amber cut their eyes at each other. It was a crock of shit and they both knew it. Hughes may have done the honorable thing, but there was no way Phillips would have. Although he was a detective, he hadn't fully learned yet that being in law enforcement meant that you sometimes had to step aside and let someone else have their moment in the sun.

"Sure, you would have," Amber said smirking.

"So, do you think we should tell Captain Snyder what's going on?" Hughes asked. It was a general question among the four detectives but there was little doubt that he was speaking to Frank.

"Come on Mike. You know we can't do that. The last thing we want to do is contaminate the case by involving someone so close to the crime."

"Yeah, I know. I had to ask, though. Now Cap will be mad at someone else besides me when she finds out that we kept information about who killed her husband from her."

"Oh, so you set me up with that question, huh?"

"Something like that," Hughes said, laughing.

"It figures. Look, we'd better get to the precinct and turn this stuff in to Joe. The sooner we do that, the sooner we find out who the murderer is," Frank said.

Christopher Speight

56

Deputy Chief Clark stared intently at the monitor. A disgusted look rested on his face. He, along with Detectives Stone, Davis, Hughes, and Phillips, was shocked and utterly flabbergasted at what they were seeing. It had taken Joseph Millano less than ten minutes to hack into Donald Snyder's phone and pull the video from the picture frame. He was good at what he did. He'd been a technical support worker for the police force for ten years, and he took great pride in his work.

"Is that who I think it is?" he asked.

"Yes, it is," Amber said. Her voice dripped with disgust. Although the figure crawling into Marie's window wasn't clear enough to be recognized, that all changed once Donald struggled for his life. Once the hood came off of the intruder's head, the identity was crystal clear. Every person in the room was wondering the same thing. *What in the hell was the motive?* Frank shook his head slowly as he dropped down in a chair. He looked at Amber and both of them shared the same exacerbated look.

"Do we know if there's any history between these two?" Clark asked.

"Not that we are aware of," Amber said.

"Well, *get* aware of it! It goes without saying that we will arrest this piece of garbage anyway, but there has to be a reason this man was murdered in cold blood! Hughes, Phillip! Get out of here and go pick up Mr. Snyder's killer. Stone, Davis! Out of respect for Marie, I think you two should pay her a visit and explain the situation to her." Without saying another word, Clark stormed out of the room. He was so angry that he slammed the door on his way out.

"Wow. I have to admit that I'm at a loss for words right now," Joe said. "I've been doing this job for ten years now, and I've never come across anything like this happening before." When Joe noticed that no one was responding to him, he turned around. He looked at the hardened faces of Frank Stone and Amber Davis and noticed how focused they were on the monitor.

"Rewind it," Frank ordered.

"Excuse me?" he asked.

"You heard the detective. Rewind the footage," Amber co-signed.

"No problem."

The two detectives sat there in disbelief. Although they were seeing it again, it was still hard for them to wrap their minds around it. Simultaneously, Frank and Amber got up and moved closer to the screen. It was as if they thought being closer to the monitor would somehow change the killer's identity. Looking at it a second time, however, only made their stomachs churn more. Frank shook his head, got up, and headed for the door. Amber was right on his heels. Twenty minutes later, they were pulling into the hotel's parking lot.

"How do you think she's going to take the news?" Amber asked.

"How would you take it?"

"Good point."

The two detectives got out of the car and made their way into the hotel. Not another word was spoken until they reached the hotel room door. Frank raised his fist to knock on the door, but before he could it opened.

"Hello Detectives. Come on in," Marie Snyder said, leading them inside. "I just got off the phone with Deputy Chief Clark. He gave me a heads-up that you two would be coming by to see me. He also told me that there was some news regarding my husband's murder."

"Cap, before we tell you this——"

"Save it, Stone. I'm a big girl. Whatever you're about to tell me, I promise you that I can handle it," she said.

Frank looked at Amber, who just shrugged her shoulders. He sat on the couch and took a deep breath. He looked at his captain and quickly realized that she was tougher than even he thought. What he was about to tell her wouldn't break her, but it would surely piss her off. By the time he finished giving her the run down, she was twice as pissed off as she was before.

"What? Are you freaking *kidding* me?" Marie yelled. "You mean to tell me that my husband had been recording my living room?"

"Yes ma'am. The evidence of the crime was right up under our noses," Amber said.

Marie rubbed her head.

"I can't believe this," she mumbled.

Frank walked over and put his hand on Marie's shoulder.

"It's okay Cap. At least we know who murdered your husband, and we can prove it now. That asshole is going down!"

Seemingly in a daze, all Marie could do was stare at the floor.

Christopher Speight

57

It took Hughes and Phillips ten minutes to arrive at their destination. Silence dominated the car, as each detective was immersed in his own thoughts. With a frown on his face, Phillips stared out the window. Even though he wouldn't admit it to Hughes, he was highly pissed off that he'd been wrong about Timothy Jordan. He didn't have to, however. Hughes knew his younger partner like the back of his hand.

"You good over there, partner?" Hughes asked.

"Yeah, I'm all right. I just can't believe we were wrong about Timothy Jordan being guilty. I would have bet my last dollar that he was the murderer."

Hughes cut his eyes at his partner.

"You know better than to jump to conclusions in this job. You've been a detective too long to do that. I still can't believe this, though. We're about to go in here and arrest Donald's killer and we have no idea what the motive is. Most of the time, we have a hunch about the killer did what they did, but this time, I don't have a clue."

"Neither do I, so let's go in here and cuff this piece of scum."

The two detectives got out of the car and entered the lobby of the apartment. The apartment was a two-story building located in Cleveland Heights, Ohio. It was a quiet neighborhood that housed mostly professional workers. This particular building was full of tenants who worked as teachers, barbers, and beauticians among other professionals. Hughes pulled out a piece of paper and looked at it.

"4C," he said to his partner. "Let's go."

Hughes and Phillips headed for the elevator and patiently waited for it to arrive. The longer they stood there, the more the gravity of the situation started to sink in.

"This feels weird. I've seen a lot on this job, but I have to admit this is a first for me," Phillips said.

Hughes slowly nodded. He'd been on the job longer than Phillips and had only encountered such an occurrence once. He wasn't involved in that case, so it didn't dig at him the way this one did. This one involved someone he cared about getting hurt. That made it personal. The elevator door opened, allowing the detectives to step inside. As the elevator ascended toward its destination, the two detectives got angrier and angrier. By the time they got off the elevator and made their way to 4C, they were downright livid. The husband of one of their own had been murdered and someone had to pay. The unusual circumstances however, made this situation different. Because they were there to arrest a killer, the detectives weren't about to take any chances. They both pulled their weapons and hid them behind their backs just in case they needed them. Hughes knocked on the door and waited. Ten seconds later, the door opened.

"Detectives? What's going on? Has there been a break in the case?" the person who answered the door asked.

"You could say that. We're going to need you to come with us?"

"Is this about Officer Jordan?"

"Actually, no. It's about you," Phillips said as he aimed his gun.

"Carla Johnson, you are under arrest for the murder of Donald Snyder."

58

Judge Joanna Tripp peered over her wire-framed glasses and cast an evil glare in Carla Johnson's direction. In her twenty-eight years on the bench, Judge Tripp had presided over nearly every type of case imaginable, but she could honestly say that this was a new one for her. After staring at Carla for what seemed like forever, Judge Tripp cast a cool glance at Beverly Hubbard. The lawyer had a stoic look on her face as she stood beside Carla, who, after being locked up for the last seventy-two hours, looked disheveled and raggedy. In all honesty, Beverly didn't want to take the case, but her superiors insisted that she did. Beverly had a reputation of taking cases that were slam dunks. She didn't like the challenge or the hard work that came along with trying to prove a client was innocent when they appeared to be guilty as sin. She would rather just take the cases she knew she could win, win them, and collect her paycheck. In this instance however, she had to play the hand that was dealt to her.

"Counselor, how does your client plead?" Judge Tripp asked.

"Not guilty, Your Honor. The defendant is a police officer and poses no flight risk. We request that she be released on her own recognizance."

Judge Tripp then looked at the assistant district attorney, Derek Weaver. Weaver was a short, heavyset, African American man with a baldhead and zero facial hair. Many lawyers often took one look at him and underestimated his ability to get a conviction. The ones who had done their homework, however, knew better. Weaver was a shrewd man who had a ninety-seven percent conviction rate, which meant one thing. When he took the case, more than likely, the person on trial was going to jail.

"Mr. Weaver?" the judge said.

Christopher Speight

"Your Honor, we request remand for the defendant. She killed her boss's husband in his own home and then planted evidence to frame one of her co-workers."

"Allegedly," Beverly Hubbard countered.

"Allegedly, my foot. The Euclid Police Department has video of the actual murder and someone planting evidence."

Carla's heart nearly stopped. This was the first time she'd heard about any evidence the police may have had. She cut her eyes at Beverly, who simply ignored her.

"I haven't seen any video, Your Honor. For all I know, this so-called video could have been doctored by someone," Beverly said.

"Give me a break, Counselor. That's weak, and you know it," Weaver contended.

"Okay, you two, that's enough. Bail will be set at two hundred-fifty thousand dollars, cash or bond."

"But, Your Honor——"

"Save it for the trial, Mr. Weaver. Next!" the judge yelled.

59

Two hours after her bail was set, Carla walked out of her cell a free woman. At least, for the time being. As soon as she left her cell, she made a beeline for her locker. Since no shift changes were coming up, she could do what she needed to do without being interrupted.

Carla quickly opened her locker and pulled out the small tape recorder she kept in there. After making a sweep through the locker room to make sure that she was alone, Carla sat down in front of her locker, hit record, and left her partner a message. She had a slim hope of returning to work, but if not, she knew her partner needed this information. She then grabbed a piece of paper and an ink pen and wrote a short note.

It began,

Listen in private . . .

When she was finished, she got up and exited the precinct. Since she wasn't allowed to bring her cell phone with her, she couldn't even call for an Uber to take her home. She had just gotten to the bus stop when a car pulled up beside her. As soon as it came to a stop, the passenger's side window rolled down.

"Get in the car," Timothy Jordan said.

Carla looked from her right to her left before finally getting in. The flow of traffic was light as Jordan pulled into it.

"So, tell me Carla, how does it feel to be accused of something that you didn't do?" he asked.

Carla's head snapped around.

"You believe I'm innocent?"

"Of course I believe you're innocent. You're my partner. I think I would know if my own partner was a killer. I believe in you just like you believed in me when I was accused," he said, condescendingly.

"I never said that I thought you were guilty," she responded.

"No, you just stood there and let everyone stare at me like I was a damn criminal."

"Timothy, I——"

"You know what? Don't even worry about it. I just came down here to give you a ride home after finding out that you'd made bail. Who bailed you out?" he asked.

"I have no idea," Carla lied. She knew exactly who had put up her bail money.

"Well, I heard that they had you on tape. I haven't seen it, but I know that couldn't be you, right?"

"Of course not, partner. And thanks for giving me a ride home. I appreciate it. But look, if this all goes wrong, I need you to clean out my locker for me, okay?"

Timothy gave her a sidewards glance.

"Why would it go wrong?" he asked, suspiciously.

"I didn't say it would. I'm just saying *in case* it does. Please Tim. This is important to me, partner."

"No problem." The two officers said their goodbyes as Carla got out of the car and made her way inside her building. A million thoughts ran through her head as she got on the elevator. The three days she was in jail before she was bailed out left a stench on her that she couldn't wait to wash off.

When she got to her door, Carla noticed an envelope sticking under it. She bent down, picked it up, and looked at both sides of it. There was no writing on either side. She did a quick look around before opening her door and going in. Luckily for her, her keys were still in her pocket when she was arrested, or she would have had to contact the building's superintendent to get into her own apartment. When she got inside, she opened the envelope. Inside of it was a note.

Don't worry about it. Everything will be OK, it read.

After reading it, Carla balled the note up and threw it in the trash. She couldn't get to her shower fast enough. She jumped in and scrubbed her skin for thirty minutes. Feeling better, she got out of the shower and threw on her robe. She then went to her kitchen, took a bottle of wine out of her cabinet, and corkscrewed it open. She then poured herself a glass and wondered how in the hell everything was going to be okay.

Carla took a deep breath and tossed down a large gulp of her wine. Her greed now had her in an unenviable spot. After finishing off her glass of wine, Carla went into her bedroom and retrieved her cell phone. Now that there was a video of her committing murder, there was no reason for the other end of the bargain to be held up. She was on her own. It took Carla forty minutes to polish off the entire bottle of Lambrusco. After she was finished, she came to a decision. Carla had no idea if or when she would enjoy the flesh or another man again, so she decided to call Timothy. Her decision was based on lust but rooted in the guilt of trying to frame him. She picked up her cell phone and began dialing.

"Hello?" Timothy answered.

"Hey. You busy?" she asked.

"Not really. Just making some rounds. What's up?"

"Well, I was wondering if you wanted to keep me company for about an hour?"

Timothy was speechless.

"Really? I thought you said before——"

"I know what I said before. Do you want what I'm offering or not?"

"I'm on my way," he said, before hanging up.

By the time he got to her apartment, Carla was lying naked in her bed. Roughly an hour later, she was ushering Timothy out the front door. She didn't want to cuddle. She didn't want to talk. She'd gotten what she wanted. Now, she just wanted him to leave. Although he was disappointed, Timothy didn't argue. He was just happy that she'd allowed him into her bed. As soon as he left, Carla lay back in her bed and cried her eyes out. More and more the severity of her situation was beginning to hit her. While the tears flowed down the side of her face, Carla made another decision. She reached onto her nightstand and picked up her cell phone. If she was going down, she was not going down alone.

Christopher Speight

60

"Bailed out? What the hell are you talking about? How in the hell was she able to get bail? She killed my damn husband, and you mean to tell me that this murdering slut is out of jail? Who in the hell bailed that slut out of jail? How the hell did this happen?"

Marie's breathing was heavy as she continued to rant. Frank, Amber, Deputy Chief Clark, Hughes, Phillips, and Timothy Jordan, all knew that she was going through a very traumatic time, so they let her have her moment. She was pacing back and forth across the floor so hard that she had begun to wear a groove in the carpet. When no one answered her, Marie stopped in her tracks. She looked around the room and made eye contact with everyone there. Her head stopped moving when her eyes landed on Timothy Jordan. Slowly and with a purpose, she walked up to him. Her head tilted back as she looked up into his eyes.

"Was it you? Did *you* bail that murderer out?" she asked, tears now dancing in the corner of her eyes.

"Me? No. I had nothing to do with her getting out of jail. But to be honest with you, I just don't think she did it."

Marie looked at him like he'd lost his mind.

"Are you insane? Apparently, you haven't seen the video! I have, and that's her!"

"Come on Captain. How do we know that the video wasn't altered?"

"Well, we don't, which is why we have the techies working on it now! If it's been altered, in any way, they'll discover it!"

"Okay, Captain Snyder. Calm down. I know you're upset about this, but we need to make sure this is right. The last thing we want is for some slick-assed lawyer to get her off on a technicality."

"What technicality, Chief? We have her dead to rights! Video doesn't lie," Amber said.

"Davis, you know as well as I do that nothing is always wrapped up in a neat little bow. Things go wrong. Let's just hope that the techies find that video to be authentic. Then we'll have her ass."

Their meeting was abruptly interrupted by the loud ringing of someone's cell phone. All eyes landed on Timothy Jordan as he reached into his pocket and pulled his out. He was just about to press the answer button when Phillips snatched it out of his hand and did it for him. He then pressed the speaker function on the phone and motioned for Timothy to answer it.

"Hello?" he said, sheepishly.

Being a trained officer, Carla immediately picked up on the fact that she was on speaker.

"Okay, since you have me on speaker, I have to assume that other people are present. I'm going to make this short and sweet. I want to come in tomorrow and make a statement."

Surprised looks filled the room. Did Carla want to come in to confess to the crime?

"Carla, this is Detective Amber Davis. Are you sure you want to do that? Maybe you should talk to your lawyer first."

"Screw my lawyer! I have something to say! I'll be in tomorrow at nine a.m.!"

Without saying another word, Officer Carla Johnson hung up the phone. In her mind, there was no need for her to carry on a long conversation. When it all went down, she was going to make sure that her head wasn't the only one on the chopping block.

61

After being sexually satisfied and finishing off another bottle of wine, it still took Carla nearly an hour to fall asleep. She may as well have stayed awake because she tossed and turned all night thinking about what she had to face the following day. Jail time was inevitable, but she wouldn't be the only one doing time. The plan had seemed to be fool proof, but now that she'd been caught on video there was nothing stopping her from becoming the only sacrificial lamb.

By the time her alarm went off, Carla had tossed and turned so much that her sheets were on the floor. Feeling like she'd only been asleep for twenty minutes, Carla sat upright in her bed. With a yawn, she reached over and hit the snooze button on her cell phone. Afterward, she immediately fell back in her bed. Eight minutes later, it went off again. This time she rolled off the side of her queen-sized mattress and stood up. She stared at her beeping cell phone for ten seconds before silencing the alarm on it.

Carla then jumped in the shower. When she got out, she took her time getting dressed. When she finished, she sat down on the edge of her bed and texted her lawyer.

I need you to meet me at the police station at nine o' clock. I'm ready to make a deal with the D.A.

After doing that, she shut down all her social media accounts. Carla looked at the time and saw that she had roughly an hour before she had to be at the precinct. She figured that she had just enough time to scramble herself a couple of eggs and fry some sausage. After doing so, she sat down at her kitchen table and enjoyed what she figured would be her last free meal. Thinking about what she had gotten herself into, Carla wanted to kick her own ass. For as long as she could count, she'd always been consumed by the almighty dollar. When the opportunity presented itself to earn a cool twenty-five thousand dollars to commit cold blooded murder, she jumped at the chance.

While other cadets at the academy looked forward to fighting crime and making the city safe for civilians, Carla joined for one reason only. To do drug busts and pocket the cash hoarded by drug dealers. She was a dirty cop in every sense of the word, and now her lack of morals was coming back to haunt her.

After finishing her meal, Carla got up to prepare for her day of reckoning. She walked into her bedroom and headed for her closet. She thought about wearing her uniform to the precinct but decided that if this were going to be her last day of freedom, she would dress like the diva she felt she was.

Reaching into her closet, Carla took hold of a black wrap around dress that she'd been saving for a special occasion. Unfortunately, this was as close as she was going to come to that affair. She laid the dress on her bed, went to the bathroom, and jumped in the shower. She knew that she didn't have that much time, so she quickly washed, got out, and got dressed. After that, Carla applied a generous amount of make-up to her face and let her hair hang to her shoulders. After applying her lip gloss, she took a deep breath and headed for her front door.

As she approached the door, the severity of her situation finally hit her. Tears welled up in her eyes. When she reached the front door, her hand trembled as she reached down and grabbed the knob. Carla's head turned and she took one last look at her apartment. She then opened the door and headed for the elevator. She didn't even bother to lock the door. What was the use?

As she trudged toward the elevator, each step felt heavier than the last. Normally, it seemed like the elevator would take forever to get to the first floor. Not today, though. It got there in what Carla felt was record time. She shook her head as she made her way through the lobby and into the crisp air. Carla took her time. When she finally reached her car, she could barely breathe. Her legs felt like cement. She opened the door and got into her vehicle. After closing the door, Carla took another deep breath and leaned back against the head rest. She closed her eyes and said a short prayer.

"Lord, please forgive me for all of my sins."

"That's the good thing about God. He forgives almost anything," a cold, steely voice said from behind her.

Carla's eyes snapped opened the exact moment that a gun was being pressed against the back of her head.

"Tell him I said hello," was the last thing Carla heard before a bullet entered the back of her head and crashed through her skull. She slumped forward onto the steering wheel as her blood splattered against the windshield. The horn began to blow before her head was violently snatched back. She was then slung unceremoniously onto the passenger's seat. Her eyes were open, but they would never again focus on anything other than the afterlife.

62

Detective Franklin Stone sat at a table in Starbucks, staring down into his coffee. It had been two weeks since Officer Carla Johnson had been murdered. The fact that it had taken place in her car was giving Frank some sleepless nights. Carla was a trained police officer. It would have taken someone with a high level of skill to get the drop on her like that.

"You okay over there, partner?" Amber asked, biting into a chocolate doughnut.

"I guess. Just thinking about the Carla Johnson murder."

"What about it?" she asked callously.

Frank looked up at her.

"What? Am I supposed to feel sorry for her? I'm sorry, Frank, but that's not easy for me. She killed our captain's husband and the messed up part about it is that we don't even know why."

"That's what I mean, Amber. No one kills without a motive. There has to be some reason that Carla killed Donald Snyder."

"I agree, but I think the explanation died with her."

"You may be right. But that doesn't stop me from wondering."

"Me neither," Amber admitted. "But it doesn't look like we're ever going to find out, so—

Amber let the sentence remained unfinished as she shrugged her shoulders.

"Well, if Captain Snyder has anything to say about it, we will. She's dispatched every available detective to the case."

"Really? Why?"

Amber was surprised. Had it been her, she wouldn't have given two shits about a woman who had killed her husband.

"Simple. She feels that if we find out who murdered Carla, it will lead to finding out why Donald was killed."

Amber stared at Frank for a few seconds. She then took a deep breath and let her chin rest in the crevice of her thumb and forefinger.

"Let me ask you something Frank. You haven't given any thought to the possibility that Carla and Donald were having an affair? And that's why she killed him? Maybe he tried to break it off with her, and she was too far gone to let go of him."

"Yes, I've thought about it once or twice, but it just doesn't fit. Carla was in her twenties. What could she possibly see in a man nearly twice her age?"

"Hmmm. Good point, partner."

The two of them then sat quietly for around ten seconds before Amber once again broke the silence.

"Were you surprised that Captain Snyder didn't attend the funeral?" she asked.

Frank thought on for a few ticks before saying, "No, not really. I mean, I do believe that she's going to do everything in her power to find out who killed Carla but attending the funeral of a woman who killed her husband was probably too much to ask."

"Yeah, I guess so. Concerning Carla's murder, though, I am surprised that no one saw anything, especially since it was in broad daylight."

"That's what bothers me. Someone should have seen something. But then again, maybe someone did and just doesn't want to get involved."

"You know how it is, Frank. No one ever wants to get involved but get pissed off when it happens to them and other people won't get involved."

"Yep, that's the way it usually goes," he said, before pausing a brief second and then continuing. "Amber, I don't know if you've thought about this, but we have another problem on our hands."

Amber's face scrunched up. She had no idea what Frank was talking about.

"Oh yeah? What's that?"

"We still have two other murders that remain unsolved. If you remember, we thought that Donald's murder was tied to those because we believed that the killer was targeting interracial marriages and mixed couples. But now that we know Donald's murder had nothing to do with the other two, we still have a killer on the loose."

Amber closed her eyes and rubbed her head. With everything that had been going on, she hadn't even thought about that.

"Damn, Frank, you're right. We'd better get back on that before two more bodies pop up."

"You're right."

Frank reached into his pocket and pulled out a few crumpled-up bills. After that, the two detectives got up to leave when they were approached by a tall, burly looking man with a square jaw and thick beard. He placed a hand on Frank's shoulder and smiled at him warmly.

"Frank! How the hell are you?" he asked.

Frank took one look at the man and broke into a large smile. He hadn't seen him in quite some time, but the two of them had always been pretty good friends.

"Well as I live and breathe, if it isn't Jarvis Green! How the hell are you?"

"Doing good man. I just got back in town."

"Work?"

"Nah man. I needed a vacation. That last case I was on wore me out. Hey, you're not about to leave, are you? Have a quick cup of joe with me."

"Well, since my partner didn't have the courtesy to introduce me, I guess I just have to do it myself," Amber said, sticking out her hand. "I'm Amber Davis."

"Jarvis Green. Nice to meet you."

Amber cut her eyes at Frank, who had an embarrassed look on his face.

"Sorry about that Amber," he said, sheepishly.

Amber was about to respond when her cell phone buzzed. She looked at the screen and rolled her eyes.

"Give me the keys Frank. I'll take this in the car."

"New boyfriend?" Frank asked.

"Please. It's Roger's annoying behind."

As Frank and Jarvis sat down, Amber scurried toward the exit. She had no idea what her ex wanted but, unless it had something to do with her son, she was sure that it was some nonsense.

"So, how's it been going, my friend?" Jarvis asked Frank.

"Not too good lately, man. I know you've heard about what happened to Captain Snyder."

"No. Like I said, I've been out of town for the last couple of weeks. After she—never mind. Like I said, I've been lounging on a beach in Miami. What happened?"

Frank raised an eyebrow. He didn't know what Jarvis had to say, but something. In his gut told him that he needed to hear it. He let it slide . . . for the moment.

"Well, for starters, her husband was murdered in their living room."

"Murdered? Donald Snyder was murdered?"

"Yes, he was. Apparently, Captain Snyder came home and found him dead on the couch. From the look of it, he'd been strangled from behind with some type of wire."

"Oh, wow."

"That's not all. We thought we'd nabbed the killer. An Officer Timothy Jordan."

"Wait, hold up. You guys thought a police officer killed you captain's husband? What made you guys think that?"

Frank went on to tell Jarvis about the altercation between Donald Snyder and Timothy at the restaurant. He then told him about how Timothy was conspicuously the first person to arrive on the scene after Donald was found dead, saying that he was going to Marie and Donald's house to apologize to him for the argument. Frank punctuated the story by informing Jarvis that Timothy's wallet was found outside the window of the home, although the officer had previously stated that he had not searched the perimeter.

"I see. That does make him look guilty."

Frank held up his hand.

"Hold up, my friend. It gets better . . . or worse depending on how you look at it."

Jarvis leaned forward. Frank's story was fascinating to him.

"When we brought him in for questioning, he maintained his innocence. We really didn't have anything other than the wallet to charge him on, so we had to let him go because, quite frankly, that's not enough to hold him on."

"So, the killer is still out there?" Jarvis asked.

Frank took a deep breath, as he slowly shook his head.

"It turns out that the killer *was* a cop. On a hunch, I went back to the house to look around. While doing so, I noticed a picture sitting on the mantel that looked different from the rest of them. Well, it turns out that the frame holding the picture had a miniature camera in the bottom of it. Apparently, Donald didn't trust what was going on in his own home and kept video surveillance on it."

"How do you know that he was the one doing that?"

"Because the video was attached to his cell phone."

"Jesus," Jarvis said, rubbing his head.

Frank thought his reaction was on the strange side, but he continued with the story.

Black Viper

"Now, here's the part that broke the case wide open. After finding the picture, I was about to go back to the precinct and see what the techie could do with it. We already had Donald's phone so all we had to do was go through the phone and see if it was connected to the video. But before I could even get in my car to leave, I heard a woman calling me and running toward my car from across the street. She told me that she has something important to show me. I tried to blow her off, but she said that it's important. There was something in her voice that told me she was telling the truth, so I followed into her house. She proceeded to show me footage from her security camera. The first thing she showed me is someone sneaking around the side of Marie's house. I'll give you one guess what they were doing."

"Planting evidence."

"Exactly. I asked her why she didn't come forward with this video sooner. Apparently, she'd been in Hawaii for the last couple of weeks."

"Did you get a good look at the suspect?"

"Hell no. They had a hood covering most of their face. What it did do however was, exonerate Timothy Jordan."

"How so? I thought you just said that you couldn't really see their face."

"We couldn't, but from the physical stature of the person, it was obvious that it wasn't Officer Jordan."

"Is that all? Or is there more?" Jarvis asked.

"There's more. After showing me that, she went back even further and showed me footage of the day Donald Snyder was killed. The same figure was seen climbing through the window just moments before he was murdered. Now," Frank said as he leaned across the table. "Here is the thing that broke the case wide open and left no doubt as to who the guilty party was. When I got back to the station, I had Joe work his magic on connecting the cell phone to the camera on the frame. Imagine our surprise when we saw Officer Carla Johnson strangling Donald Snyder from behind."

Jarvis's mouth fell open.

"Wow. That's quite a story."

"You're telling me."

"So, this Carla Johnson, is she in custody? And just what the hell was her motive?"

"To be honest with you, we have no idea what her motive was. As far as her being in custody, we had her in custody until someone bailed her out."

Jarvis's face twisted.

"Bailed her out? The judge gave her bail? On a capital murder charge? That's hard to believe."

"My thoughts exactly. But from what I heard, the judge didn't want a police officer in jail for fear of her safety."

"Even so . . . The bail had to be set pretty high. Who in the hell put up that kind of money?"

"Beats the hell out of me. But get this, Carla called the next day wanting to make a deal."

"Really? What kind of deal?"

"She didn't say. Just said she wanted to talk to the DA."

Just then, a young-looking woman came over.

"Excuse me. You two looked like you were in deep conversation, so I didn't want to interrupt, but my manager told me I needed to come over and see if you wanted anything."

"Yes, we'll have two coffees," Jarvis answered. "So, this Carla Johnson, what deal did she want to make?"

"We never got the chance to find out. Carla was found dead in her car."

"Wait . . .what?"

"You heard me. She was getting ready to come to the station and tell us what kind of deal she was looking for, and someone murdered her."

Jarvis was stunned. This had to be one of the strangest cases he'd ever heard of.

"Something stinks here, Frank."

"I agree. Hopefully, I can find out what it is."

Jarvis stared at Frank for a few seconds before looking down at the table. It was clear that he had something on his mind.

"Jarvis, what's up, man? Ever since we started this conversation, it seems like you've had something on your mind."

Jarvis took off his glasses and ran his hand down the front of his face. With his eyes closed, he bit the bottom of his lip. When he opened his eyes, they immediately met Frank's piercing gaze.

"Frank, I had some information I think you need to know."

"I'm listening."

Jarvis paused as the waitress came and set two cups of coffee on the table. He waited until he was sure that she was out of earshot to begin talking again. Taking a deep breath, he leaned forward on the table and laid out the situation to Frank. By the time he finished, Frank was thoroughly shocked.

"Oh my God," he said, standing up to leave. He was just getting ready to head for the door when Amber came power walking toward the table.

"Frank, we may have a problem. We need to leave right now."

Christopher Speight

63

Timothy Jordan sat quietly in the police station parking lot. A river of tears streamed down his face. The secret feelings he had for Carla Johnson were pushing their way to the surface. Although he had never admitted it to anyone, Timothy had an enormous crush on Carla. The two of them had shared a night of passion that resulted in him falling hard. He wanted to pursue a relationship, but Carla was vehemently opposed to it. She blamed their sexual slip up on the bottle of wine the two of them had consumed on Carla's birthday. She also reminded him that personal relationships were not allowed within the department. Timothy didn't like it, but he had to accept it.

His feelings for Carla remained strong, which is why doing what he'd promised her he would do was so difficult for him. It had been days since Carla's funeral, and Timothy still couldn't bring himself to open up her locker. Even though he'd promised her that he would clean it out for her, so far, it had been too painful for him to do so, but he knew that he needed to do so before his superiors ordered it to be cleaned out. Today was the day he'd decided to find his resolve. Today was the day he decided to man up. Today was the day that he'd decided to honor her wishes.

Because of the extremely hard way he'd taken Carla's death, the powers that be decided that it would be better for him to take a few days off. Timothy didn't want to do it, but Sergeant Moore had insisted. He himself had just returned from vacation and was shocked to find out what was going on. Since Marie Snyder was still on leave, he made the calls on how the precinct was being run. She'd been allowed to return to her home, but not the precinct.

Timothy wiped his eyes and got out of his car. He closed the door and stood there for a few seconds before taking a deep breath and heading into the precinct. His steps were hurried. He determined that the faster he did what he was there for, the faster he could get over it.

Timothy kept his head down as he walked through the station. He didn't want to talk to anyone. That was the main reason he came in early. This way, he could avoid his co-workers. His chest tightened when he got to the locker room and came upon Carla's locker. After taking another deep breath, he opened her locker and looked inside. He was surprised to see that it was relatively empty. All that sat inside was a small voice recorder. Lying underneath it was a folded slip of paper. Timothy slid the paper from under the recorder and opened it.

Listen in private, it simply said.

Timothy picked up the recorder and looked at it curiously. Not wanting to take the chance that someone else might overhear it while he listened to it, he decided to take it back to his car. He was so curious that he literally ran to his vehicle. Could it be that she was professing her love for him? Timothy nearly ripped the handle off the door, trying to get inside of his car. His heart fluttered as he pressed *play* and listened for the sound of her sweet voice.

Hello, Timothy. There are some things that I need to confess to you . . .

Timothy smiled warmly as she began speaking. However, the more she talked, the more his smile metamorphosized into a bitter frown. By the time she finished, his emotions were scattered, mostly dominated by shock and rage. Knowing that he needed to relay the information he'd just received to someone he felt he could trust, he called Detective Amber Davis. When she didn't answer, she called back. Again, there was no answer. He called a third time. By this time he played the recording and left it on his voice mail.

Black Viper

"I'm on my way to get to the bottom of this," he said, just before hanging up and starting his engine.

Christopher Speight

64

Frank and Amber sprinted from the coffee shop and jumped in their vehicle. As fast as humanly possible, Frank started the engine and peeled off down the street. He clicked the switch for the siren, alerting cars in his path that he was on his way to attend to official police business. His mind whirled around the information that the private investigator, Jarvis Green, had just given him. Every bit of it held massive importance to the puzzle he was trying to piece together. It paled in comparison however, to the bomb that Amber was about to drop on him. Frank's mouth was wide open as he listened to her. When she finished, he instantly knew that if he didn't step on it, the message she'd received could have disastrous consequences.

While Frank was zipping through traffic, Amber was on the radio calling for back up. Hopefully, they wouldn't need it, but it was better to be safe than sorry. When they arrived at their destination, Frank skidded to a stop at the curb. Amber looked at the car parked in front of them and held her breath. Praying that they weren't too late to intervene, they made their way inside the fence and up the steps. An earsplitting bang caused both detectives to draw their weapons. With no time to follow announcement protocols, Frank rammed his thick shoulder into the door. Wood splintered as the door detached from its hinges. Both detectives came to a sudden halt when they got to the living room. Utter shocked was plastered on their faces as they stared down at the bleeding corpse on the floor.

"Drop that gun!" Amber shouted as she cocked her weapon and pointed it at Timothy Jordan's head. Timothy slowly turned his head and looked over his shoulder at the two detectives. The crazed look in his eyes caused a cold shiver to run down Amber's spine. Although her gun was still trained on him, she took a cautionary step back.

"You heard her, asshole! Drop that gun!" Frank shouted, backing up his partner.

"She killed Carla."

"You don't know that," Amber said.

"Yes, I do. She admitted it. She admitted the whole thing," he said softly. "Didn't you listen to the voicemail I left you Detective?"

"Yes, I did."

"Then you know all about her paying Carla to kill her husband. You know all about the million-dollar life insurance policy she took out on him a year ago. And I guess you know all about——"

"We know about everything! Now drop that gun, Officer Jordan. I'm not going to ask you again," Frank said, cocking the hammer on his .45 caliber pistol. Timothy Jordan smirked as he tossed the gun on the floor beside Marie Snyder's dead body.

"She laughed at me. She thought it was funny that she killed Carla." Timothy then looked at Amber. "Did you tell Detective Stone why she had her husband killed?"

Frank looked confused. From the moment Amber had told him about the one-million-dollar life insurance policy, he assumed that Marie had killed her husband for the money.

"The money was only part of the reason Detective," Timothy said to Frank, reading his mind.

"Timothy, you have no idea what you just did," Amber said.

"Yes, I do. I came over here and killed a woman who murdered someone who I cared very deeply about."

"No, you came over here and killed a woman for a woman who tried to frame you for murder."

A look of shock fell across Timothy's face. He couldn't believe what he'd just heard.

"What did you say?" he asked in astonishment.

"You heard me. But just in case you're confused, I'll explain it to you. Remember when you couldn't find your wallet at the bar? Well, you couldn't find it because Carla had pick-pocketed you. Then she planted it right next to that window," Amber said, pointing toward the window.

Timothy's heart shattered. Once again, he couldn't believe what he was hearing. He started shaking his head rapidly.

"No! That's bullshit! I don't believe it! Carla would never do that to me!"

"Well, whether or not you believe it, your ass is going to jail," Amber said.

Frank stared at Timothy for a long while before instructing Amber to handcuff him and read him his rights. As she ushered Officer Timothy Jordan out of the house and into the back of a waiting squad car, Frank walked across the floor and stood over his now deceased captain. His emotions were all over the place. This woman who he'd come to know and respect had turned out to be a cold-blooded murderer. Sadly, it dawned on him that he hadn't really known her at all.

Christopher Speight

EPILOGUE

A driving rain pummeled Frank's umbrella, nearly causing it to collapse. For the second time in the last two weeks, he'd had to stare down into the casket of another slain law enforcement officer. It was a feeling he had no desire to get used to. He was still amazed at how easily Captain Marie Snyder had fooled he and the entire police force. Never in his wildest dreams could he ever imagine that she could be such a cold-blooded murderer. He couldn't help but feel a measure of contempt for her. She was a cop—and not just a regular cop. She was a captain. She was in an authoritative position and instead of using it to protect and serve the public, like she'd taken an oath to do, she used it to try to get away with killing her husband.

The longer he'd looked down at her, the angrier he became. This was not only his boss. This was a woman that he considered to be his friend, and she had deceived him. The only thing stopping him from hating her was the ultimate reason she'd hired someone to kill her husband. When Amber had played the voice mail of Carla's recorded message to Timothy Jordan, all the pieces fell into place. Frank Stone was heartbroken. He was also disappointed in himself. He'd been trained to tell when someone was lying to him. He'd been trained to notice when someone was trying to deceive him. Maybe if he had figured out what was going on earlier, he could have done something to stop it.

The burial service was barely ten minutes old when Frank decided he'd had enough. He abruptly turned and headed back to his car. His shoes made sloshing sounds as his frame sunk into the mud. By the time he got back to his car, they were so filthy he had to wipe them off.

After doing so, he shook off his umbrella, threw it in the backseat, and closed the door. Five seconds later, his passenger's door opened. He looked to his right to see Amber getting in. Instead of wiping off her shoes, however, she took them off and put them inside a plastic bag.

"You weren't going to leave me, were you?"

Frank responded by slowly shaking his head.

"You okay?" she asked.

"I just can't believe that Marie did this."

"Neither can I."

Frank put his hands on his head and shook again.

"I'll tell you what though, partner. I know some women who would think she's a damn hero."

"What?" Frank asked, his head snapping around.

"Not me, partner," Amber said, raising her hands. "But the asshole did give her a death sentence."

Frank sighed. If he were being honest with himself, he would have to admit that, deep down inside, Donald Snyder got what he deserved.

"Play the recording again," Frank said, silencing his cell phone.

"What?"

"Play it again. I think I'm going to have to hear it again to believe this bizarre incident, honestly."

Amber hesitated for a brief second before reaching into her pocket and taking out her cell phone. She accessed her voicemail, increased the volume to its fullest, and pressed play.

Hello, Timothy. There are some things that I need to confess to you, but before I start, I would like to say that I am very, very sorry. I never meant to lie to you. If you are hearing this, it means that I am probably on my way to prison. The fact of the matter is that I am the one in the video. I killed Donald Snyder. His wife promised to pay me fifty thousand dollars to do it. She said that she had a one hundred-thousand-dollar life insurance policy on him, but I'm not stupid enough to believe that she was willing to give me half of her life insurance policy.

Nevertheless, fifty thousand dollars is a lot of money. I have always been money hungry. I'm not proud of it, but that's the way I am. The life insurance policy is just part of the reason Marie Snyder killed her husband.

She also told me that she had a private investigator follow him and discovered that he'd been cheating on her. She told me that I had no idea how hard it was to pretend to still love a man who had put her in the position her husband did. When I asked her what she meant by that, she looked me straight in the eye and revealed that Donald had given her HIV. I am telling you this just in case something sinister happens to me. In that event, the first person you should look at is Captain Marie Snyder.

Just so you know, Timothy, I would have never allowed you to go to jail. I would have come clean about what I had done before I let that happen. Timothy, I realize that you have feelings for me and if by some miracle, my lawyer gets me out of this jam, I would like to discuss our relationship. I know that's not proper protocol, but at this point, I really don't give a shit. Once again, I want you to know how sorry I am. Please forgive me. Carla.

As the voicemail ended, Amber glanced over at her partner.

"I don't know about you, but I don't believe one word of that."

"Which part?"

"The part where she says that she would have come clean. I don't believe that crap for a second."

"Neither do I. She would have let that man burn in hell to save herself if she had to. I have to admit though, it shocked the hell out of me to learn that Captain Snyder had HIV."

The two of them sat in silence, watching the people around the burial site until they began to disband. Not wanting to be bothered with anyone, Frank started the engine and pulled off. Both he and Amber decided that they weren't going to attend the repast. They were tired, disgusted, and had no desire to be asked a thousand questions. After dropping Amber off, Frank drove as fast as safety would allow. All he wanted to do was go home, sit on his front porch, and sip a cold beer. He pulled into the driveway, cut the engine, and sat there. It was he first time in two weeks that he was able to decompress. After taking a few deep breaths, Frank got out of his car and went into his house. He was greeted warmly by Frank Jr. and Rhonda ran up to him and wrapped her arms around him. Although she and Frank Jr. were teenagers, they sensed that their father was torn apart by what had transpired.

"Are you okay, daddy?" she asked. "I'll be okay, baby girl," he said, kissing her on the forehead.

"You're doggone right you will. Your last name is Stone. We don't fold," Frank Jr. proclaimed, holding out his fist for a pound. After slamming his fist down on top of his sons, Frank Sr. wrapped his arms around his kids and pulled them close to his chest.

"Thanks for the welcome kids. I really appreciate it. But what I want right now is to grab a beer out of the fridge, sit on the porch, and relax." "No problem, Pop," Frank Jr. said and scurried into the kitchen. When he returned, he had an ice-cold Heineken in his hands.

"Here you go," he said, extending the bottle toward his father.

"Thanks son." After receiving the beer from his son, Frank went on the front porch and dropped down into his chair. He shot a sideways glance towards Sadie's residence and for once, he was happy to see that she wasn't outside. It wasn't that he didn't want to see her. He just didn't want to see her at that particular moment. The rain was still coming down and it seemed to make him drowsy. He took one sip of his beer and sat the bottle down beside him. Frank had just about nodded off when Amber pulled into the driveway. She got out and slammed the door, causing Frank to jerk awake.

"Hope you're not too tired, partner."

"Why? What's going on?" he asked, rubbing his eyes.

"We have to go. Another interracial couple has been murdered."

The End

Turn
the
page
for
a
thrilling
except
from:

The Grey Killings

Christopher Speight

<u>The Grey Killings</u>

Bright stars overlooked the city as Jerome and Kelly walked hand in hand along the uneven sidewalk. The only thing brighter were the smiles glued to their faces. The young couple, both seniors in high school, had been pretty much inseparable since they'd began dating. Their parents believed they were simply infatuated with each other. After all, they were only seventeen years old. In their young minds, however, there was no doubt they were in love. Kelly shivered slightly as a cool breeze pelted the light jacket she was wearing. The jacket was so thin; the air seemed to penetrate it and soak into her skin. Jerome snickered as he felt her hand shake slightly from the chill. Kelly responded by yanking her hand free of his.

"What's so funny punk?" she asked, punching him in the arm.

"I wasn't laughing."

"Liar. I heard you snickering."

"Okay. I was."

"I know you was, jerk. Just for that, I'm not going to give you what you want," she said, flirtatiously. The young man's hormones began to stir. Although they'd told their parents something to the contrary, the couple had been sexually active for the last three months.

"Oh, so you're going to be like that, huh? Maybe I should change my Facebook status to single," he countered.

"You do and I'll kick your ass," she threatened.

Jerome laughed out loud.

"Come on, baby. You know I wouldn't do that."

"You'd better not."

Another gust of wind blew their way, causing them to shiver.

"Oh, I know you're not cold. Not after you was laughing at me."

"Whatever. You know what? Let's just cut through here."

Kelly looked at where he was pointing, and then back at him.

"Have you lost your ever-loving mind? I know you don't think I'm about to walk through a graveyard!"

"Don't be such a scardy cat. Come on."

Kelly looked inside the cemetery and then back at Jerome. "I don't know about this," she said.

"What in the hell do you think is going to happen? Can't nobody out there do anything to you."

Christopher Speight

<u>The Grey Killings</u>

"How do you know?"

"Because everyone out there is dead, that's how. Now come on."

Before Kelly could protest any further, Jerome grabbed her hand and pulled her along. Kelly's eyes darted from right to left, zeroing in the tombstones. In her mind, they seemed to stare back at her. Instinctively, she gripped Jerome's hand tighter. Jerome glanced down at her and smiled.

"Ain't no need to be scared, baby girl. I'm not going to let anything happen to you."

Jerome turned Kelly toward him and hugged her tightly. After breaking the embrace, he leaned down and kissed her deeply.

"Ah, puppy love. You gotta love it," a voice sounded from the shadows.

Jerome and Kelly looked around. Although they could hear the voice clearly, no one seemed to be there.

"What the hell? Who said that?" Jerome asked, nervously. His head continued to whip around until he came to a tall, slim figure coming towards them. A Cleveland Indians baseball cap was pulled down on the figure's head. In his hand was an aluminum, thirty-six inch baseball bat. Jerome instinctively stepped in front of Kelly. Out of fear, she gripped the back his shirt tightly.

"Who are you, man? What do you want?" Kelly asked, her voice trembling.

The figure ignored Kelly and continued walking forward.

"Isn't that nice. He's protecting you."

Jerome balled up his fist. He was scared shitless but the last thing he wanted, was to look like a wuss in front of his girlfriend. The figure looked down at Jerome's balled up fists and smiled sinisterly.

"So, tell me. Do you two love each other?"

The figure threw the bat over his shoulder and smirked as he awaited the couple's reply. Jerome and Kelly looked at each other, curiously.

"What?" Jerome said.

"I asked you if you two loved each other, dammit!"

The figure was getting impatient. He wanted to finish his business and be on his way.

"Yeah, we do love each other," Jerome said defiantly.

324

<u>The Grey Killings</u>

"That's all I needed to know," the figure said.

"What's that supposed to——"

Jerome never got to finish his sentence. In a flash, he was lying on the ground, semi-conscious. Blood poured from the top of his head. The screams he heard coming from Kelly's mouth seemed like they were far away. The last thing he remembered seeing was Kelly's skull being crushed by the baseball bat.